SWEET MERCY

Books by Ann Tatlock

SWEET MERCY

ANN TATLOCK

BETHANY HOUSE

a division of Baker Publishing Group
Minneapolis, Minnesota

© 2013 by Ann Tatlock

Published by Bethany House Publishers
11400 Hampshire Avenue South
Bloomington, Minnesota 55438
www.bethanyhouse.com

Bethany House Publishers is a division of
Baker Publishing Group, Grand Rapids, Michigan

Printed in the United States of America

Library of Congress Cataloging-in-Publication Data
Tatlock, Ann.
    Sweet mercy / Ann Tatlock.
        pages ; cm.
    Summary: "When Eve discovers her uncle's bootlegging operation, she knows it's against Prohibition law. But can she really condemn the only thing supporting her family?"—Provided by publisher.
    ISBN 978-0-7642-1046-4 (pbk.)
    1. United States—History—1919–1933—Fiction. 2. Prohibition—Fiction. 3. Alcoholic beverage law violations—Fiction. 4. Family-owned business enterprises—Fiction. 5. Life change events—Fiction. 6. Ohio—Fiction. I. Title.
PS3570.A85S94 2013b
813′.54—dc23   2013002076

Scripture quotations are from the King James Version of the Bible

This is a work of historical reconstruction; the appearances of certain historical figures are therefore inevitable. All other characters, however, are products of the author's imagination, and any resemblance to actual persons, living or dead, is coincidental.

The internet addresses, email addresses, and phone numbers in this book are accurate at the time of publication. They are provided as a resource. Baker Publishing Group does not endorse them or vouch for their content or permanence.

Cover design by Dan Pitts. Cover illustration by William Graf

Author is represented by MacGregor Literary, Inc.

13 14 15 16 17 18 19   7 6 5 4 3 2 1

For my sisters,
Martha Shurts and Carol Hodies,
because you've been my best friends from the beginning

Prologue

MAY 1981

No one has been by this way for years, but as I step up to the porch of the old abandoned lodge I'm certain I hear music. Music and laughter. Footsteps and telephones ringing. And a thousand voices coming not from far away but from long ago, reaching me now the way the light of a burned-out star reaches Earth thousands of years after the star itself is gone.

I turn to Sean. He is gazing at me quizzically, head cocked, fingers kneading the flashlights he holds in each hand. He is eager to get inside.

"What's the matter, Grandma?" he asks.

"Nothing," I say. "I'm just listening."

"To what?"

But of course he doesn't hear what I hear. He can't. He doesn't have the memories.

I turn the key in the lock and open the front door. It was

last closed in 1978 by Stuart Marryat, my first cousin once removed and the final owner of the Marryat Island Ballroom and Lodge. When I told him why I wanted to go back, Stu gave me the key and said I could go in and look around before the wrecker's ball did its work.

Not much has changed in fifty years. When I step into the spacious front hall and breathe deeply of the musty air, time snaps shut like a paper fan and I'm young again. Young and idealistic. And smug, though back then I didn't know it.

My grandson walks through the front hall, head bobbing like a pendulum, looking left and right. On the one side is the vast dining room, still furnished with tables and chairs and the large buffet table from which we served and refreshed drinks during meals. Across the hall is the sitting room, where guests reclined to read, converse, play cards or board games, or simply to rest. Straight ahead is the front desk, the mail slots, the rows of hooks that still hold an odd assortment of room keys.

"Wow," Sean says. "Cool place. Why are they going to tear it down?"

"Too old to pass code," I say.

"Too bad." He shrugs.

"Yes, it is."

"So how old were you when you lived here?"

"Well, I was seventeen when we moved here from Minnesota." Seven years older than Sean is now. He probably thinks I was all grown up. I thought so too, at the time.

"So what are we looking for?"

"Something I left behind when I moved away. I'm pretty sure it got packed up with some of my other things and was stored away in the attic."

"But what is it, Grandma?"

"A wooden box. My parents gave it to me for Christmas one year, when I was very young."

"Just a box? After all these years, why do you want it now?"

I pause and smile. "I'm a sentimental old fool."

He laughs lightly. "No you're not, Grandma."

"Well, there's something in the box your grandfather gave me. I'd like to have it again."

"All right. So how do you get to the attic?"

"Follow me."

The attic is a large room with a low slanted ceiling and windows across the front and on both sides. With the electricity off in the lodge, the attic is dim and stuffy and smells heavily of must and of things that have been stored for decades. Sean and I go about unlocking and opening the windows to let in both sunlight and fresh air. Then we turn to the task at hand. We are surrounded by an eclectic collection of dusty furniture, old steamer trunks, floor lamps with tasseled shades, wooden crates, and cardboard boxes.

"Where do we start, Grandma?"

I turn on my flashlight; he follows suit. "Well," I say, "we might as well start with these boxes right here." I shine my light to indicate the pile.

Sean shrugs. "Okay." He settles his flashlight on the seat of a ladder-back chair and pulls one of the boxes off the pile. He opens the flaps. "While we're looking through all this stuff, why don't you tell me about what happened here?" he says. "You know, the summer you moved in."

I step to the box and move my flashlight beam over what's inside. "Do you really want to know?" I ask.

"Yeah. You've never told me the story, Grandma. Tell me now."

I think about that a moment. I suppose it is time for him to know. "All right, let's see," I say, searching for the place to begin. "You know we moved here in 1931, right?"

"Yeah. But that's about all I do know."

I nod. He pulls another box off the pile. Taking a deep breath, I say, "Well, I'll tell you what, had I known what was waiting for me in Mercy, Ohio, I might not have been so eager to leave Minnesota. . . ."

Chapter 1

Had I known what was waiting for me in Mercy, Ohio, I might not have been so eager to leave Minnesota. But of course I could never have imagined what lay ahead, so for weeks I happily anticipated the sight of St. Paul in the rearview mirror of Daddy's 1929 Ford sedan. It was May 30, 1931, when we finally packed up the car and made our great escape from the Saintly City, refuge of fugitives and gangsters.

Something else I didn't know then was that the furnished apartment we'd just vacated, #205 at the Edgecombe Court, would in two days' time be rented out to bank robber Frank "Jelly" Nash, lately of Leavenworth Federal Penitentiary. He'd managed to escape the year before and had taken a circuitous route to Minnesota's notorious haven. Like most criminals, he knew that once he reached the state capital, it was "olly olly oxen free!" That's just the kind of town St. Paul was in those days.

The sun was starting its ascent over the eastern edge of the city as Daddy started the car and pulled away from the curb. The morning offered enough light to showcase the wondrous array of spring blossoms that had unfolded like a miracle after another harsh winter.

In the passenger seat in front of me, Mother sighed. "We're leaving at the very best time of the year," she said.

"It can't be helped," Daddy replied. "At any rate," he added, "there's spring in Ohio too."

"Do you suppose they have lilacs there the way we do here?"

"Probably. If not, we'll have some imported."

Mother laughed lightly at that before sighing again. Truth be told, Mother and Daddy weren't happy about leaving St. Paul. I was the only one among us who wanted to go.

I felt a quiet satisfaction as we drove down Lexington Avenue for the last time, winding our way through the otherwise fashionable streets of the city, filled with stately Victorian houses and luxury hotels, among them the Commodore where rich and famous luminaries like F. Scott and Zelda Fitzgerald had partied away much of the Roaring Twenties. It might have been a nice town, this midwestern metropolis nestled along the banks of the Mississippi River, had its wheels not been oiled by corruption.

We'd lived there seven years, having arrived in 1924 when Daddy got a job as a spot welder at the Ford Assembly Plant. Before that, we'd been living in Detroit, where I was born, and where Daddy also worked for Ford. But Mother and Daddy didn't like Detroit, and eventually Daddy applied for a transfer to Minnesota.

When we arrived in St. Paul, the city was already rife with criminals, and yet it was a surprisingly safe place to live. This was a result of the layover agreement established by former Police Chief John O'Connor. Gangsters, bootleggers, bank robbers, money launderers, fugitives—all were welcome as long as they followed the agreement's three simple rules.

First, upon arrival in St. Paul, they had to check in with "Dapper Dan" Hogan, owner of the Green Lantern speakeasy and supervisor of O'Connor's system. He was himself a hoodlum, a money launderer, and an expert organizer of crime who was known as the Irish Godfather.

Second, all incoming criminals were to make a donation to Dapper Dan, who distributed it among the lawmen with pockets open to payoffs: police detectives, aldermen, grand jury members, prosecutors, and judges.

Third, once settled in the life of St. Paul, these active felons had to swear never to commit a crime within the city limits. Bank robbers could rob banks, murderers could kill, and gangsters could blow each other to kingdom come without interference from the law, so long as they conducted their business elsewhere.

John O'Connor died the year we moved to Minnesota, but Hogan went on instituting the agreement until he himself was hurled into the hereafter by a car bomb in 1928. After that, without Hogan around to keep the peace, things started going downhill. Harry Sawyer, Dan Hogan's assistant as well as his probable assassin, took over both the Green Lantern and control of the O'Connor system. Sawyer wasn't nearly as interested in keeping the peace as he was in making money, and right after Hogan's death, crime spiked and crested in a five-year wave. Sawyer's friends from all over the country started rolling in—public enemies like John Dillinger, Alvin Karpis, and Fred and Doc Barker. When we left in 1931, the worst was yet to come, and yet I'd already seen one man gunned down in the streets. That one murder was enough for me and the reason I was glad to see St. Paul in the rear-view mirror.

Daddy sat behind the wheel, his face wan and pinched. Of the three of us, he was the one who wanted least of all to go back to his home state of Ohio. We were going only because we had no choice. A year and a half after the stock market collapse, more than a third of the country's Ford dealerships had closed, and men were being laid off in droves. Daddy's turn had come a few weeks back. The night Daddy told us the news was the first time I'd ever seen my father cry.

Mother and Daddy prayed to God for help, and God's unforeseen and somewhat bewildering answer came in the form of a call from Cyrus Marryat, Daddy's brother, the one who owned the Marryat Island Ballroom and Lodge. There were plenty of rooms and plenty of work at the lodge, Uncle Cy said. He even sent us the money to make the trip, which was quite remarkable, since Daddy and Uncle Cy hadn't seen each other since 1926 when we went to Ohio for Uncle Cy's wedding to Aunt Cora. Daddy and Uncle Cy had had a disagreement, but I never knew what it was about. It was a wonder Uncle Cy invited him back, since they'd never really gotten along since childhood. But blood was blood, and in desperate times, family took care of family no matter what.

As we headed east on Grand Avenue, Mother said, "Pull over onto Victoria one last time, will you, Drew?"

"Oh now, darling—"

"Please, Drew, for me."

Sighing, Daddy turned left onto Victoria Avenue. In another moment, we approached a familiar house. "Stop just for a minute," Mother said.

"Now Rose . . ."

"Please."

Daddy reluctantly eased the car to a stop in front of the clapboard house where my sister lived with her husband and their two little girls. Mother pulled a handkerchief out of her pocketbook and brushed away tears. "Oh, Cassandra," she moaned.

I moaned too and rolled my eyes.

Daddy patted Mother's arm. "She's a big girl. She'll be all right."

"I can't help thinking she still needs me."

"She's made her bed, Rose, and so far she's adjusted pretty well to lying in it. You worry too much."

I knew Mother was thinking about all the years that had brought Cassandra to where she was now. All the tumultuous and heartbreaking years.

I crossed my arms and slunk down impatiently in the back seat. All I wanted was to be on our way.

Mother reached for the door handle, but Daddy stopped her. "We said good-bye last night, Rose. And anyway, they're probably still asleep."

"I suppose you're right." Mother dabbed at her eyes again.

"And just think, we'll be seeing them in a couple months," Daddy reminded her. "August, they said. They'll take their vacation in August and come on down and see us."

Mother turned to Daddy and tried to smile, but it was little more than a ripple of sorrow passing over her lips.

Daddy put the car in gear and we moved on down the road. Finally. I would miss my brother-in-law and two young nieces but, like Uncle Cy and Daddy, Cassandra and I didn't get along. She was the older sister I had never admired and never wanted to be like. I was just as content to leave her behind with the criminals and gangsters in St. Paul.

The sun had fully risen by the time we reached the eastern edge of the city. An equal measure of anticipation rose in my heart. *Good-bye, St. Paul! Good-bye and good riddance!* The town of Mercy lay ahead of us, the place I had loved as a child but hadn't visited in years.

"Daddy?" I asked.

"Yes, darling?" He glanced at me in the rearview mirror. His brown eyes looked weary, and his narrow handsome face was still without color.

"What did you and Uncle Cy fight about?"

His brows went up. "When?"

"The last time we were in Mercy. You know, when we went down for the wedding. Whatever it was, it's kept us from going back for five years."

Daddy was quiet a moment. He looked at Mother, who shrugged. Then he gave another glance at me in the mirror. "Did we fight about something? I honestly can't remember."

"Then why haven't we gone back? To visit in the summer like we did when I was little?"

Daddy sniffed and scratched at the cowlick on the crown of his head. His brown hair was thick and unruly. "That's a good question, Eve," he said. "I'm not sure I have an answer."

"I do think you argued about something." Mother pulled one corner of her mouth back and shook her head. "Though for the life of me I can't remember what."

"Well," Daddy said, "it's water under the bridge. And you know what I always say, right?"

"Don't tell me," I said. "Let me guess. First Peter 4:8. Right?"

"That's it." Daddy nodded. "'For love shall cover the multitude of sins.'"

"That's *charity*, Drew," Mother said. "'For charity shall cover the multitude of sins.'"

Daddy chuckled. "You correct me every time, Rose, but you know very well I say love because it made more sense to the girls when they were little. And anyway, charity, love—same thing pretty much, don't you think?"

"So, Daddy," I interrupted, wanting to get us back on track, "whatever you and Uncle Cy fought about, we'll forgive him and love him anyway."

Daddy hesitated just a moment before saying, "That's right, darling."

"Well, that's easy," I said. "It's easy to love Uncle Cy." After all, he was my ticket out. He was my ticket to a new life. We were leaving the city of sin behind. No more bootleggers, brothel-keepers, gangsters, corrupt lawmen, kidnappers, or murderers. We were on our way to Marryat Island Ballroom and Lodge in Mercy, Ohio, on the Little Miami River. We were on our way to the Promised Land.

Daddy gave me one more glance in the rearview mirror before settling his eyes on the road for the long haul ahead. Mother wiped at tears one last time before resignedly stuffing her handkerchief back into her pocketbook. She turned her face to the window, her features delicate and gentle in profile, her soft brown hair pulled into its usual knot at the back of her head.

I too settled back for the ride. As the newly awakened Minnesota landscape rolled by, I noticed the morning edition of the *St. Paul Pioneer Press* on the seat beside me. Clear of the city limits and facing the long stretch of open road toward

Wisconsin, I picked up the paper to pass the time. When I saw an advertisement on page six for Wilson Tailors, I shook my head and clicked my tongue softly. Even the tailors were making money from the fallout of St. Paul's sleazy underworld. In bold type the proprietor, Mr. Edmund Wilson, boasted: *Bullet holes rewoven perfectly in damaged clothes.*

Chapter 2

Late in the afternoon of the third day of our journey, we arrived in Mercy. We climbed out of the car stiff and weary, our clothes sticky with sweat, our ears ringing from the churning of the engine and the rattling of the tires over the roads. But even as I stepped into that sweet Ohio air, I felt at once refreshed.

I breathed deeply, glad to have arrived. As we moved from the graveled parking lot to the lodge, I listened to the happy cries coming up from the river, from the dozens of people swimming, boating, and picnicking on Marryat Island. Even the grounds around the lodge were bustling with visitors, some moving to or from the island, some strolling along the riverbank, others taking part in a game of croquet on the expanse of green lawn. I stopped just a moment to watch the game. The women looked stylish in linen chemises with matching cloches pulled low over their ears. The men wore neatly pressed slacks, cotton shirts, and straw hats or caps; one of them was pulling on a pipe. Their laughter and chatter rose and fell like winged creatures at play. I wanted to join them, to be part of this simple pleasure.

But smiling, I turned away and moved on to the lodge. It was much the same as I remembered, though even more beautiful now because it was home. Far larger than any Victorian mansion in St. Paul, it was a mammoth two-story affair, probably the largest structure in town aside from the Mercy Milling Company up on the north side. Part fieldstone, part clapboard siding, Marryat Island Ballroom and Lodge sat enthroned on the banks of the Little Miami like the fortress I wanted it to be.

I fairly floated up to the porch where vacationers reclined in a neat row of rocking chairs. I was hardly aware of Mother's and Daddy's heavy footfalls behind me as I stepped into the expansive front hall and looked around, trying to take it all in. To the right was the dining room. Even now dinner was being served on linen tablecloths. To the left, the spacious sitting room, filled with comfortable chairs and couches, walls of books, a phonograph, a fireplace. Straight ahead was the front desk and behind that the large circular staircase leading up to the twenty or so guest rooms on the second floor.

Uncle Cy was behind the desk, facing away from the door. With the telephone handset pressed against his right ear, he spoke loudly into the mouthpiece while his left hand stayed busy hanging up room keys on the rack and sliding letters into the myriad mail slots lining the wall. I walked to the desk and waited. And listened, as he was unaware that I was there.

"That's right, Charlie, he's done it again. Plowed up Williams Street and planted oats. Four neat rows, straight as six o'clock, all the way from Third to Fifth. What's that? Another warning. Naw, that's not good enough. It's time to talk to the solicitor. I'm telling you, Ralph has got to be prosecuted. For what? Defacing public property, for one. Ignoring the law, for another. Yeah, that's right. I know it's not a main thoroughfare, but people have got to drive their cars down that street, and that's hard to do when you've got oats growing under your wheels. If we could just get that stretch paved, this wouldn't happen."

Uncle Cy sighed. I remembered then how, as a very young child, I thought his name was Uncle Sigh because he sighed so often. It was as though at regular intervals all the worries in the world squeezed the air right out of his chest.

"And then there's the matter of his wife's chickens," he went on. "Yeah, the neighbors are complaining again. What? Well, how would you like it if you woke up and found Trudy Mae's chickens pecking their way through your flower bed?"

At that point, Uncle Cy turned around and saw me. He looked at me quizzically a moment as though he didn't know who I was, and I don't believe he did, till he saw Mother and Daddy standing a ways off behind me. "Listen, Charlie," he said, the flash of recognition lighting up his eyes, "I've got to go. Yeah, we'll bring it up at the meeting tonight. All right, yeah. See you then."

He settled the handset back in the cradle and leaned forward on the front desk with both palms down. "Drew, Rose," he said. "And this can't be . . ." He stopped and shook his head.

I laughed. "Yes, it's me, Uncle Cy. Eve."

"Well, I'd have never known. Listen, sorry about that." He nodded toward the desk phone. "Town council business. I'm president this year. So hey, welcome, huh?"

He smiled and walked around the counter with one beefy

arm extended. He went to Daddy first and shook his hand, then gave Mother a hug. Turning back, he leaned forward, and I stood on tiptoe so we could exchange pecks on the cheek. He was a tall man, the tallest of the three brothers and big as a linebacker. Though he was somewhere over fifty years old, he still had a full head of hair that he combed straight back from his ruddy face. His hair was streaked with gray now, though, and he was beginning to lose his chin and gain jowls instead. Crow's feet fanned out from his eyes, and even his brows had turned gray. Time was catching up with Uncle Cy.

"Well, you made it," he said, and while he waited for one of us to respond, the air was filled with an awkward silence. I looked at Daddy who, after three days, still held that same pinched expression I had seen reflected in the rearview mirror as we headed out of St. Paul. He didn't want to be here.

"Looks like business is good, Cy," Daddy said at last, feigning an interested glance around the place.

"Nothing like a couple years ago," Uncle Cy said. "Or even a year ago. People have been hit hard. But we have enough of a crowd to keep us afloat."

While Daddy nodded, Mother asked, "How's Cora, Cy?"

Uncle Cy sighed again. "She's about the same. I've got her at the best place in the country, though. If they can't get her better, nobody can."

"She'll get better," Mother assured him.

"Yes." He nodded, but his dark eyes said he wasn't sure at all. "She's been there only a month. I don't expect her back before Christmas."

Another awkward moment followed in which I thought about Aunt Cora. I'd met her only once, at the wedding. She was Uncle Cy's second wife, his first having died in 1919 in the final days of the great flu epidemic. They'd had no children. Uncle Cy met Cora some years later and married her in 1926. Now Aunt Cora was convalescing in a tuberculosis sanitarium at Saranac Lake in upstate New York.

I shivered at the thought of the dread disease and hoped none of the tainted air from Aunt Cora's lungs still lingered in the nooks and crannies of the lodge. Consumption would be an unwelcome guest in Paradise, and I wanted nothing of it.

"Well," Uncle Cy rubbed his large hands together. "Let's get you settled. Have you eaten supper?"

Daddy looked toward the dining room with reluctant eyes. I knew what he was thinking, that eating Uncle Cy's food was as good as taking a handout. And that meant, to Daddy, that he was little better now than the drunks and the prostitutes down at the St. Paul Mission where he'd spent so many years helping out. I'd heard him say as much to Mother when he thought I wasn't listening, back during one of their late-night talks about whether or not to come down here after Daddy lost his job.

Before Daddy could respond to Uncle Cy's question, I jumped in and said, "We're starving, Uncle Cy. What's cooking?"

He smiled at me. "All your favorites, I bet. We'll go see, soon as we get you settled in your rooms. Where's your luggage?"

"Out in the car," Daddy said.

"I'll have someone help you carry it in."

We were given adjoining rooms, connected by a bath. The rooms were at the very end of a long hall. Mine was a corner room with windows overlooking both the river in front and the side yard where the croquet game was still under way. The only true apartment in the lodge was on the ground floor in the back. That was where Uncle Cy lived, and Cora too, when she was there.

Having no kitchen of our own, we would take all our meals in the dining room, which is what we did that evening. It was a brief and solemn meal, punctuated by the small talk of two brothers who hadn't seen each other in years, and Mother, who in her own quiet way always tried to make everything right. I said little and instead satisfied my hunger with huge helpings of roast beef, boiled new potatoes, and corn on the cob. Other guests came and ate and left; their chatter merged and mingled with our own. A couple of waitresses bustled about, carrying trays of food and pouring glasses of tea and water. I knew then that all our meals would be taken in the midst of constant motion, and yet, the busyness of the room was tempered by the lazy flow of air from the open windows and the slow churning of ceiling fans overhead.

Shortly, Uncle Cy excused himself to go to his town council meeting, and when he left, I did too, called out to the island by the breeze wafting up from the river. A small steel bridge, humped like the back of a frightened cat, extended from the riverbank over the tributary to the island. I walked across, and a rush of childhood days came at me like a giant wave cresting and rolling over the shore. I welcomed them—welcomed the remembrance of that innocent time when life's greatest wonders were as simple as a shovel and a pail of pebbly sand, an hour of splashing with Mother in the cool clear water, an afternoon of rowing on the river with Daddy. Even Cassandra was friendly toward me then. She'd play with me, keeping me entertained by twirling me around on the dance floor when the bands played in the pavilion on summer nights. Those were good days, and I embraced them now like long-lost friends. Words could not describe how glad I was to be there, where neighbors weren't fugitives, nor the local drugstore a front for a money-laundering business, where the greatest problems to be dealt with were ill-planted oats and wayward chickens, and where I wouldn't have to worry about seeing anyone sliced up by a hail of bullets the way we saw the man murdered near the St. Paul Mission.

That was the thing that haunted me most—that murder. Mother, Daddy, and I were walking downtown, on our way to serve soup at the mission, when a Lincoln sedan drove past us and slowed down. In the next moment the long black barrel of a Thompson submachine gun appeared in an open window. Shots rang out, and little sparks of flame, and a man not half a block ahead of us rose up from the sidewalk like a rag doll tossed by a child, his arms upraised as though in surrender. He seemed to hang in the air a moment in a shower of his own blood before he crumpled in a lifeless tangle on the front steps of a Jewish deli. The next moments were pandemonium—women screaming, tires squealing, two men rushing to the body to feel for a pulse and, finding none, removing their hats and shaking their heads. And I . . . I stood speechless while the final moments of my childhood slipped away. The next day, after reading about the killing in the paper, Cassandra told me that's what happened to hijackers who interfered with another man's bootleg business. I'd had nightmares about that murder ever since.

Taking a deep breath to clear my mind, I strolled along the path leading to the picnic tables and the small pebbled beach where a section of the river was cordoned off for swimming. Dusk was settling and families were beginning to pack up their picnic baskets and head out for the night. As it wasn't the weekend, I doubted that a band would play, but that was all right; the air was filled with the night songs of crickets and tree frogs, and when I put my head back I could see the faint glow of Venus and the pale wafer of a full moon.

I was finally here and I was safe. I knew this was a safe place because the temperance movement had begun right here in Ohio. It was Ohioans who wanted the drinking to stop, all the dreadful drinking that ruined so many lives, tore apart so many families, left so many destitute. It was here in small towns that bands of women gathered and prayed in front of saloons until the owners agreed to close. Maybe something of those prayers remained, making Ohio a sacred place of sorts, protected from the evils of drink.

I'd read all about the temperance movement for the essay contest sponsored by the St. Paul chapter of the Women's Christian Temperance Union. My essay was awarded first prize for the year 1930. By then, Prohibition in America was ten years old. I spoke glowingly of Prohibition and firmly believed everyone should keep all its laws.

What I didn't include in my essay was how badly Prohibition had failed, how as soon as it was signed into law, the law began to be broken, how it had opened the floodgates to illegal liquor distribution and organized crime, ruining perfectly good cities like St. Paul. I'm sure I was unwilling to admit it, even to myself.

But none of that mattered now. Kicking off my canvas shoes, I stepped barefoot into the river, just up to my ankles. The water was cold and tingly. A few people were swimming farther out; one of them, a girl about my age, rose up out of the water and moved toward shore.

"Hello," she called to me in passing as she ran to grab a towel. She lifted it to her head and began vigorously rubbing her short curls.

"Hi," I said. "Nice swim?"

"Yes," she said, "but now I'm freezing." She shivered as she wrapped the towel around her shoulders. "You going in?"

"No." I laughed lightly. "Not right now. Maybe tomorrow. You staying at the lodge?"

She shook her head. "No, we live in town. We just came over for a few hours. How about you? You up from Cincinnati?"

"No. Actually I live here now. I live in the lodge." I suppose I sounded proud, but I couldn't help it. "My uncle owns it."

"Lucky you!" she said, wide eyed, and I was pleased that she was impressed. "How long have you lived here?"

"We've only just arrived. Just this evening. We moved down from Minnesota."

"Lucky you," she said again.

"Marlene!" A woman at one of the picnic tables raised a hand and waved. "We're packed and ready to go. We're waiting on you."

"Coming, Ma!" The girl turned back to me. "Well, maybe I'll see you here again sometime."

"Oh yes," I said. "We could go swimming or rent a boat or something."

"Sure." She shrugged. "Now that summer's starting we'll be here a lot. Not much else to do in Mercy."

"Marlene!"

"I said I'm coming!"

"Well," I said, "nice to meet you."

"Yeah, you too. Oh, and welcome to Ohio, I guess. But listen, just watch out for the red-eyed devil."

"The what?"

"Marlene!"

"I said I'm coming!" She started to go, and then turned back. "But don't worry. You're pretty safe as long as it's daylight. He mostly comes out at night."

I wanted to ask her what she was talking about, but before I could say another word she had run off, laughing, to join her family.

Chapter 3

Standing in the hall, I tapped lightly on Mother and Daddy's door, opening it only after Mother said, "Come in." She closed the book she'd been reading aloud, using one finger as a bookmark. "Well, Eve, how was the island?"

"As beautiful as ever," I said dreamily.

"Are you off to bed now?"

"I don't know. I'm not tired at all. Maybe I'll read awhile too."

Daddy, who was sitting in the overstuffed chair across from Mother, gestured toward the footstool. "You can join us, if you'd like. We've just started *Great Expectations*. I know you like Dickens."

I nodded, thought a moment, shrugged. "I think I'd like to get acquainted with my new room."

Daddy chuckled. "You're glad we're here, aren't you, darling?"

"You know I am, Daddy. This is going to be the most wonderful place to live. I've already met a girl who lives in town. Her name's Marlene. I think we're going to be friends."

"How nice," Mother said.

"Except . . ."

"Except what?"

I thought of her comment about the red-eyed devil, still not quite sure what to make of it. Maybe it was a joke or a bit of local color, a story told around the campfire at night. I decided not to mention it. "Except, I want you both to be happy here too," I finished.

Mother and Daddy exchanged a glance. "We're going to make the best of it," Mother replied.

"At least until the economy gets back on its feet," Daddy said. "This is only temporary, after all."

Mother must have seen the worried look on my face, because she hastily added, "But of course we'll be here through your senior year of school, Eve. Don't worry about that."

I tried to smile. Their not wanting to be in Mercy dampened my spirits and made me sorry for them, for what they thought they had lost. I hoped all that would change once we got settled into a daily routine. They would see that life in Mercy was good. How could it not be?

"Well, I'll let you get back to reading," I said. "Good night. See you in the morning."

"Good night, Eve."

"Sleep well, darling."

I kissed them both, then slipped through the bathroom to my own room. I closed the bathroom door on my side gently, shutting off the sound of Mother reading. Mother had always read to Daddy, as long as I could remember, and as soon as I was old enough I'd started reading to him too. He loved stories but he was unable to read them to himself, or at least not without great difficulty. The letters kept turning around, he said; they didn't stay where they were supposed to be. No one really knew what a page of type looked like to Daddy and why it looked different than it did to everybody else, but I did know it was one of the reasons he'd left Ohio at age eighteen without finishing high school. He had never felt good enough to be a Marryat. He wasn't like his brothers Cyrus and Luther. They were both honor-roll students who were being groomed for positions of leadership in the family businesses. Daddy would never have a place among them. He had to make his own place, and it wasn't going to be in Mercy. In the middle of their senior year, Daddy and his pal Stan Brewster ran away to Detroit, where they'd managed to get assembly line jobs at the Ford Motor Company, a journey that by happenstance, some twenty-nine years later, brought Daddy right back to the place he didn't want to be. Because he had ultimately failed to keep his job, he was back in Mercy.

I stood in the middle of my room and slowly turned around, taking it all in. It was much smaller than Mother and Daddy's room, but that was all right. A single bed, a wardrobe, a mirrored dresser, a desk and a reading chair—what else did I need? My clothes were hanging in the wardrobe, my shoes were under the bed, my photo albums and scrapbooks were tucked away in a drawer, and my treasure box was on top of the dresser. Already, I felt the place was mine.

Stepping to the dresser, I began untangling my long blond braid in front of the mirror. Unlike Cassandra, I had refused to cut my hair when the short bob came into fashion. I had no desire to be like my sister, who was eight years older than I and who had long ago made a pretty mess of her life.

I was serious about this one shot at living while she went

at it like a professional partier. I worked hard in school and tried to acquaint myself with the best of literature and art while Cassandra, awakened in adolescence to the intoxicating mix of crime and romance, devoured *True Detective* magazines. Though she was married now to a man who would no more break the law than Eliot Ness, once upon a time she had dreamed of being a moll, the girlfriend of an outlaw! She aspired to marry a man who robbed banks by day and came home to his lady at night to shower her in diamonds and dough, a man who dodged bullets and evaded arrest and was somehow invincible, a devilish Dick Tracy, a Bad-boy Buck Rogers.

She was nothing but a typical St. Paulite, always glamorizing the bad guys and longing to hang around the fringes of their world. As I brushed my hair, I remembered the time Cassandra and her friend Susan had run off giggling to the Hotel St. Paul. George "Bugs" Moran had been spotted there, and they thought if they hung around the lobby long enough they'd catch a glimpse of him. And they did.

They came back to our apartment and found me reading in the bedroom I unfortunately shared with Cassandra. Now my sister entered the room with her hands clenched in front of her heart. "Well, it was him," she said.

"Who?" I asked.

"Bugs Moran, silly. We saw him walk right through the lobby and go out the front door of the Hotel St. Paul."

"So?"

Susan leaned up against the doorframe, as though weak-kneed with longing. "Eve, you wouldn't believe how good-looking he is in real life. Even more handsome than he looks in pictures."

"So?"

"So don't you want to see him?" Susan asked.

"Why would I want to go look at one of the biggest gangsters in Chicago?"

"*Because*," Susan exclaimed, "he *is* one of the biggest gangsters in Chicago! And so much better looking than Al Capone."

"You guys are crazy."

"And you're just no fun," Cassandra snapped.

"And if you're not careful, you'll end up a moll!" I yelled.

"And if you're not careful, you'll end up an old maid!"

"Better an old maid than a gangster's girlfriend!"

Even as a very young child, I viewed my older sister as silly and shallow, a party girl tailor-made for the twenties. The years were to prove me right. The flapper craze sucked her up a willing participant and spat her out a reluctant wife and mother when, at age twenty, after years of speakeasies, bad boys, and hip flasks, she found herself pregnant and alone. Perhaps worst of all, she wasn't even sure who the father was. Mother and Daddy were horrified, though luckily several of Cassandra's former beaus suddenly materialized on our doorstep proposing marriage. These hapless suitors knew they were getting a two-for-one deal, but each was nevertheless willing to make an honest woman out of her. I could never understand that, except that Cassandra was uncommonly beautiful and perhaps her beauty knocked all the sense out of otherwise sensible men.

I leaned closer to the mirror and gazed judgmentally at what I considered my own plain face. My lips were too thin, my forehead too high. My nose was narrow and perhaps a bit too long, leaving it looking pinched and pretentious. I longed for cheekbones but they hadn't yet appeared. The only good feature was my eyes. They were blue and bright, just like Mother's. And Cassandra's. But that was the only family resemblance I shared with my sister. As I studied myself in the mirror, I wondered briefly whether I would ever turn sensible men into fools, and decided it was unlikely.

But the beautiful Cassandra had her choice of men, and she chose Warren Lemming, which all in all was a wise decision, since Warren's father had made his fortune in the railroad and had barely felt the aftershocks of the recent stock market crash. Warren was set to inherit an enviable estate and in the meantime was doing quite well as a junior partner in his father's business. On top of that he was genuinely nice, always even-tempered, and not bad looking either, if you didn't mind a receding chin and an unfortunate mole or two. He gave Cassandra's baby his name and immediately afterward gave Cassandra another baby. Effie and Grace were four and three now and lucky to have Warren as a father.

While I think Cassandra loved Warren in her own way, she resented having to settle down into marriage and motherhood before she was ready. I didn't feel sorry for her, though. In fact, her quiet misery filled me with no end of secret delight; I figured she'd got what she deserved. She had drunk and danced her way toward what she herself called drudgery. Like Daddy was known to say, she'd made her bed.

I for one wasn't going to be making any beds. I was going to make something of myself. Not just for me but, more importantly, for the two people in the room next to mine. I was going to do something important, something that made a difference. Mother and Daddy didn't have anyone else to do good in the world and to make them proud. Certainly not

Cassandra. And not the son who'd been stillborn between Cassandra and me. I was the only one they had and I wasn't going to let them down.

Laying down the brush and turning away from the dresser, I didn't know what to do next. Sleep was out of the question; I was far too excited for that. I thought about reading or writing a letter to my best friend Ariel back in St. Paul, but I had too much pent-up energy for sitting. I needed to move, to walk somewhere, or I'd end up pacing the room.

I tied my hair back with a ribbon and stepped out into the hall, quietly tiptoeing past Mother and Daddy's room and descending the stairs to the front hall below. A man I didn't know was behind the front desk; Uncle Cy must have still been talking oats and chickens with the members of the town council. The dining room was dark and empty, but the spacious sitting room was well lighted and cheery with the presence of guests. I walked through, smiling and nodding at a few people, but my feet, as though by their own will, carried me on through the sitting room and down the short narrow hallway that led to the ballroom.

As wide as the lodge itself, the ballroom was a cavernous place, with a high ceiling and a glossy hardwood floor that even now shimmered faintly in the dim electric lighting. On the far side was a stage where surprisingly big-name bands came to play, bringing in the crowds from Cincinnati, Dayton, Columbus, and even Louisville and Lexington, Kentucky. The air seemed to reverberate with the music that had bounced off these walls for years, and as I stood there staring, I could sense the presence of carefree couples dancing the Charleston and the Lindy Hop, the waltz and the fox-trot.

I had often gone to school dances with my friends, where

we were asked to dance by boys we didn't like. We accepted anyway and spent the time looking over their shoulders at the boys we longed to have ask us, but who never did. Nevertheless, I enjoyed dancing. I'd learned how to waltz along with everyone else as part of the physical education requirement in school. Once I was paired up with Scott Hampton, one of the handsome boys I contemplated from afar. I didn't want the song to end. I wanted to go on feeling what it was to have my hand on his shoulder, his arm around my waist, our other hands meeting palm to palm as we slid around the freshly waxed gym floor. Scott Hampton had never spoken to me before, and he didn't speak to me even then, but that was all right. While the song lasted I could pretend he had asked me out to the floor, that the look on his face had been one of delight rather than agony when my name was called with his.

A portable phonograph sat on the edge of the stage and, curious, I went to it. It was a big wooden box of a player, an RCA Victrola that looked brand-new, a far cry from the old gramophone back in our Edgecombe Court apartment that pumped out scratchy music through an ancient morning-glory horn. I looked at the record on the turntable. *Viennese Waltzes*. Perfect.

I turned the knob and lowered the needle. I shut my eyes, raised my arms, and imagined myself in Scott Hampton's embrace. I began to twirl, slowly at first, but then more rapidly, knowing the whole room was mine. Alone yet not alone, I moved with my imaginary lover in wide circles around the floor.

Oh, Scott! Oh, darling! You dance divinely. . . .

Oh! With a jolt, I found myself tumbling face-forward and

landing with a thud on the floor. I'd backed into someone or something, but I couldn't imagine what. Stunned, I shook my head and pulled in a deep breath. I let the air out in a quiet moan as I turned over and sat.

An extended hand slipped into my field of vision. When I looked up, I fell back on one elbow and stifled a scream. Marlene had been telling the truth. The red-eyed devil was standing over me, looking for all the world as though he was ready to pounce.

Chapter 4

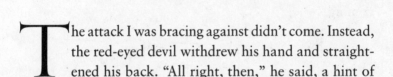

The attack I was bracing against didn't come. Instead, the red-eyed devil withdrew his hand and straightened his back. "All right, then," he said, a hint of annoyance in his voice, "you can just get yourself up."

My muscles relaxed, except for those between my eyes that pulled my brow into a frown. "I . . ."

"You're not hurt, are you?"

"Um, no, I don't think so. I—"

He lifted his chin and started to move away. I knew what he was, but I'd never seen one before and I hadn't expected to see one now. That's what startled me. I pushed myself up from the floor.

Abruptly, he swung around. "Just who are you anyway? And what are you doing here in the ballroom? It's off-limits during the summer season, you know. You can do your dancing on the island like everyone else."

"Listen," I said, "I'm sorry. I'm Eve Marryat. I just came in here because I couldn't sleep and—"

"Oh yeah," he said. "I know the name." He nodded

slightly, the dim light in the room illuminating his pale skin, his stark white hair. Combed straight back without a part, his hair was a ghostly halo on top of his narrow face. Central to that face were the two crimson eyes, glowing like rubies on a bed of lambs' wool. He wore a washed-out gray shirt that was several shades darker than his skin and a pair of weathered denim pants held up with black suspenders. It was hard to tell, but I guessed him to be a few years older than I was.

When he didn't go on, I said, "I'm Cyrus's niece."

"Yeah." He nodded again. "I know. He said you were coming."

"And you are . . . ?"

"Jones."

"Jones?"

"That's right. Jones."

My frown returned. I was trying not to stare at those strange red eyes, but the sight of them unnerved me. I slowly became aware that my thumbs were rubbing my index fingers like worry stones. "What's your first name?" I asked.

"That *is* my first name. It was my mother's maiden name." He said this as he walked to the phonograph and lifted the needle from the record. The room was suddenly, jarringly quiet. He turned off the phonograph and put the lid down as though to tell me it was off-limits.

But I wasn't paying much attention. I was trying to connect the dots as I followed him to the stage. "Your mother?" I said. "Wait. You don't mean Cora?"

"Yeah, I do. So?"

"You're her son?"

"That's right. What about it?"

"How come I never heard of you?"

He lifted his shoulders, seemingly indifferent. "Beats me."

"You weren't here for the wedding. You weren't here when she married Uncle Cy."

"That's right, I wasn't. I was still in Chicago. I was staying with relatives because I had pneumonia."

"So when did you come down?"

"About a month later, I guess. I don't really remember. Why?"

"No one ever mentioned you."

"So?"

"Well, it's a pretty big secret, isn't it? I mean, you've been here five years and Uncle Cy never told us about you?"

"It's no secret, just because you don't mention someone."

I found myself momentarily speechless. My fingers were becoming sore from the rubbing. I willed myself to stop but wasn't sure what to do with my hands. "Well, I mean, you're family, right? Isn't Uncle Cy your stepfather?"

He shrugged. "Sure. If you want to put it that way."

"Then that means we're step-cousins. Right?"

"I suppose we are," he said, though he sounded reluctant to agree.

"And you live here? At the lodge?"

"Yeah." He nodded toward Uncle Cy's apartment behind the ballroom. "I live and work here. What do you expect?"

"Well, I'm just wondering . . . what else don't we know?"

"What do you mean?"

"What else hasn't Uncle Cy told us?"

"Beats me. And if I knew, I wouldn't tell you."

We locked eyes a moment, his growing narrow as I slowly moved my head from side to side. "Listen," I said, "I'm sorry

I was afraid at first. It's just . . . well, I wasn't expecting to run into anyone."

"Yeah? Especially not someone like me, huh?"

"Well, I . . ."

"You've probably never even seen someone like me before, have you?"

I hesitated only a moment before answering truthfully. "No, I haven't. Not that I haven't heard of people like you. That is, I know there are people like you, even though I've never seen one or seen a picture or even thought very much about them. I . . ." I stopped. This wasn't going well. My nervousness was tying my tongue up in knots. I took a deep breath. "Look," I said, "why don't we start over? It's very nice to meet you, Jones."

His features stiffened into a sneer. He took one step back. "Yeah," he said. "I bet."

He turned and walked away without saying another word.

Chapter 5

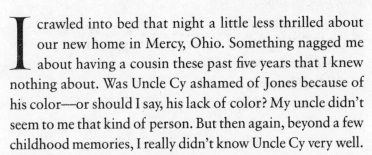

I crawled into bed that night a little less thrilled about our new home in Mercy, Ohio. Something nagged me about having a cousin these past five years that I knew nothing about. Was Uncle Cy ashamed of Jones because of his color—or should I say, his lack of color? My uncle didn't seem to me that kind of person. But then again, beyond a few childhood memories, I really didn't know Uncle Cy very well.

I slept a fitful sleep and awoke the next morning to the sound of Mother tapping on the bedroom door. "Time to get up, Eve," she called softly. "They're starting to serve breakfast now."

Twenty minutes later, I found Mother and Daddy sipping coffee at one of the tables in the dining room. Daddy smiled at me. "Sleep well, darling?"

"Not really." I snapped open the linen napkin at my place and laid it across my lap.

"What's the matter? Too excited to sleep?"

"No." Leaning forward, I shook my head and lowered my voice. "I found out something you're not going to believe."

Mother settled her coffee cup in the saucer and looked at me warily. "What is it, Eve?"

In my best conspiratorial whisper, I informed them, "Uncle Cy has a stepson and he lives here at the lodge." I topped off my announcement with a nod.

Mother and Daddy glanced at each other. Daddy said, "Do you mean the boy Jones?"

I leaned back in the chair, dumbfounded. This was not the reaction I had expected. "You know about him?"

"Well," Daddy said, "we don't really know anything about him, but I remember hearing him mentioned at the wedding. He's Cora's son."

"That's right. So how come no one ever told me?"

Daddy's brow went up as he shrugged. "I suppose we thought you knew."

"Well, I didn't."

Mother poured herself more coffee from the pot on the table. "We're sorry, honey. We weren't trying to keep any secrets from you. It's just that we haven't been in touch with Daddy's side of the family very much. Not like we should have been these past few years."

I looked from Mother to Daddy and back again. "Then why are we here?"

Daddy frowned at that. He picked up his spoon and began stirring imaginary sugar in his coffee. "All I can tell you," he said, "is what you already know. Your Uncle Cy was good enough to help out—temporarily—until things get better for us. Now the honest truth is, it seems like Cyrus, Luther, and I have been fighting about one thing or another since the day we were born. Maybe that's just the way it is among brothers sometimes. I don't know. But maybe too this is a chance for us to mend some fences. Heaven knows if that happens, our parents would die from the shock of it, if they hadn't passed on already. But I'm at least willing to give it a try."

"But I just don't understand it, Daddy," I said, shaking my head. "You're the best man I know. You're good to everyone. How could you and Uncle Cy ever argue about anything?"

"Well, darling," Daddy said, putting down the spoon and patting my hand, "no one's perfect. Not even your old man."

"Maybe not, Daddy, but you're as close to perfect as anyone I know."

While Daddy and I shared a smile, Mother said, "So how did you happen to find out about Jones, Eve?"

My smile slipped away as I turned to Mother. "Last night I decided to look around the lodge, and I just ran into him." *Quite literally,* I thought, but I wasn't about to admit to Mother and Daddy that I was dancing with an imaginary lover in the ballroom.

At that moment a young woman showed up at our table with an icy pitcher of fresh-squeezed orange juice. She bade us good morning and chatted amiably as she poured us each a glass. I took a long swallow; it tasted heavenly, so much better than the canned orange juice the milkman brought to our door in St. Paul.

"Will I be waitressing here like she is?" I asked after she left.

"You might," Mother said, "if they need someone to fill in. But not today."

"Cyrus told us this morning that he's opening the Island Eatery today," Daddy explained. "Summer's here and it's time to get it under way. You can help us with that. Looks like the Eatery is where Mother and I will be spending most of our time this summer, serving up hamburgers and soda pop. Sounds like fun, huh?"

"Sure," I said with a nod.

"The rowboats and canoes will be coming out of storage too. We'll be responsible for the rental of those."

As Daddy spoke, the romance of the island came back, and I forgot about family squabbles and my strange and previously unknown cousin named Jones. I was glad once again to be living at Marryat Island Lodge, where families came to play and life was good and surely some faint scent of Eden still lingered in the sweet clean air.

We spent the day, along with a couple of other workers, cleaning and stocking the Island Eatery, a cinderblock building painted pale green and fronted by a breezeway, where patrons could eat at concrete tables. We polished the grill, readied the soda machine, oiled the popcorn maker, laid out condiments, filled the walk-in freezer with hamburger patties, hot dogs, and tubs of ice cream. Folks came to the counter looking for refreshments; we had to turn them away with the promise we'd be ready for business by five in the evening.

While I was sweeping the breezeway sometime in the early afternoon, an overturned canoe passed by, carried on the shoulders of two young men. One of the men was wearing only a swimsuit, the trunks a solid black, the top a black-and-white stripe. In contrast the other fellow was fully clothed; he wore the long-sleeved gray shirt, denim pants, and black suspenders I'd seen in the ballroom the night before. When the men heaved the boat off their shoulders and onto the boat rest, I saw that Jones was also wearing dark glasses and a broad-brimmed safari hat. Other than his hands, very little of his skin was exposed to the sun, not even his feet, on which he wore a pair of white tennis shoes.

"Mother, come here a minute," I hollered. She looked up from one of the tables where she sat stuffing paper napkins into aluminum holders. She put the napkins aside and joined me where I stood. "That's Jones," I said with a nod toward the boat rest. "The one in the hat and suspenders. He's—" I stopped. For some reason I was finding it difficult to say the word.

"He's what, Eve?" Mother asked.

I let the word escape on a sigh. "He's albino. Did you know that? His hair is completely white, and his eyes are the fieriest shade of red you could imagine. Did Uncle Cy tell you?"

Mother shook her head slowly. "No, he didn't. He never said a word. Then again, Cy never told us much about Jones at all." She gazed at Jones and seemed deep in thought. Finally she said, "Pity. His eyes might have at least been blue, like some of them."

"Blue?" I echoed.

"Some albinos have blue eyes," she said absently. After another moment, she shook her head again, as though to shake away her thoughts. "But it doesn't matter, does it? That he's albino, I mean?"

"Of course not," I answered dutifully.

She smiled at me. "We can look forward to getting to know him."

Good luck, I thought, remembering my encounter with him the night before.

Mother stepped away, then turned back. "You know, Eve, he probably has a hard time of it, being different the way he is."

"I know, Mother. Maybe that's why he's so . . ."

"So what, Eve?"

I wanted to say rude, but Mother wouldn't like it. "Shy," I said. "He seems rather timid."

"Well, then, we'll make sure to let him know he's part of the family, won't we?"

I nodded. Sometimes it was hard to be my parents' daughter, but I wanted to think I was up to the challenge.

At about nine o'clock that evening I was passing by the front desk on my way up to my room when Uncle Cy stopped me. Another man, one of the night clerks, was behind the desk with him.

"Wait just a second, will you, Eve?" Uncle Cy dropped a stack of thick manila folders into a cardboard box and closed the flaps. He handed the box to the night clerk. "Okay, Thomas," he said, "this old tax stuff is ready for storage. Take it on up to the attic, will you? One more box to add to the clutter." He winked at me. "But we've got to keep it in case the IRS ever starts breathing down our necks. Got to have all our ducks in a row for the feds, you know."

Thomas, bald and bespectacled, nodded and took the box. Without a word, he slipped around the desk and headed up the stairs.

"How do you get to the attic, Uncle Cy?" I asked.

Uncle Cy, already busy gathering another pile of papers, didn't look up. "You know where the VIP suite is, right?"

I thought a moment, reaching back into childhood memories. "It's at the opposite end of the hall from my room, isn't it?"

"That's right." He nodded. "That's where I stick the big-wigs and the people who think they're bigwigs. Well, the door to the right of that door, that's how you get up to the attic. I don't recommend you going up there, though, especially if you're allergic to dust."

I shrugged. "I'd rather spend my time in the suite. From what I remember, those are the prettiest rooms in the lodge."

"Smart kid. And don't worry. You'll see the suite plenty, once you start helping the maids clean the rooms."

"That wasn't exactly what I had in mind, Uncle Cy!" I tried to sound stern but laughed instead.

Uncle Cy smiled good-naturedly as he bundled the papers with a clip. "Now, listen, Eve honey"—he waved the papers at me and looked annoyed when the phone rang—"do me a favor, will you? Take these invoices to Jones."

"To Jones?"

He nodded and picked up the receiver. "Good evening. Marryat Island Lodge. Cyrus Marryat speaking."

He listened to whoever was on the other end of the line. I took the invoices and whispered, "But where is he?"

Uncle Cy put his hand over the mouthpiece and nodded over his shoulder. "In the apartment."

"But—"

Uncle Cy cut me off with a wave of his hand, pulled the guest register from beneath the front desk, and started flipping through it.

I frowned at the invoices. I really didn't want to carry them to Jones. So far, he wasn't anybody I liked very much, and besides, I had worked hard at the Eatery all day and I was tired, too tired to deal with anyone as surly and ill-mannered as this newfound cousin of mine. But I remembered what

Mother had said, that we needed to make him feel like part of the family, so I resolved to deliver them willingly and perhaps even wish Jones a good-night.

I clenched my teeth as I made my way through the sitting room, down the hall, through the ballroom, and into yet another hall that led to Uncle Cy's apartment. The door was open, so I paused to look inside. From what I could see of the room, it was sparsely furnished with a couple of wing chairs, a bookcase, and a long dining room table pushed up against one wall. The hardwood floor was dull and rutted with scrapes and scratches. Dark heavy drapes hung in the window. A few paintings and framed photographs adorned the walls. Other than that the room was nearly devoid of a woman's touch, and I wondered why Aunt Cora hadn't tried to make it more homey and cheerful.

Jones sat at the dining room table in one of its accompanying ladder-back chairs. Every inch of the tabletop was consumed by clutter: coils of wire, vacuum tubes, batteries, dials, and any number of unidentifiable parts belonging to an odd collection of radios in various stages of assembly and disassembly. On the upper left corner of the table was a small pile of books. Wearing a pair of dark-framed glasses, Jones leaned over a pad of paper. In his right hand was a pencil poised for note taking, but instead of writing he appeared to be listening. A woman's singsong voice drifted from the large cathedral radio directly in front of him; I strained to hear and caught something about sugarplums and teddy bears and the noontime train to Wonderland. As she spoke, Jones intermittently scribbled a few words before pausing to listen again.

I wasn't sure what to do, but after a moment Jones snapped

off the radio and continued scribbling. When I knocked on the doorframe, he sat up so abruptly his chair jumped several inches. He turned to look at me with his crimson eyes greatly magnified by the glasses.

"What do you want?" he asked.

My jaw clenched again. I stepped into the room. "A little old for bedtime stories, aren't you?" I said.

He looked at the radio and back at me. "I was just testing the clarity. I've been teaching myself about electronics, mostly radio, as you can probably see. I'm not going to work at the lodge the rest of my life, you know." A few seconds passed in which neither of us spoke. He took off his glasses and laid them on the table. "So did you want something?"

I had almost forgotten my reason for coming. "Uncle Cy said to give you these."

"Invoices?"

"Yes."

He nodded toward a rolltop desk on the other side of the room. "You can add them to the pile there."

I moved to the desk and laid the invoices down among several stacks of bills, receipts, and ledgers. "Do you keep the books for the lodge?"

"Yes," he said. "Among other things."

"Like carrying canoes?"

He almost smiled. "Whatever needs doing."

"A jack-of-all-trades, then?"

"I suppose. Though mostly I'm here taking care of paper work."

We locked eyes then, and for several long seconds we seemed to be sizing each other up. Finally he said, "Anything else?"

I started to shake my head and turn away, but I stopped. "Yes," I said. "I wanted to tell you I'm sorry your mother's sick and I hope she gets better soon."

Where that sentiment came from, I didn't know. Jones looked suspicious as well. But after a moment his face seemed to relax and he said, "Thank you. I'm sure she'll be better before long."

"You must miss her."

He nodded but didn't reply.

"So you're learning how to put radios together?" I stepped closer to the table, and when I did, Jones closed up the notepad and pushed it aside.

"Yes," he said. "I have a knack for things like that."

"I see." My eyes swept the table as I tried to think of something else to say. I wanted to learn more about this mysterious person, but my mind was a blank slate, and I couldn't find any words. "Well," I said at length, "I'd better go. Good night, Jones."

He looked at me another moment. Then he nodded, one small lift of his chin. "Yup," he said. He turned back to the table, put on his glasses, picked up a tool of some sort, and went to work. Our conversation was finished, and I had been dismissed.

Chapter 6

Several days passed and Mother, Daddy, and I quickly became accustomed to our new life. The local public schools let out and summer settled into full swing, meaning Marryat Island was hopping. People came from all over Ohio and Kentucky and even farther away to spend a weekend or several days or maybe a week at the lodge. Poverty was on the rise in a way the country had seldom seen, but plenty of people still had money.

With the official arrival of summer, our jitney bus added several runs to its usual back-and-forth route between the lodge and the train station. Sometimes I'd ride along to greet the guests and make them feel welcome, one of my favorite jobs. I enjoyed chatting with our jitney driver, a kindly Negro man by the name of Morris Tweed. He was the husband of one of our cooks, Annie Tweed, whose infectious laughter permeated the kitchen, sweet as the cinnamon rolls she baked up fresh every morning.

I didn't have any one job at the lodge; each day I simply did what needed doing. I helped Mother and Daddy in the

Eatery. I washed dishes with Annie; I waited tables, cleaned rooms, put freshly washed linens away in the linen closet. I swept the front porch, made change for boat rentals, showed guests to their rooms. When those who had driven to the lodge asked about a car wash, I directed them to the service station across the street, owned and operated by an old friend of Uncle Cy's by the name of Calvin Fludd. In my spare time, I was allowed to enjoy the island or walk into town or join a game of croquet or volleyball on the lawn.

Never had I been so happy and at peace. Occasionally I thought about my old life and the friends I'd left behind, especially my best friend Ariel, who wrote me weepy letters about how much she missed me. I missed her too, and yet, that life seemed far away and like the torn edges of an early morning dream. The lodge and the island were my real life. This was the place I was meant to be, and I had little desire to look back at what I'd left behind.

On our first Saturday in Mercy, I was enjoying an early afternoon swim when I saw Marlene. She waved at me from the shore and then splashed her way to my side.

"I see you've finally braved the water," she said with a laugh.

"Yes. It's wonderful!"

"I'm afraid I can't remember your name."

"I don't think I ever told you. It's Eve. Eve Marryat. And you're Marlene, right?"

"Yes, Marlene Quimby. For a little while, anyway."

She took a deep breath and sank beneath the surface then came up shaking water off her curls. She threw up her arms and said, "You know what's really wonderful, Eve?"

I had to smile at her enthusiasm. "No, what?" I asked.

"I'm free!" She pushed up on her toes and floated on her back, her face lifted to the sun.

"What do you mean, you're free?"

"I have officially graduated. The ceremony was yesterday. I am finished with school forever!" She kicked her feet and paddled around in circles.

"Good for you," I said. "So what will you do now?"

"Get married, I hope."

"Get married?" I echoed. "Are you crazy?"

"Yes, yes, yes, I'm crazy!" she cried, emphasizing each word with a splash of her arms. "Crazy for my boy Jimmy."

"But you're too young to get married."

She stopped paddling, looked at me, and laughed again. "I'm eighteen! I'm old enough. How old are you?"

"Seventeen."

"So you haven't graduated?"

"No, I have one more year."

She poked out her lower lip playfully. "Poor you."

I shrugged. "After high school, I intend to go to college."

"Whatever for?"

"To earn a degree."

"A degree in what?"

"I don't know yet. Something that helps people."

"Phooey!" she said. "You'll end up getting married like everyone else."

I frowned and shook my head. "I don't think so. I don't want to get married. I intend to have a career."

She sank under the water and popped up again. "Well, Eve Marryat," she said, "I've just learned something about you."

"What?"

"You're a liar!" She laughed loudly and down she went again.

I wasn't sure whether to be offended or to laugh along with her. I decided to let it go. When she broke through the surface of the water, I asked, "So when are you getting married?"

She sighed an exaggerated sigh. "I don't know for sure."

"Well, are you engaged?"

"Not officially, no."

"So whoever this Jimmy is, he hasn't asked you to marry him?"

"Not yet. But he will. And soon, I think."

"Well, if that's what you want, then I hope you get it." I was telling the truth. She seemed incredibly happy and her joy was infectious. We shared a smile. "By the way, Marlene, I met the red-eyed devil."

She stopped splashing and gave me a disbelieving look. "You did? What happened?"

"Nothing. We talked."

"You talked? What did he say?"

I thought about her question, my mind flipping through the catalogue of what Jones had said: *You can just pick yourself up off the floor. . . . Don't dance in the ballroom. . . . I'm learning to fix radios. . . . I bet you've never seen anyone like me. . . .*"

Nothing seemed right. So I simply said, "We're cousins."

Her wide eyes grew even wider. "You're what?"

"Well, step-cousins."

"You mean . . ." She looked around at the others splashing in the water near us and lowered her voice. "You're related to that freak?"

I drew back. "He's no freak. He's very nice. Well, mostly, anyway."

"But how can he be your cousin?"

"My Uncle Cy is married to his mother."

"You mean that Cora lady?"

"Yes, Cora. She's my aunt."

Another glance around, another whisper. "She has the consumption, you know."

"I know. But Uncle Cy has sent her to the finest sanitarium in the East. She'll be all right."

Marlene eyed me warily. "Well," she said, "this *is* a surprise. Who knew the devil was Mr. Marryat's stepson? He's only seen around here once in a blue moon, you know, and even then he's all covered up from head to toe. Only a few people have seen his eyes. I never have and I hope I never do." She paused long enough to shiver dramatically. "Most people assume he's some sort of hired help. You know, like Mr. Marryat feels sorry for him, so he allows him to work here and sleep in the attic or something."

"He doesn't sleep in the attic," I said, rolling my eyes at her.

"How was I to know? No one really knows anything about him."

"Maybe you would, if you talked to him."

"He's the one who won't talk to anybody. He looks at the ground when he walks, like he wants to pass people by without being seen."

"Listen, Marlene, he has a name, you know. It's Jones, and I bet he'd talk to you if you said something to him. Anything. Just hello. You could give it a try."

She smiled, shrugged. "Well, maybe. If I ever run into him."

"You're not afraid, are you?"

"Of course not." She laughed, but it didn't sound convincing.

Before I could say anything else, Mother appeared on the shore and called my name. "We could use your help for a minute in the Eatery," she hollered. "We have a question about the supply list."

"All right," I hollered back, "I'll be right there."

Before I could take a step toward shore, Marlene leaped toward me and grabbed my hands. "Listen, Eve, we're going to be great friends. I just know we are. And I want you to meet Jimmy. Tonight!"

"Tonight?"

"Yes. There's going to be a band playing in the pavilion, isn't there?"

I nodded. Uncle Cy was bringing in the first band of the summer season, a well-known group from Cincinnati.

"I'll bring Jimmy and you can meet him, all right?"

"Sure," I said.

"And he can . . ." Her face grew animated and she laughed.

"He can what?"

"Nothing," she said, shaking her head. "You'll see. Just come looking pretty and be ready to dance."

"With Jimmy?"

She laughed again and swam away. I shook my head and moved toward shore.

Chapter 7

At dusk, Alonzo Martin and His Band assembled in the pavilion and, with one quick wave of Alonzo's hand, broke the quiet of the night with the first jump-crazy notes of "Keep a Song in Your Soul." Those horn-blowing, banjo-strumming, piano-pounding musicians pumped out some kind of dynamism, because all at once the dance floor was rushed by a fox-trotting crowd of couples bebopping all over the place.

I stood off to the side, tapping my foot and nodding my head as I waited for Marlene and her boyfriend to show up. Twenty minutes went by before I felt a hand on my shoulder and knew she had finally arrived. She was dressed in a shiny orange chemise with a string of knotted pearls around her neck and a pair of black strapped heels on her feet. She was arm in arm with a young man wearing a casual shirt and slacks, his thick blond hair slicked back with pomade. He had a narrow face with pleasant blue eyes, a slightly too-large nose, and a smile that formed heartthrob dimples in his cheeks.

"Eve," Marlene said, speaking loudly over the music, "I want you to meet Jimmy. Jimmy, this is Eve, the one I told you about. Her uncle owns the lodge."

Jimmy nodded and said, "Nice to meet you. So Cyrus is your uncle, huh?"

"That's right," I answered. "Do you know him?"

The young man laughed. "Sure I do. Everybody knows Cyrus. Him and my dad go way back. My dad owns the gas station across the street."

"Oh yeah. He's—"

"Calvin Fludd. Yup. Me and Marcus work for him."

"Marcus?"

Marlene stood on tiptoe and scanned the crowd. "Speaking of which, where'd he go?"

"There he is." Jimmy pointed with a thumb. "Talking with Spencer Girton over there. Probably up to their usual no-good."

"Oh, hush, Jimmy. The son of the sheriff is hardly going to be up to no-good. Marcus!" Marlene hollered, waving one long white slender arm. "Marcus!"

The young man heard his name, said a parting word to Spencer Girton, and headed toward us. As he weaved his way through the crowd, I felt my breath come up short and my heart pump itself into a momentary spasm. If he had stepped right out of a Hollywood film, he couldn't have been any more good-looking. He was an easy shoo-in for Rudolph Valentino, tall and lean, with a face so achingly handsome I had to fight the urge to turn and run. I knew what was happening. I was being set up. *He* was being set up. With me. And that could only spell disaster.

"There you are, you rascal," Marlene said coyly.

"Sorry about that." He smiled apologetically.

"I want you to meet Eve Marryat."

When those two dark eyes settled on my face, it all came raining down, all the things Cassandra had said to me over all the years. I had tried to tamp it down into some unused corner of my soul, but under the gaze of this Greek god I knew every word was true. I was the typical ugly duckling, the mean-faced little rat, the luckless wench who would inevitably hurl headlong into a lost and lonely spinsterhood.

"And Eve, this is Marcus Wiant."

I lifted my eyes to his then and felt a burning crimson creep up my neck and fan out across my face. I became keenly aware of my dress, not a clingy orange flapper slip like Marlene's but a simple blue cotton going-to-church dress with a white eyelet collar and a fringe of matching eyelet around the sleeves and hem of the skirt. When I'd put it on, it was fine, but now it was all wrong. What would Marcus think?

"Very nice to meet you, Eve," he said politely.

"You . . . you too." *Bumbling idiot!* I willed myself to stay, though my feet were still yearning to flee.

"Well, what are we doing standing around?" Marlene cried jubilantly. "Come on, Jimmy, let's dance!"

I was left alone with Rudolph Valentino or Marcus Wiant or whoever he was, someone who would undoubtedly give Marlene the business come morning for setting him up on this miserable blind date. Shame, fear, and dread came over me, and I wanted to apologize for what Marlene had done, but before I could form the sentence in my mind and deliver the words to my lips, the young man shrugged, flashed a shy smile, and said, "Shall we?"

He held out a hand and waited to escort me to the floor.

I looked at that hand and wanted to take it with my own, but I was paralyzed by a deep sense of inadequacy. "I don't know any fancy steps," I said, and even as I said it I heard Cassandra laugh, which made me want to scream loud and long into the clear star-studded sky.

Marcus, still smiling, shrugged again. "Perfect," he said. "I don't know any fancy steps either."

The next thing I knew I was in his arms and we were moving around the dance floor like we'd been dancing together all our lives. Before the song was over I fancied myself the happiest girl on Marryat Island. And before the song was over, I saw Jones standing in the shadows, shoulders hunched and hands in his pockets, staring at me with his piercing red eyes like fiery arrows hurled across the night.

Chapter 8

Sunday evenings were quiet on Marryat Island. After supper, in the cool of approaching dusk, I wandered down to the island and stepped into one of the rowboats tied up to the dock. It bobbed gently under my weight as I sat on the seat between the oars. I lowered my chin to the palms of my hands and drifted into thoughts about Marcus.

We'd danced till the end, till the band laid down their instruments and everyone headed toward home. We danced for three hours thinking only minutes had gone by, and then he walked me to the lodge and said good-night. I wondered whether that was what it was to be in love. Was it being so thoroughly happy that the joy seemed unbreakable?

Never having been in love, I didn't know. And I wasn't sure I was going to find out, because I didn't know whether the night was a one-time affair or whether I'd see Marcus Wiant again. He was unfailingly polite and a proper gentleman, thanking me for a good time and then letting me go with neither a kiss nor a promise of anything more to come. The kiss I was relieved to do without, but I would have liked to know whether he might come around another time.

So lost was I to thought, I didn't hear the footsteps on the dock, nor see anyone approach till someone said, "If you're taking that thing out, you might want to find someone to go with you."

Startled, I looked up to find Jones standing over me, his safari hat pulled down over his brow, its long strap dangling low beneath his chin. He wore dark glasses, a long-sleeved button-up shirt, and a pair of cotton slacks, minus the suspenders. His startlingly white feet were bare. I looked from him, to the river, and back again. "Well," I said, "I don't guess I was planning on taking it out."

"Then why are you sitting in it?"

Why indeed? Because it seemed a good place to think about Marcus? I shrugged. "I don't know," I said. "Does someone need it?"

"Yeah."

"Who?"

"I do."

"You do?"

"I enjoy rowing the river in the evenings, if that's all right with you."

"Well, of course it's all right with me," I said testily, "but there are plenty of other boats." I waved a hand at them to prove my point.

"I like this one."

I sighed, started to stand. "All right. You can have it."

"No, don't get out."

"Don't get out?"

"Just move up to the bow and let me sit there."

I hesitated a moment. "You mean, you want me to go with you?"

"Don't you like boats?"

"Sure I do."

"Then sit down."

I moved to the bow and sat down. For one brief moment I wondered what Marcus would think if he saw me out on the river in a boat with Jones, but I dismissed the thought. Jones was my cousin, after all. My cousin of a sort, anyway.

Jones untied the rope anchoring the boat to the dock. He stepped in and settled onto the seat I had just vacated. "I can get more exercise if I have somebody weighing down the boat," he said.

"Oh." So that was it. "Well, I'm glad I can help out by being your dead weight."

He nodded, as though I was serious. Fastening the oars into the oarlocks, he pushed us away from the dock and began to row. Because I was at the front of the boat, he was sitting with his back to me, as if I weren't there at all. If he'd told me to sit on the other end of the boat, we'd have at least been facing each other, though perhaps that wasn't how he wanted it.

For several minutes he moved us along at a generous clip. I watched, mesmerized as the oars dipped in and out of the river. Every time they came up, they dripped great pearls of river water before they quickly sank down again. Their sweeping motion formed small whirlpools that circled momentarily on the surface of the water before drifting off and dying out. I dipped one hand over the side of the boat and let it linger in the water; my fingers cut a small wake into the river.

"This is really nice," I said, "being out here like this."

He didn't answer. After a time he rowed less vigorously, and we moved at a more leisurely pace down a long stretch of river. I hugged my knees and breathed deeply of the cool air. I watched as a trio of sparrows soared on an upward draft. I searched the sky for the first sign of stars, but it was too early yet for anything other than a translucent hint of the moon.

We slowed down enough that we were overtaken by a couple of punts, flat-bottom boats with square-cut bows. Each was navigated by a man standing on the deck of the stern, pushing the boat along with a pole. The men wore unseasonably warm jackets and tweed caps, and in the hull of both boats were several wooden boxes labeled castor oil.

As they passed us, one of the men touched the brim of his cap and gave a nod in greeting. Jones nodded in return. I watched as the punts moved on down the river ahead of us.

In an attempt at conversation, as heaven knew Jones wasn't very good at it, I said, "Now where do you suppose they're going?"

Jones pushed his hat back a notch and looked over his shoulder after the two boats. "The Little Miami meets up with the Ohio River not too far from here," he said. "That's probably where they're headed."

"Funny that they're taking a bunch of castor oil down the Ohio River."

Jones turned again to look at me. I couldn't see his eyes, but somehow I sensed they held amusement. My suspicions were confirmed when he shook his head and laughed. "Castor oil, nothing," he muttered. "They're hauling moonshine."

For a moment I was speechless. I frowned and wondered whether I had heard him right. "Moonshine?"

"Sure. People like them are up and down this river all the time."

It can't be, I thought. This was Ohio, after all, birthplace of the Temperance Movement. I knew. I had done the research. I had won first place in the essay contest. "Are you sure?"

"Of course I'm sure."

"Don't they know moonshine is illegal?"

Jones laughed again, louder this time. "You're kidding, right?"

"I'm not kidding, Jones. I can't believe they're hauling that stuff right out here in the open. They could be arrested and go to prison. They *should* be arrested."

"Yeah? And who's going to turn them in? You?"

I drew back. I didn't know how to respond. "You mean, nobody does anything about it? Nobody tries to shut down the stills?"

"And just what would people drink if they shut down the stills?"

"But that's the point! People shouldn't be drinking anything at all. Aren't there any Prohibition agents around here?"

"Of course not. There aren't enough agents for the big cities, let alone a little Podunk town like Mercy. Anyway, it's a losing battle. There's stills all over the county. Too many to count."

"But Prohibition is the law!"

"A stupid law, itching to be broken."

"It's not a stupid law. It's one law that makes completely good sense."

"And who are you? Carrie Nation? You go around with an axe chopping up saloons?"

"Maybe I would if there were any saloons to chop up!"

"Well, there aren't. They've all gone underground and turned themselves into speakeasies and blind pigs. And believe me, someone like you would never get in."

"I wouldn't want to get in! I don't believe in drinking. All it does is ruin people's lives."

He stared at me a moment, brows turned down, nostrils flaring. "I guess Cyrus forgot to tell me you were a saint."

"You don't need to be sarcastic just because I believe in obeying the law. But then, I wouldn't drink even if the country were wet again. It's just a sin, plain and simple, and it leads to no good."

"You're all-fired sure about that, are you?"

I lifted my chin. "I am."

"And how do you know so much about it?"

I thought about Cassandra. I thought about the drunks down at the St. Paul Mission. I thought about the gangsters that wreaked havoc, killing each other and even innocent bystanders over the selling of illegal booze. "I've seen it," I said. "I've seen what it does to people. But folks keep on drinking because other people, terrible people, keep on making illegal liquor and selling it."

"Now hold on just one minute there, St. Eve," Jones spat out. He pulled the oars into the boat and turned around on the seat to face me. "I'd wager those two men who just went by aren't terrible people. I'd wager they're not bad people at all. They're just a couple of men trying to feed their families, and they got no other way to do it except to sell spirits to people who want an occasional drink. If it's between making moonshine and letting their kids starve, they're right to choose moonshine, and you're wrong to judge them."

Looking away, I could taste the disgust at the back of my

throat like something sour. "There are other ways to make a living," I said.

"It's not all that easy, especially now, times being what they are."

"The times being what they are isn't an excuse to do what's wrong. If everybody would obey the law and work together, I'm sure we'd be able to find jobs for everyone. Or at least make sure no one goes hungry. People don't have to resort to crime to stay alive."

"Selling liquor wouldn't be a crime if we got rid of the law. Then people could just go about their business and take care of their families."

"But it's the law and—"

"You sound like that man who said he believes the law can regulate morality and make upstanding citizens out of everybody."

"His name is Volstead, and that's right, I do agree with him. If people acted decent and nobody drank, this country would be a whole lot better off."

He looked at me a long time. Finally he said, "You mean, if everybody was as perfect as you, this country would be a whole lot better off."

"I didn't say that."

"No, but that's what you meant." He sighed, turned around on the seat, and took up the oars. "You've got a lot to learn about being human, missy," he concluded.

My mouth dropped open. How dare he admonish me when the law was on my side? I was glad he had turned his back to me again, because that way he couldn't see my tears of frustration as we rowed toward home.

Chapter 9

I climbed the stairs to my room with leaden feet, feeling as though my heart had cracked in two. In the short time I was on the river with Jones, the luster of Marryat Island had begun to tarnish. Something was amiss in Paradise. St. Paul was the devil's playground, and I'd left it for a safe place, but the serpent had found its way even here.

Passing by Mother and Daddy's door, I decided to knock and see if they were in for the night. They were. They sat in the room's two overstuffed chairs, drinking tall glasses of iced tea. *Great Expectations* was open facedown on the table between them.

"Going to bed, darling?" Daddy asked.

"Soon, I guess."

Mother gave me that knowing look. "What's the matter, Eve?"

I took a deep breath and let it out slowly. "I just found out something terrible."

"What is it?" Daddy asked, leaning forward in his chair.

Deep furrows cut across his forehead as he gazed up at me with concern.

"I found out . . ." I paused and squeezed my hands together in front of me, "there are stills all over the place around here. People are making moonshine and selling it down the river."

Mother and Daddy were quiet for a long moment. Finally Daddy said, "Well, that comes as no surprise, does it?"

"What do you mean?" I cried, my voice climbing a notch. "Did you know about it before we came here?"

"I think we just assumed . . ." Daddy shrugged. His face relaxed as he leaned back in the chair. "People are making their own liquor all over the country. They have been for years. Even more so since Prohibition started, you know."

"But I didn't think . . ." I squeezed my hands till my knuckles hurt.

"What, darling?"

"I thought it would be different here."

"Why would things be any different here?"

"Well, because . . . because . . ." How to explain? I thought it would be different because I wanted it to be different. I didn't want to be afraid, like I had been in St. Paul.

Mother must have seen the fear in my eyes. "Nothing bad is going to happen here at the lodge, Eve," she said gently.

I looked at her and nodded my reluctant agreement. Surely Mother was right. Surely here we wouldn't see someone mowed down on the sidewalk in front of us, like the man who haunted my dreams. So there were moonshiners moving their goods on the river, but at least there weren't hordes of gangsters killing each other, or robbing banks, or kidnapping the wealthy for exorbitant ransoms.

"Daddy?" I said.

"Yes, Eve?"

"Why can't people just obey the law? Why can't they just be good?"

Daddy thought a moment. "Because there's something deep inside that won't let them, darling."

I shook my head. "But *we're* good. We don't break the law. It's not that hard."

"Well . . ." Daddy paused. He rubbed the side of his face with an open palm. "If you're talking just about Prohibition, then no, it's not that hard for you and me to keep the law. We're not tempted by liquor like some are. That doesn't mean, though, we won't meet temptation in some other way. There's not a man since Adam who hasn't had his share of troubles."

I sighed; I didn't want Daddy to get started on Original Sin. If we were all so bad, why did I find it so easy to be good?

"Well, I guess I'll go to bed," I said. I gave Mother and Daddy each a kiss and wished them sweet dreams. Then I went to my own room, cradling my sense of self-righteousness like a rare and beautiful gift.

After lunch the next day, a couple of Rolls-Royces eased over the graveled drive and came to rest in the far corner of the parking lot. I stopped sweeping the porch and watched slack-jawed as the driver of one of them jumped out and hurried to open the back passenger door. He stood erect as a soldier, eyes away from the lithe figure emerging from the car. The young woman wore a white dress, sleek and clingy, with a fur collar and a filmy waist-length cape. Her bleached blond hair was a ripple of tight marcelled waves that hung just to her jawline. As she lifted a broad-brimmed hat to her head, the gemstone jewelry on her fingers and wrists sparkled and shimmered in the sun.

The driver hurried around to the other side of the car and held open the door for the woman's companion. He was a large fellow wearing a dark double-breasted suit and black-and-white wingtip shoes. A pink carnation was tucked into the buttonhole of his jacket, and a gold watch chain stretched across his ample waist. As he lifted his fedora and dabbed at his forehead with a handkerchief, his bejeweled hand sparkled too like the woman's. He poked the handkerchief—surely it was silk—back into his breast pocket and then held out his arm to the white vision of loveliness that was walking around the car to meet him. They sauntered together toward the lodge as the driver turned back to the car to retrieve their luggage.

Two men from the other Rolls-Royce, well dressed, though not quite so flamboyant, followed behind, each carrying a suitcase.

What, I wondered, were these people doing here?

The lodge was a nice place to visit, so far as that goes, and many of our guests were well off, but surely this man and his wife were used to the kind of luxury that most of us only dreamed of. They belonged in New York, Chicago, London, Paris. Why would they vacation on a tiny provincial island in the middle of an unremarkable river?

I clutched the broom handle and, feeling very much like Cinderella, watched this man, his wife, and his entire entourage—including the suitcase-laden driver—climb the porch steps and enter the front hall. Not one of them so much as glanced at me in passing. I was an insentient part of the scenery, no different from the rocking chairs that lined the porch.

Resting the broom against the railing, I moved to the door and stood just inside the threshold. Uncle Cy was coming around the front desk with his hand extended. "Mr. Sluder! Delighted to see you again." He shook the man's hand vigorously, then turned to the woman and actually offered a small bow. "Mrs. Sluder. I trust your stay with us will be comfortable."

He turned abruptly to the young fellow behind the counter. "Charlie," he snapped, "help Mr. Sluder and his party with their luggage, will you?"

"Yes, sir!" came the quick response. Charlie was someone I'd been introduced to but didn't know well, a college student who helped cover the front desk for Uncle Cy part-time.

"I'm assuming you have Mrs. Sluder and me in our preferred room, Cyrus?" the man asked stiffly.

"Oh yes, indeed," Uncle Cy answered. "The suite, of course. It's ready and waiting for you."

"That's fine." Mr. Sluder patted his wife's hand. "Come along, dear."

"But, George," his wife said, "you haven't asked about refreshments."

"Ah yes. Cyrus, send up some fresh fruit in about thirty minutes, will you?"

"Of course, Mr. Sluder."

I watched our newest guests ascend the stairs like the King and Queen of England. Once they disappeared, I moved across the hall and leaned my arms on the front desk. "Who in the world *is* that man, Uncle Cy?" I asked.

"George Sluder and his wife, Ada. They're regulars here."

"They are?"

Uncle Cy nodded disinterestedly and turned aside to the mail slots. He picked up a pile of letters and started sorting them into the proper cubbyholes.

"Well," I said, "doesn't he have to sign the guest register like everyone else?"

"He can sign later."

"I bet he's got enough money to do whatever he wants, huh? How'd he get to be so rich, anyway?"

Uncle Cy paused and turned back to me. "You ask too many questions, Eve. Don't you have something you're supposed to be doing?"

"I was sweeping the porch before His Highness arrived."

"Then I suggest you get back to it. And Eve, rule number one around here: We don't ask questions about the guests."

I narrowed my eyes at Uncle Cy, but he'd already gone back to sorting the mail. Reluctantly, I finished sweeping the porch then wandered to the kitchen to see if I could do anything for Annie.

"I believe you can, child," she said when I found her. She was wiping a frying pan with a dish towel while she stared out the side window. "I'm going to make up a plate of lunch for that young man out there. You can carry it out to him."

When she stepped away from the window, I took over her spot to see who she meant. A stranger sat on the low stone wall separating the drive from the side yard. He wore tattered overalls, a button-up shirt with the sleeves rolled up, and a pair of weathered boots. I looked quizzically at Annie. "I don't recognize him," I said. "Is he one of the maintenance men?"

Annie shook her head. She lifted her apron to her brow to wipe away the shiny beads of sweat. The faded red kerchief tied around her hair was moist with perspiration. In spite of the heat, her brown eyes danced merrily while she reached for a plate, as though she relished the task at hand. "I haven't seen him before neither," she explained, "but I'm sure he's one of the men from the camp down the river. They got a way of knowing where they can find a hot meal and a cold drink."

"There's a camp by the river?"

"That's right. Been one there for a while now."

"You mean, like a shantytown?"

"That's what it is, child. A shantytown. The railroad runs right by here, you know. That's where the men come from, the rails. Looking for work. Far too little of that, these days." She shook her head again and clicked her tongue as she ladled a thick helping of beef stew onto the plate. She added a piece of bread and butter and handed the plate to me, along with a glass of iced tea. "Tell him just to leave the dishes on the wall when he's finished. Morris knows to bring them in."

"You mean, other men come by here to get a plate of food?"

"All the time." She smiled then, her perfect teeth a sudden flash of white against her russet-colored skin. "They know we'll give it to them. Your uncle's generous that way. Anyone comes looking for food don't go away hungry."

"Really? Uncle Cy says you should feed these people?"

"'Course he does. Mr. Marryat not going to let anyone starve. No sir, not Mr. Marryat. He's different that way."

"What do you mean, Annie?"

"I mean, he pays no mind whether a man is white or Negro, young or old. If that man needs help, Mr. Marryat helps him. Everyone here in Mercy knows that. He's a good man, your uncle."

A small thrill of pride moved up my spine. "I know he is,

Annie," I said. After all, he had taken me and Mother and Daddy in, even when he hadn't seen us in years.

Annie smiled at me again as she nodded toward the door. "Now get on out there 'fore the stew gets cold and the tea gets warm."

I pushed open the kitchen's screen door with my foot and stepped outside. I made my way to the man on the wall and handed the food to him shyly, without a word. In that moment, the difference between him and George Sluder weighed on me heavily. Such wealth in the world, and such hardship. It didn't seem quite right.

He took the plate of food with a nod. "Thank you kindly, miss," he said.

"You're welcome."

He balanced the glass on the wall and started scooping up the stew with the bread.

"I forgot to bring you a fork," I said.

"Don't need one."

"You sure?"

He nodded, swallowed. "By the time you got back, I'd be done."

I studied him quietly while he ate. He was a young man, somewhere just past twenty, I guessed. Though he appeared to have shaved that morning, he was badly in need of a barber. His fair hair hung over his forehead in a tangle of curls and, in the back, crept like stray tendrils over his frayed collar. Other than that, he had pleasant features and clear gray-blue eyes that seemed to sparkle and dance while he ate. He was obviously enjoying the stew and was glad to have it.

"Is it true you live in a shantytown?" I asked, my curiosity trumping common courtesy.

"It's true," he said, not even pausing as he shoveled the stew into his mouth.

"Where is it?"

"Up that way." He indicated the direction with a nod of his head. "Past the mill."

"Oh." I looked up the river, though the mill was too far away to be seen from the lodge. "My uncle owns that mill," I said.

"Yeah? Busy place. You must be rich."

I shook my head. "We're not rich. We're just regular folk."

"You work here?" Now he nodded toward the lodge.

"No. Well, yeah."

He rolled his eyes up from the plate and looked squarely at me. "Well, which is it? You work here or don't you?"

"Yes, I work here but I don't get paid. I live here. My uncle owns the lodge."

"Same uncle as owns the mill?"

"No, a different one. They're brothers."

"Guess you got this town sewn up, huh?"

"What do you mean?"

He tore a hunk off the bread and chewed while he studied me. Then he shrugged. "What's your name?"

"Eve Marryat. What's yours?"

"Everyone just calls me Link."

"Link?"

"That's right."

"You got a last name, Link?"

"Sure. I got a last name like everybody else."

"Can I know what it is?"

He didn't answer. He wiped up the last of the stew with the bread, ate it, and licked his fingers. Leaving the plate and the still-full glass of tea on the wall, he hopped off and stood in front of me. He was so tall I had to put my head back to look up at his face. He picked up the tea and downed it in one long swig. He was wiping his mouth on his sleeve when Morris Tweed drove by in the pickup truck he used for hauling goods from the railroad station.

Link gazed at the truck then looked back at me. I thought he was finally going to tell me his surname, but he must have forgotten I'd asked. "Listen," he said. "You don't happen to have any alky in any of those rooms, do you?"

"Alky?"

"You know." He stuck his thumb to his mouth and tilted his head back as though he were drinking from a bottle. Then he winked.

I took a step backward. Alcohol again! Bad enough to have it floating down the river, but to have someone come around the lodge looking for it—that was even worse. "Of course we don't have alcohol here," I said sternly. "That stuff's illegal."

Link laughed. "So it is," he said. "Not that that ever stops anybody."

"Well, it stops us."

"Does it?" He sat back down on the wall, as though he were expecting dessert. He shrugged. "Now, don't get your feathers all in a ruffle. Just thought I'd ask."

"This is a respectable place."

"I'm sure it is."

"If you're looking for liquor, you can go look somewhere else."

"I wasn't looking for liquor when I came here. I was looking for a good meal and I found one. Give my compliments to the chef, will you? And don't go off in a huff."

I'd started to walk away but I turned back. "You're nothing but a bum, aren't you?"

He smiled. "I'm a bum and a good one, at that."

"Why don't you get a job instead of going around looking for handouts?"

"Plenty of men looking for jobs, little lady. In case you haven't noticed, they're kind of hard to come by these days."

"But you could be out asking around, instead of sitting here doing nothing," I argued.

At that, he glanced one way and then the other, as though looking for an opportunity right there on the grounds of the lodge. To my dismay, he found one. "Tell you what," he said. "Looks like your hired man there is carrying crates down to the cellar. How about if I give him a hand? No charge, of course. Would that make you happy?"

I looked over to where Morris was lifting crates out of the truck and loading them onto a dolly. "Well," I replied, "I'm sure Morris would be happy for the help, but frankly, I don't care what you do."

He hopped off the wall and began scissoring across the driveway in great strides. About halfway there he turned back to me, bowed, and tipped an imaginary hat. "And a lovely day to you too, little lady," he said with a laugh. And then he ran off to help Morris.

Chapter 10

A couple of evenings later, Uncle Cy held a fish fry on the island for our extended family and a number of his friends from town. Uncle Luther was there with his wife, Suellen, and their sons Earl, Jason, and Denny. The mayor of Mercy, Granville Drake, came with his wife and children, as did several members of the town council. Reverend Ralph Kilkenny of Grace Presbyterian Church showed up and invited us to services on Sunday, an invitation Mother and Daddy accepted gratefully.

Mother mingled with Aunt Suellen and the other ladies while Daddy spent most of the evening in quiet conversation with Mercy's Chief of Police, a ruddy-faced bear of a man named Neal Macnish. He and Daddy had been friends all the way through school but had lost touch when Daddy left Mercy back in 1902. The intervening years had left them with a lot of catching up to do.

As for me, I wasn't feeling very sociable. Uncle Cy said he'd invited the sheriff of Warren County, Jerry Wiant, which meant Marcus should have been there, but he wasn't.

For whatever reason, the sheriff and his family weren't able to attend. I was trying to come to terms with the idea that there would be no more dances with Marcus. I hadn't heard from him since Saturday, and here it was Wednesday. The passing of the days told me he wasn't interested in coming back.

After eating, I stood barefoot along the river's edge, my toes in the water. I looked up and down the river for bootleggers, but the only boats out on the water were our own rowboats and canoes. Down the shore from where I stood, my teenaged cousins competed to see who could spit a watermelon seed the farthest into the Little Miami. I was thinking about getting another helping of watermelon myself when Uncle Cy sauntered over and joined me.

"Having a good time, Eve?" he asked.

"Yes," I lied.

"Want me to introduce you to some of the young ladies?"

I looked over my shoulder at the crowded picnic tables and felt my stomach turn. "Not right now, Uncle Cy. But maybe later."

He nodded, pulled a cigar out of his shirt pocket, and lighted it. I rarely saw him smoke; most of the time he was simply too busy. He inhaled deeply, let it out. "You and your family doing all right? I mean, you feel like you're settling in all right?"

I smiled. "Oh yes. I love being here, Uncle Cy. I really do. I have so many good memories of the island from my childhood."

He took another pull on his cigar. Even the scent of tobacco brought back warm memories of earlier times. "I'm glad you do, darling," he said.

"I think it's a shame we didn't come here for so many years."

Another nod. "I do too. Wish you'd gotten back sooner."

"Really, Uncle Cy?"

He looked at me with his large brown eyes. "Of course."

"Well." I picked up a pebble and tossed it in the water. "Why didn't we? I mean, I know you and Daddy had a fight about something at the wedding, but it seems like it shouldn't have kept us away."

"Did Drew say that?"

"What?"

"Did your father say we'd fought?"

"Yes. Although he doesn't remember what the fight was about."

Two long pulls on the cigar. Then, "Funny. I don't remember fighting."

"Really?"

Uncle Cy shook his head. "We've had plenty of arguments in our time, but I don't remember a fight at the wedding. Doesn't mean it didn't happen, though. But as far as you not getting back here sooner, I think there might be something else involved. Drew . . . your daddy . . . he never really felt like he fit in here. He was always comparing himself to me and Luther and feeling like he came up short. Of course, it's a bunch of poppycock, his feeling that way. Drew's as good a man as ever lived and better than most. He just doesn't believe it."

For a moment I couldn't speak. I felt a rush of love for Uncle Cy that sent me up on my toes so I could plant a kiss on his sweaty cheek.

"What was that for?" he asked with a smile.

"For believing in Daddy."

"Well, he's a Marryat, isn't he?"

I nodded. We Marryats, with a few exceptions like Cassandra, were cut from good cloth. "Uncle Cy?"

"Yes, darling?"

"The other day when I was out boating with Jones, we saw a couple of bootleggers on the river. Did you know there are bootleggers around here?"

"Sure." He squinted against the setting sun as he looked upriver. "But we don't have anything to do with them. We mind our own business, and they mind theirs. It's best that way."

"They won't bother us?"

"Of course not. Why would they?"

I shrugged, trying to look nonchalant, trying not to let Uncle Cy sense my fear. "Where *is* Jones, by the way?" I asked. "Shouldn't he be here?"

"Jones?" Uncle Cy frowned as he exhaled a long stream of smoke. "He doesn't much care for social gatherings like this. Last I saw him he was working on his radios."

"Oh." Of course, I thought. Had I really needed to ask? "Maybe I'll take him some watermelon. Do you think he'd mind?"

"I think he'd like that. He—"

"Cy!" A heavyset man approached us, waving an arm. His unkempt moustache wiggled like a caterpillar while he spoke. "Beg pardon for interrupting, but I got a bit of business for the town council. We can bring it up at our next meeting, though I'm not sure it can wait that long. Granville tells me we've got the gopher problem again."

"The gopher problem, Stan?"

"They're back digging their tunnels in the graveyard and scattering bones around the grounds. Someone found a shinbone far away as Water Street. We all got family buried there, and we can't have them being dragged hither and yon, Cy. We got to get this thing under control."

Uncle Cy sighed. "All right, Stan," he said. He tossed what was left of his cigar on the pebbled beach and ground it out with his shoe. "Maybe we can call an emergency meeting. . . ."

As Uncle Cy drifted off with a hand on Stan's shoulder, I went to get a plate of watermelon for Jones.

Chapter 11

He was sitting at the table with all the radios. None of them was turned on and the room was quiet. Jones was bent over some papers spread out on the table, one index finger guiding his way as he read.

I knocked on the doorframe with my free hand. "Jones?"

"Yeah?" He looked up, white brows raised.

"I brought you some watermelon."

He didn't move, not even his eyes. They stared at me from behind his dark-framed glasses.

I said, "You don't like watermelon?"

"No," he said. "I mean, yes. I do."

I lifted the plate a little higher. "Want it?"

"Um, sure." He turned the papers over on the table, then took off his glasses and laid them aside. "Come in. Have a seat." Rising, he pulled a chair around from the end of the table and waved me into it. "I'll be right back."

I sat and looked over the tangled mess spread out before me. The gutted radios, the coils, tubes, and wires all made me think of Dr. Frankenstein putting together his monster. The only orderly section of the desk was the upper left corner where Jones had neatly stacked a half dozen books—a couple of encyclopedias, volumes A and R; some books on radios and radio repair, and an illustrated book about the Alaskan Territory. I was about to reach for the Alaska book when Jones returned with another plate. I withdrew my hand and smiled at Jones as he sat down.

"So how's the fish fry going?" he asked as he divided the watermelon between us. He picked up a slice and took an enthusiastic bite, unmindful of the seeds.

"Everyone's having a good time, I guess." From where I sat, I could see out the window to the service station across the street. I wondered whether Marcus was there working, but no cars were at the pumps, and the place looked quiet. "What have you been doing?"

"I've just been reading another letter from my mother." He nodded toward the stationery he'd turned upside down. "She has a lot of time on her hands. She writes me a lot of letters."

"I see." I tried to take dainty bites of watermelon, but it was hard to keep the juice from running down my chin. I had to wipe it away with the back of my hand. "How's she doing?"

He shrugged. "She's all right. She misses me and Cy. She's anxious to get home."

"I hope it's soon."

He nodded, said nothing. We ate in silence a moment. Finally he said, "Listen, about the other day, I didn't mean to make you cry."

I looked away. "I wasn't crying."

"Yes, you were."

"No, I wasn't."

"I heard you sniffling."

I felt the color creep up my cheeks. "Forget it," I said. "It doesn't matter."

"Yeah, well, I'm sorry. I'm . . . I don't spend a lot of time with people. I probably say stupid things sometimes."

"It's okay. I understand."

"I don't think you can. Understand, I mean." He stared at me intently then. "I mean, you're . . ."

"What?" I asked.

But he didn't respond. He lifted his shoulders again, dropped his eyes, and took another bite of watermelon. I think he wanted to tell me that I was like other people, that I *looked* like other people, but he couldn't say the words.

I said, "I guess, out on the river, I probably sounded silly and idealistic to you."

He smiled at that. "Silly, no. Idealistic, yes."

"Well . . ." I looked toward the window again. Jimmy was out at the pumps washing the windshield of a Chevy, but still no Marcus. "I don't know, Jones, I just feel like the whole country's gone crazy. A whole lot more people drink now than before Prohibition." I turned back to Jones. "Why do you suppose that is?" I asked.

"Simple," he replied. He spat a seed into the juice on his plate. "You know what they say about forbidden fruit."

I cocked my head. "No. What?"

He looked at me, amused. "It's the sweetest, of course."

I thought about that a moment. "You mean, tell people they can't have something, and all of a sudden everyone wants it?"

He nodded. "We're a stubborn lot. We won't be told what to do."

"Not even if it's for our own good?"

"Especially then." He laughed. But only briefly. In the next moment the amusement slid off his face and he looked serious. "You know, you're a strange bird, Eve. I don't think I've ever known anyone quite like you."

"Is that good or bad?"

"Good," he said. Then he added, "I think."

"Well, thank you, then. I think."

"You know that saying about lips that touch wine will never touch mine?"

"Yeah. What about it?"

"You're probably the only person around who would say that and mean it."

I glanced away. "Maybe I am," I said quietly.

"In a way I feel sorry for you."

"You do? But why?"

"Because that makes you all alone in the world."

Until that moment, I wouldn't have put it that way, but I knew Jones was right. I harbored a sense of aloneness, of being different, of not fitting in. But surely Jones . . .

"Maybe that's one thing we have in common," I said.

He opened his mouth, closed it, looked away. He finished the watermelon and wiped at his mouth with the sleeve of his shirt.

"Jones?"

"Yeah?"

"You grew up in Chicago. Right?"

He nodded. "Till I was fourteen. Then I moved here."

"When you lived there, did you ever see any gangsters? Did you ever see Al Capone?"

Jones sniffed at that. "Al Capone? No, I never saw him. Why do you ask?"

"Just wondering."

He gingerly pushed his plate aside on the table, careful not to spill any of the juice. "Well, let's see. I did know a guy who was arrested a couple of times for burglary and safecracking. He always got off on time served, though."

"Oh yeah?"

"Yeah. But he made most of his money from bootlegging, and he was never once arrested for that."

"Really? How'd he get away with it?"

Jones shrugged. "Beats me," he said. "He must have had connections."

I chewed thoughtfully as I pushed the watermelon rind around on the plate. "Where did he make moonshine in the city?" I asked.

"Moonshine? Oh no, he never made his own stuff. He dealt in the real deal—Scotch that came in from Canada, rum that came up from the Bahamas, sometimes even champagne from Europe. The good stuff, none of this bathtub gin or rotgut that's made out in the woods like the stuff around here."

"It seems funny you would know a man like that."

"Yeah? How so?"

I shrugged. "I don't know. I've never known a bootlegger personally. How did you know him?"

"He was a friend of the family."

"You didn't . . ." I dropped my eyes to my plate. "You didn't buy booze from him, did you?"

Jones laughed loudly. "No. Though sometimes we bought flowers from him."

"Flowers?"

"Yeah. He was a florist. That was his legit profession. He owned a flower shop that served as the front for his boot-legging business. Funny thing about him, though, was that he really did love flowers. I mean, he was crazy about them. He was all the time saying his second biggest joy in life was making floral arrangements. You'd almost always find him wearing a sprig of lily of the valley in the buttonhole of his jacket. He was funny that way."

"If that was his second biggest joy, what was his first?"

"His family. He had a wife and son, and he was crazy about them both. Never cheated on his wife. Was a good father to the boy. Every evening when he closed up the flower shop he went straight home. He didn't go out to the saloons after work like other men. Far as I know, he didn't drink. He even went to Mass every day."

"He did?"

"Yeah."

"He sounds like two people in one. You know, like Dr. Jekyll and Mr. Hyde, where the same man is both the good doctor and the crazed killer. They just made a movie of it with Fredric March. Have you seen it? That's what your florist sounds like."

"No, he's not like that at all." Jones shook his head. "A lot of gangsters go to Mass and even have a great respect for the church. A lot of them are faithful to their wives, and there's not a one of them that doesn't love their kids. When it comes right down to it, they're just like anybody else, really."

I thought about that but couldn't make sense of it. "What was his name?"

Jones pressed his lips together, as though he didn't want to tell me. Finally he said, "Why do you ask?"

"I don't know," I said. "Just curious."

"Oh." He lifted his chin in a small nod.

"Never mind," I said. "You don't have to say."

Jones wiped his mouth again on the sleeve of his shirt. "His name was Michael O'Brannigan."

I thought a moment, shrugged. "Never heard of him."

"He wasn't one of the big gangsters like Al Capone or Bugs Moran."

"Are you still in touch with him?"

"No." He paused. He picked up a pencil and tapped the eraser on the desk. "He's dead."

My eyes grew wide at that. "Dead? What happened?"

"Shot by a rival bootlegger."

At once, I saw the man walking ahead of me, heard the shots, saw the man rise up as his blood rained down over the sidewalk. Squeezing my eyes shut, I tried to rid my mind of the dreaded image. "That was a terrible thing to happen," I whispered.

"Yes it was."

I wanted to add, *but maybe if he had stuck to the business of flowers instead of booze, he'd still be alive.*

But I didn't say it.

Evening was giving way to nighttime. The streetlamp came on over by the service station. Somewhere in the apartment, a clock struck nine. Jones sat up straight, looked at me, reached for a radio, and turned it on. He picked up his glasses and carefully slid them over his ears.

"Listen, will you excuse me? I've got work to do."

"Um, sure."

I stood. He reached for a notebook and opened it to a clean page. I started to pick up the plates, but he objected. "I'll take care of those later. I'll see you tomorrow, Eve."

"All right. Good night, Jones."

He didn't reply. A woman's soft voice drifted out of the radio as I made my way out of the room.

Chapter 12

Eve!"

  "Yes, Uncle Cy?"

  "Someone here to see you."

I paused in my task of setting the tables for Friday's lunch. My hands were full of flatware. I dropped the knives and forks in a clattering heap and headed for the front desk.

I couldn't imagine who had come to see me, though never in a million years would I have guessed Marcus Wiant. Yet there he stood, in grimy overalls, his cap in his hands, a smear of grease over his left brow.

Breathless, I stopped in the archway of the dining room and stared. He misunderstood what surely must have been my shocked expression. Running a dirty hand through his hair, he said, "Sorry. I didn't have time to clean up. I just ran over from the station for a minute."

I nodded as I searched vainly for my voice.

Marcus glanced hesitantly at Uncle Cy, who at that moment turned away and pretended to be busy behind the desk. "Well, see . . ." He turned his cap around and around in his hands.

"Yes, Marcus?" I said, my tongue loosed at last.

"Well, the carnival has set up a few miles outside of town. Me and Jimmy and Marlene are going tomorrow, and I was wondering whether you'd like to come along."

"Oh?" Something was knocking at my rib cage. It took me a moment to realize it was my heart.

"We're going to head out around noon. We can pick you up here, if you'd like."

I nodded again. "Yes. I'd like to go. Thank you."

His eyes brightened and he smiled. "Great," he said. He took one step backward. "Well, I'll see you tomorrow, then."

"Yes. Okay."

Settling his cap back on his head, he took off out the door. My own feet were motionless, as though stuck to the polished threshold between the rooms. I heard Uncle Cy clear his throat. When I looked at him, he was grinning playfully.

"Got yourself a date, do you, darling?"

My cheeks burned and my lips quivered as I tried to suppress the shout of joy that was rising in my throat. I didn't tell Uncle Cy that it was not just a date but my *first* date. I was seventeen years old, and I'd never once before been asked out by a boy.

Uncle Cy gave off a happy sigh. I turned away from him and floated back to work.

Jimmy drove the four of us to the carnival in the old Model T he'd bought third-hand with money earned at his father's gas station. He and Marlene sat shoulder to shoulder up front while Marcus and I kept a modest amount of air between us in the back. Marcus had cleaned up since the day before, the only grease visible a few stubborn smudges embedded beneath his nails. He wore a white button-up shirt and a neatly pressed pair of brown slacks. He smelled of something good, though whether it was the pomade he used in his sleek dark hair or a type of cologne he'd patted on his cheeks, I couldn't be sure. I made a mental note to ask Mother if I could buy some perfume. Wearing some now might have drawn Marcus's attention away from the faded yellow dress and the white straw sun hat Mother insisted I wear. With my long braid and that silly hat, I felt childish and unattractive. I wasn't nearly as stylish as Marlene, whose rose-patterned summer dress and broad-brimmed hat both looked brand-new. I noticed too that she wore lipstick, something else I'd never used.

I squeezed my hands together in my lap as we rode a few awkward moments in silence. Marcus tapped his fingers on his knee as though keeping time to music no one else could hear. Finally he turned to me and asked, "So, do you like living here in Mercy?"

I felt myself brighten. "Yes, I like it very much. I think it's a wonderful place to live."

Ahead of us, Marlene laughed and said over her shoulder, "You wouldn't think so if you'd grown up here."

"Oh, I'm sure I would, Marlene. Why do you say that?"

"Because it's so boring. Nothing ever happens in a small town like Mercy. Nothing fun, anyway. That's why Jimmy and I are going to get out as soon as we can. Right, Jimmy?"

Jimmy nodded. I sat directly behind him and could see nothing but the back of his blond head. "That's right, honey," he said agreeably.

"We're going to go where life is exciting!" Marlene waved one arm like a cheerleader. "Right, Jimmy?"

Another nod. "You got it, honey."

Marcus sniffed at that and shook his head. Turning back to me, he said, "So, you say you moved from St. Paul? As in Minnesota?"

"That's right." We had exchanged small talk on the night we danced, but not much. We'd found it too difficult to hold any real conversation over the music and the hubbub of the crowd, and so we'd been content to slide silently together around the dance floor.

"I've never been to St. Paul," Marcus said.

"Don't bother to go."

"Why not?"

"Too much crime. It's where all the gangsters hole up when they want to get away from the law."

The cheerleader arm flew up. "Jimmy, let's go to St. Paul!"

Jimmy shrugged. "Whatever you want, baby."

Marcus laughed. "You two are going to end up in trouble, if you're not careful."

"Well, *somebody's* got to have fun, Marcus, and it's probably not going to be you," Marlene said. "Tell Eve what *you're* going to be doing in the fall."

Marcus and I looked at each other. He lifted one shoulder in a lopsided shrug. "I'm going to college."

"You are? You've been accepted?"

"Sure, I've been accepted."

"He even got a scholarship," Marlene said. "Tell her, Marcus."

"Partial scholarship," Marcus corrected.

"Academic?" I asked.

"No." Marcus shook his head. "Athletic."

"Oh." I would have been much more impressed with an academic scholarship, but free tuition was free tuition.

Marlene said, "Eve told me she's crazy about sports. Didn't you, Eve?"

I'd said no such thing. But I was willing to pretend I was crazy about sports for a day. Or for the summer. Or for the rest of my life, if need be.

"Really?" Marcus was smiling now.

"Sure," I answered.

"What's your favorite?"

I thought a moment. "Oh, I like all sports equally," I said, which was true, as I didn't like any of them at all. "So you want to play a sport professionally?"

"No. I'm going to study civil engineering. I want to build things. Roads, bridges, dams. You know, things like that."

"I think that's wonderful," I gushed, though even as I spoke, it dawned on me that Marcus would be leaving Mercy at the end of the summer. Nervously, I asked, "So where are you going to school?"

"The University of Cincinnati." And then, as though he could read my thoughts, he added, "It's close."

I smiled. Up ahead, over the next rise, the carnival appeared. First the Ferris wheel, then the larger spread of rides and colorful canopies, the sounds of calliope music and barkers calling, the scent of popcorn and warm dust and grease. If the carnival workers had hoped for a profitable turnout, their wish had been granted. It looked like the population of several counties had converged on those few acres outside of Mercy. We took our place among them, and for the next several hours we strolled about the grounds, riding rides, playing games, drinking sodas, eating popcorn and candied apples.

From time to time I looked at Marcus, not quite believing I was with him. I longed for Cassandra to see me now. The girl she'd called the "luckless wench" had finally stumbled upon a bit of handsome luck! I had a date with Marcus Wiant and that meant, at least for the moment, I wasn't alone. That was the amazing thing. The familiar sense of loneliness was missing as I walked through the hours with Marcus. Instead, I was surprised by a sense of satisfaction.

And that too brought me around to Cassandra. For the first time in my life, I stood with my eye to a peephole into my sister's existence, and I understood that maybe this was why she had relentlessly run with the wrong crowd—to dance halls, to speakeasies, to parties. She'd yearned for this very feeling, this sense of connectedness, however fragile and brief, a blessed reprieve from solitude. It was lovely being outside of oneself, lovelier than I might have imagined.

While Marcus and Jimmy went for hot dogs and drinks, Marlene and I sat down at a picnic table to wait for them. She leaned forward on her elbows and winked. "I didn't do too bad a job at matchmaking, did I? You like Marcus, don't you?"

I nodded shyly. "He's wonderful, Marlene."

"Good. I'm glad you like him because he obviously likes you."

"Do you really think so?"

She looked at me askance. "Really, Eve? Is the Pope Catholic?"

I couldn't help smiling. "But," I asked, "how come he doesn't already have a girl? I mean, a guy like Marcus ought to have plenty of girls after him."

Marlene adjusted her hat and applied fresh lipstick from a tube plucked out of her dainty handbag. "Listen," she said, "there's something you have to understand about Marcus.

He's a looker but he doesn't have a clue. He's way too shy. I mean, yeah, he's had a girl or two, but nothing serious. I think it's because his father's the sheriff."

I frowned at her. "What's that got to do with anything?"

"Oh, just that Sheriff Wiant thinks he's the most important man in Warren County. Maybe even Ohio. He expects so much of Marcus, and Marcus never seems able to live up. There's a couple of daughters in the family, but Marcus is the only son. It's a tough break."

"But I don't get it. Marcus is going to college on an athletic scholarship! What else does his father want?"

"A full scholarship, I suppose, instead of a partial."

"But some kids don't get anything!"

Marlene shrugged. "Like I said, nothing's ever good enough for Sheriff Wiant. I think he's also disappointed Marcus has a mind of his own and wants to be something other than the next sheriff. I'm telling you, Eve, the man's a real creep. He swaggers around with his guns on his hips like he's Wild Bill Hickok or something. On top of that, he's just plain mean. Like Jimmy's dad, only Jimmy's dad is even worse."

"He is?" I hadn't formally met Calvin Fludd myself, but he didn't seem like such a bad fellow to me. I'd seen him at the lodge several times, leaning his greasy elbows on the front desk while talking with Uncle Cy. Their conversation was always punctuated by hearty laughter that could be heard as far away as the kitchen. I know, because Annie always appeared with a glass of iced tea for Mr. Fludd and another for Uncle Cy. Surely if my uncle and Annie Tweed approved of the man, he had to be a good guy.

"Let me put it this way, Eve," Marlene said. Her eyes narrowed and her mouth grew small. "I hate Calvin Fludd and

I hate that he's going to be my father-in-law. But like I said, it's not as though Jimmy and I are going to hang around Mercy once we're married. No sir. Get me in front of the JP and then we're gone for good."

"Really? Do you—" I wanted to know more, but the boys showed up with the hot dogs and drinks.

Later, when we were walking through the midway, Marcus offered me his hand, and I took it. Our fingers easily entwined; his flesh felt warm and comfortable. But at the same time, we both looked shyly away and pretended to be intrigued by the games and distracted by the carnival barkers, as though our hands were their own persons and not a part of us at all.

"Would you like me to try to win you a stuffed animal?" he asked, stopping at a shooting gallery. On display in the booth was a variety of prizes: stuffed animals of all sorts, spinning tops and yo-yos and plastic swords and costume jewelry.

"Sure," I said.

He pulled his hand from mine; I reluctantly let go.

"You know these games are all rigged," Jimmy warned.

Marcus shrugged. "Sometimes they let people win. They have to. They can't cheat everyone and get away with it." He turned to the carny in the booth and asked, "How much?"

"A nickel for three shots," the carny replied. He was a weathered man with leathery skin and a mouth full of broken teeth. His arms were tattooed from shoulder to wrist, and three of his fingers were missing on his left hand. One glance at him sent a shiver down my spine.

Marcus pulled a nickel from his pocket and dropped it into the carny's outstretched hand, the one with the fingers intact. The carny handed him a rifle and stepped aside. Marcus lifted the rifle so that the butt nestled against his right shoulder. He held the barrel in his left hand while the index finger of his right hand curled around the trigger. He peered over the barrel, taking aim at the toy ducks lined up at the back of the booth. I held my breath and waited. He fired the first blank; the ducks remained unruffled. He fired the second. Nothing. Three times Marcus fired and three times not a single duck budged.

"Aw, too bad," Marlene said.

"I told you it was rigged," Jimmy added.

"Never mind," I said. "It doesn't matter."

Before Marcus could hand the rifle over, a man came up behind him and put a hand on his shoulder. "Let me show you how it's done."

When the man turned toward me I recognized him. "Link!" I cried. "What are you doing here?"

He motioned us back with a wave of his arms. "Step aside. Don't want anybody getting hurt."

"You know this guy?" Marcus asked.

"I met him once," I said. Then, more quietly, "He's just a bum who hangs around the lodge looking for food."

Link reached into the pocket of his overalls and pulled out a nickel. *How is it,* I thought, *that a bum has a nickel? And why is he wasting money on a silly carnival game when he could be using it for food?*

I reached for Marcus's arm. "Come on," I said. "I want to ride the carousel."

"All right."

Link took a shot. One duck flew off the shelf. I tugged at Marcus's elbow. "Come on," I said again.

Another shot, another flying duck.

Link turned and looked at Marcus. For a moment they held each other's gaze. I clenched my fists until my nails dug into the soft flesh of my palms.

Link fired off his last shot. One more duck flew upward. Jimmy laughed and Marlene cheered. I glared at Link.

"The game's rigged," Marcus said.

"Maybe," Link said, "but I'm still a good shot."

"Come on, Marcus." I pulled at his arm.

Finally Marcus turned away. I offered Link a parting frown as we walked off toward the carousel, trailed by Jimmy and Marlene. I had half a mind not to give Link any food next time he came around with his empty stomach and hangdog look. Anyone with spare change in his pocket didn't need to beg.

Once we reached the carousel, I forgot all about the bum from the shantytown. I'd always loved the carousel, the calliope music, the up-and-down and round-and-round of the colorful horses. Who could ride a carousel and not be happy? And now, I was all the more so because Marcus was on the horse beside me.

Every time we made the loop, Marcus reached toward the ring dispenser. On our third time around, he captured one of the rings and held it up in triumph.

"It's the brass!" he hollered, slipping it into his shirt pocket. "I'll let you use it for a free ride."

But he forgot. We both forgot, until we got back to the lodge in the early evening and he found it still in his pocket. He pulled it out and looked at it with chagrin. "I meant to let you use it," he said. "How did I get so sidetracked?"

"As soon as the ride was over," I said, "Marlene insisted

she wanted a snow cone, and she wanted it right that minute, remember?"

"Oh yeah." He laughed lightly.

"And then we forgot to go back," I added.

"Well, here." He gave me the ring. "You can have it as a souvenir."

I smiled. "It was a wonderful day, Marcus. Thanks."

He offered a shy grin and glanced around. The porch was crowded with guests relaxing, rocking, reading the newspaper, puffing on cigarettes. One little boy pushed a wooden truck around our feet. Marcus shrugged and smiled sheepishly. "Well, good night, Eve," he said. "I'll be seeing you."

"Good night, Marcus."

With a quick nod, he hurried off the porch and around the lodge to the parking lot where Jimmy waited to take him home. In another moment I heard the horn of Jimmy's Tin Lizzie cutting through the summer air to bid me one last good-night. *Aarruga!*

I clasped the carousel ring in both hands and held it to my heart. Then I stepped into the front hall and moved toward the stairs. Uncle Cy was behind the desk.

"Ah, Eve, how was the carnival?" he asked. "Did you have a good day?"

"It was the best day imaginable," I said.

"Shall we start planning a wedding?"

"Not yet."

Uncle Cy laughed. "Well, be sure to let me know so we can reserve the dining room for the reception."

"I will."

I walked up the stairs like one in a dream, my sails swelled by what I could only imagine was the breath of passion as I moved down the hall to my room.

My treasure box sat in solitary abandon on the dresser. I had ignored it lately, but now I had something to tuck inside. I picked it up and gazed momentarily at the floral pattern carved into the hinged lid. Mother and Daddy had given me this teakwood treasure box on September 21, 1923, my ninth birthday, though it would be nearly a year before I laid my first treasure inside. Now, I opened the lid, kissed the brass ring, and tenderly placed it on the velvet lining next to the only other item there.

My fingers touched the lid, but I hesitated. That other item . . . maybe it no longer belonged. Maybe I should put it somewhere else. Or give it away. Or drop it in the trash.

I picked it up and held it in the palm of my hand. Why had I kept this little ivory elephant all these years? Should I keep it now, as though it were something delightful, like the brass ring from Marcus? It had been given to me by a very bad man, an evil man. And yet, that was what had always puzzled me. I hadn't known then who he was. I'd known only that he was a stranger who stopped to show kindness to a little girl one summer day in 1924. . . .

Chapter 13

I'd begged Daddy for weeks for a pair of roller skates and, though we never seemed to have much money for extras, he somehow scraped together enough to present me with a pair of skates on the first day of summer in 1924. He said they were a reward for earning all As in the fourth grade, in spite of our move from Detroit in the middle of the school year.

The skates were a brand-new pair of Winchesters, shiny silver with bright red wheels and red leather straps to go around my ankles. I sat right down and slid the toes of my Keds between the metal clasps, then buckled the straps. Daddy tightened the skates with the key, which Mother then put on a shoestring so I could wear it around my neck. I spent all afternoon skating up and down the sidewalk in front of our apartment building and never once fell down. I fancied myself a natural athlete, so much so that over the next few weeks I dreamed of being a famous ballroom roller dancer or maybe even a movie star who skated her way through musicals, singing and dancing flawlessly on wheels.

My skates and I became inseparable. I took them everywhere, even to my best friend Ariel's party when she turned ten. She knew she'd be getting her own pair of Winchesters for her birthday, and she asked me to stay after the party so we could go skating together.

Ariel's family lived in the upstairs portion of a duplex on Arundel Street, not far from the Commodore Hotel. Since its opening four years earlier, the hotel had attracted the rich and the famous, and was particularly well-known for the wild parties thrown there by F. Scott Fitzgerald and his eccentric flapper wife Zelda. That meant little to me, as I knew nothing about being either rich or famous and was certainly not acquainted with the people who were. I was just a kid with a pair of red-wheeled skates that summer day in 1924.

Once her new skates were attached to her shoes, Ariel became timid and uncertain and so moved along the sidewalk at a cautionary pace. I, on the other hand, was a cannonball to her tumbleweed, which made me feel rather superior, since I was still nine years old to her ten.

We skated south on Arundel to Holly Avenue and turned left toward Western Avenue. That whole corner was occupied by the Commodore, a huge multistory redbrick fortress with a gated courtyard in front. By the time I'd turned onto Western, I was half a block ahead of Ariel and gleefully racing forward in a reckless blaze of glory. I was passing the wrought-iron gates that led into the courtyard when it happened. The wheels of my right skate met a buckled crack in the sidewalk, and before I even knew I was in trouble, I was airborne like a ballplayer stealing home plate. After a split-second freefall, I skidded onto the pavement, ripping the hem of my party dress and scraping the skin off both knees. I was stunned senseless. I heard Ariel calling my name— "Eve! Are you all right?"—but I couldn't answer. It took me a few long moments to gather my wits and turn over. I sat with my legs sprawled in front of me, saw the torn flesh of my kneecaps and the blood oozing out of the wounds, and that's when the pain set in, along with the humiliation. I started to cry, and through my tears I saw Ariel pawing her way clumsily toward me, pounding the sidewalk like someone smashing grapes instead of gliding on the wheels beneath her. I wanted to laugh at her but couldn't. I'd been so smug about my skating, yet here I was, on the ground with tattered knees and—I finally noticed—palms furrowed with scratches and dusty white with concrete, which made me cry all the more.

I didn't want anyone to see me like that, but, of all the rotten luck, the heavy wrought-iron gate of the Commodore squeaked open on its hinges, and three men stepped out of the courtyard and onto the sidewalk. One walked out in front while the other two shadowed him like wings. The one in front was a heavyset man smoking a newly lit cigar. He wore a white double-breasted suit, a white fedora, and black-and-white wingtip shoes. The only color on him was the black parts of his shoes and the rose-colored silk handkerchief in his breast pocket. When he saw me, he stopped and squatted down, his great weight balanced on the balls of his feet. He pulled the cigar from his mouth and tossed it aside. "Hey, kid, you all right?" he asked, his shaggy brows knit, his gray eyes tender with a kind of fatherly concern.

I tried to nod but I could do little more than stare at this oversized angel hunched clumsily beside me. I stared not just because he was there, but because his face was so badly scarred, as though a three-fingered monster had clawed him, leaving gouges from his left ear almost all the way to his mouth.

"You all right, kid?" he asked again, and though I saw his purplish lips move, I still couldn't answer. His raised his brows and gazed at me quizzically.

He must have decided my tears were the only answer he was going to get, because he shrugged and lifted a hand toward one of the dark-suited men. Though he didn't say a word, the man knew what he wanted. A handkerchief was put into the pudgy fist of my rescuer, who used it to dab at my bloody knees. It hurt, but I didn't want to say so. The tears were still flowing and my nose was leaking, and since I had nothing to wipe my face with, I tried vainly to sniff everything back inside. The sound was so pitiful, the man in white held up his hand again, and the second shadow handed over *his* handkerchief, which the angel gave to me with the word, "Blow."

I blew my nose and wiped away my tears. By now, Ariel had caught up with us; she stood slack-jawed on the sidewalk, staring at the scene unraveling before her.

"Listen," the man said, "why don't you give the skates a rest and walk home? That the key?" He pointed to the key on the shoestring around my neck.

I nodded. He lifted the key over my head and unlocked the skates. Then he slipped them off my feet and laid them aside. "Anyway," he went on, "I think the bleeding's stopped.

Why don't you go on home and have your mother put some iodine on these cuts?"

"All right," I said shakily, finally able to respond. I glanced at Ariel. I knew she was staring at the man's scars and wondering about his peculiar accent. He sounded like he'd come from somewhere out east, like New Jersey.

The man stood and adjusted his fedora. One of the shadows grabbed my wrists and pulled me up. Neither he nor the other shadow ever said a word; they simply stood there looking impatient and annoyed.

When I was back up on my feet, the angel said, "You gotta be more careful, little lady."

I nodded again, meekly. "I will," I promised.

A long sleek car pulled up to the curb, and one of the shadows opened the back door. The man in white took a step forward, then stopped and turned to me. "Say, you like elephants?" he asked.

I was so shaken by the penetrating eyes, the scars, the whole imposing white figure that I couldn't speak till Ariel nudged me in the ribs. "Sure," I said. "I like elephants."

He reached into the pocket of his slacks like he was searching for spare change, but what he pulled out was a miniature ivory elephant, hardly bigger than a radish. "Here you go, kid," he said. "It'll bring you good luck."

I held up a trembling hand, and he laid the elephant in my palm. I stared at it, afraid to lift my eyes. "Thank you," I whispered.

I was hardly aware of the men climbing into the car, but when the doors slammed shut, I realized I was still clutching the handkerchiefs. "Hey, mister!" I yelled. I knocked on the back window until it rolled down. The man's face appeared without the fedora. His thinning brown hair was brushed straight back and his forehead glistened with sweat. His right side was toward me so the scars were largely hidden.

"Don't you want your handkerchiefs back?" I held them up. They were soiled with blood, mucus, and tears.

The man looked at the other fellows in the car and laughed heartily. Then he turned back to me. "Naw, you keep them," he said. "Another little gift from your friends in Chicago."

The window rolled up and the car moved down the street. Ariel and I looked after the car until it disappeared.

Her voice lilting with awe, Ariel asked, "Who was that?"

I shrugged. "I don't know. But he was nice."

"Yeah. Let's go home. Mom will put some iodine and bandages on your knees."

Six years would pass before I could identify the man outside the Commodore Hotel. In all that time I didn't have a clue and had almost forgotten about him until his smiling face appeared on the March 24, 1930, cover of *Time* magazine. With one eyebrow raised and a rose in his lapel, he looked cocky and self-assured, as though he'd just been named Man of the Year. I'd seen smaller photos of him in the papers, but with his life-sized mug on the magazine cover, his now infamous scars were glaringly apparent. He was well-known for his dealings in bootlegging, gambling, racketeering, and prostitution. He was also a ruthless murderer, as well as the prime suspect behind the St. Valentine's Day Massacre of 1929 when seven of Bugs Moran's men were gunned down in a warehouse in cold blood. He'd been named Public Enemy Number One by the Chicago Crime Commission and nicknamed Scarface by the newspapers. By 1930 both his name and his nickname were household words, but I didn't connect him to my corpulent angel until I saw the cover of *Time*.

Ariel and I stared at that cover a good long while, unable to believe that the man who'd helped me when I fell was Al Capone.

Chapter 14

"And so we come back around to mercy, the place where we must live, if we are to live at all." Reverend Kilkenny paused and smiled pleasantly as he looked out over the congregation. In the weeks ahead I would realize that cashing in on the name of the town was a favorite tactic of the Reverend's, for with every sermon he reminded us that we lived in Mercy. "Because, as we are told in Romans, we are all sinners who fall short of the glory of God, we have no hope other than to throw ourselves on His mercy and find our salvation and redemption in His Son, our Lord Jesus Christ. Let us pray."

That Sunday morning, I, for one, was happier than ever to be living in this town called Mercy. Still gliding on giddy wings from spending the previous afternoon with Marcus, I found my mind drifting—to his shy smile, the feel of his hand in mine, the carousel ring now in my treasure box. I could scarcely concentrate on the service, and I must have been fidgeting because Mother kept glancing at me, as though searching for signs of another Cassandra. She needn't have worried. I would never make the choices my sister had made. I was stronger than that and would not be tempted.

The days of summer went by in a sweet routine. Foremost was the busyness of the lodge. I loved the simple joy of entertaining our guests. I loved their coming and going, their chatter and laughter, their obvious pleasure in spending time on the island. Morris and I made runs back and forth to the train station to pick them up and to take them back again, and whenever we took them back they were sorry to go and we were sorry to see them go, but we knew that many of them would return as soon as the upcoming weekend. I found great satisfaction in doing my chores around the lodge, watching the guests swim and boat and play croquet, and standing on the edge of the river myself, lifting my face to the sun and drinking in the warm fragrant air.

Marcus was with me every moment in thought if not in fact, though we tried somehow to see each other every day. Sometimes he simply waved at me from the station across the street. Other times he'd run over and grab a bite of lunch with me at the Eatery. We went to the movies at the theater in town with Jimmy and Marlene; we went to the ice cream parlor on Main Street and ate banana splits and shared vanilla Cokes. If life had gone on in that idyllic way forever, I would have been completely satisfied. I wouldn't have needed to ask for anything more.

Occasionally I saw punts on the river carrying what must have been moonshine, but other than that I thought little about the local bootleggers or Prohibition or outlaws. My old life drifted farther and farther away until one Tuesday morning, June 23, the memories came rushing back. The news came over the radio that Al Capone had been arrested.

He'd been indicted ten days earlier but was now in custody, along with sixty-eight other members of an alleged beer syndicate. They were charged with five thousand offenses against the Prohibition law. Five thousand! Capone himself was accused of conspiracy dating all the way back to 1922.

As I stood by the front desk listening to the radio with Uncle Cy, I was surprised at the feelings welling up inside me. Al Capone was a terrible, evil man and he deserved prison for all that he had done, yet . . .

"Hey, kid, you all right?"

His face was vivid in my mind, that fleshy moon with the gray eyes and bushy brows. I bit my lower lip, remembering the sting as he touched my tattered knees with a handkerchief.

"You gotta be more careful, little lady."

He didn't have to stop and help me. I was just one more clumsy kid who'd hit a buckled sidewalk and skinned her knees, a rite of childhood. Other grown-ups might have clicked their tongues and walked on by, but he didn't. He squatted down and looked at me the way a father looks at his own child and asked me if I was all right. And then he'd wiped away the blood and given me a handkerchief for my tears.

"Say, you like elephants?"

And he'd given me a piece of carved ivory that I'd kept in my treasure box for eight years.

"Looks like old Scarface is really in hot water this time," Uncle Cy said as he turned off the radio. "I guess it's bound to catch up with you sooner or later."

Uncle Cy sighed.

So did I.

That night I found Jones sitting on the front steps, straining to read a letter by the dim light of the porch lamps. When I saw him there I remembered what Marlene had said about Jones the first time I met her—that he came out only at night. For the most part, that was true. He rarely went outside during daylight hours, and when he did, he almost always wore the safari hat that covered his hair and dark glasses that covered his eyes. It was only at night that he looked like everyone else.

I sat down on the step beside him. "Hi, Jones."

"Hello, Eve."

"Mind if I sit here?"

"Naw. Go ahead."

He folded up the letter and stuffed it into his shirt pocket, followed by his glasses.

"From your mother?" I asked.

He nodded.

"How is she?"

He seemed to have to think about that for a while. He looked out toward the river, and I followed his gaze to the shards of moonlight glistening on its surface. When I looked back to Jones, the muscles in his face had tightened and his eyes, like the river, seemed to have picked up the flickering glow of the moon. "She's not doing well," he said at last.

I pressed my lips together. I would pretend I hadn't noticed the unshed tears. "I'm sorry, Jones," I said gently. "I'll keep praying for her, twice as hard."

He didn't respond. For what seemed a long time, we sat in silence. I had come to ask him something and I thought maybe I should leave him alone, choose another time. But no. I wanted to ask him now. Quietly, tentatively, I said, "Say, Jones?"

"Yeah?"

"Can I show you something?"

"I guess so."

I reached into the pocket of my skirt. My fingers trembled. I'd never shown anyone before, other than Ariel. I held the ivory elephant up toward the light so that Jones could see it.

With a small grimace, he plucked his glasses out of his pocket and put them on again. He gazed at the elephant for only a second before saying, "Yeah? What about it?"

"I know you won't believe me when I tell you who gave it to me."

He laughed a little. "So tell me anyway."

"Al Capone."

He turned to me sharply, his brows hanging low over his eyes. He took the elephant and looked at it more closely, turning it over and over, as though looking for a signature of previous ownership. Then he returned it to my palm. "I believe you," he said.

"You do?"

He nodded. "He collects ivory elephants. He has them all lined up on his desk."

I gasped. "How do you know that?"

Jones looked away, but not before I saw a small inexplicable smile spread across his lips. "Let's just say I know people who know things."

"You said you never met Al Capone."

"I never met him myself." He looked back at me. The smile was gone. He nodded toward my hand. "So how'd you get it?"

I told him the story. When I finished, he didn't say anything and he didn't even move, just kept staring straight ahead.

"I'm trying to understand it all, Jones," I said quietly.

"What do you mean?"

"Why was he nice to me?"

"Because you were a kid and you were hurt."

It wasn't enough. There had to be something else. "I've been thinking about that man you told me about. The friend of your family's who owned the flower shop. What was his name?"

"You mean Michael O'Brannigan?"

"Yeah." I nodded. "You told me about how he loved his son and never cheated on his wife. And how he didn't even drink and how he went to Mass."

"So?"

"But he was a criminal. Like Al Capone."

Jones narrowed his eyes at me. They looked a deep brown in the dim light. "That's right. He was a criminal, not the devil himself. No one's completely bad, Eve. Don't you know that?"

I wasn't sure. Good and evil. Black and white. I wanted them to be separate. I didn't like gray. "I'm trying to understand," I said again.

"Look," Jones said, sitting up a little straighter and stretching his legs out in front of him. "Even gangsters have a code of honor. One thing they swear not to do is hurt women and children. Not on purpose anyway. And a lot of them do nice things for people. They make a whole lot of money in crime, and then they end up giving a lot of it away to charity. Not all of them, of course, but some of them. One guy I heard about would pack his car with food and clothes and drive into the slums and hand them out. I've heard of some who go around giving money to old folks and orphans, just because they want to help in some way; you know, do something good. And why not?" Jones looked at me and shrugged. "It's not like they're incapable of being human."

I thought about that. "I heard Capone used to play Santa Claus at his younger sister's school every year."

Jones nodded. "That's true, he did. He's also financed soup kitchens up in the Chicago area since the market crashed. He's put food in a lot of hungry bellies."

"Maybe he just wants to look good."

"Maybe." Jones shrugged. "Did he stop and help you, though, just because he wanted to look good?"

I had no answer for that. I slipped the elephant back into my pocket.

Jones pointed toward it with a thumb. "Better hold on to that," he said. "It's going to be worth something someday."

Chapter 15

Marlene came over to the island on Friday afternoon, and we decided to take one of the rowboats out on the river. I volunteered to row first, so Marlene settled herself in the bow of the boat. Just as I was putting the oars into the oarlocks, someone on the dock said, "You two young ladies aren't going to take that thing out by yourselves, are you?"

Looking up, I found myself squinting against the noonday sun in spite of my broad-brimmed hat. Link stood there on the dock, towering over us and smiling. Nearly two weeks had passed since he'd shown off at the carnival shooting range, and I hadn't seen him since.

"Of course we are," I snapped. "Why not? We're capable of rowing."

"I'm not questioning your ability," he said. "Just thought you might like someone else to do the work while you sit back and enjoy the ride."

I was about to turn him down when Marlene waved an

arm and said, "Jump in, cowboy. Eve, move to the back and let this sharpshooter do the rowing."

"So you remember me?" Link asked Marlene.

"I never forget a face. Not a handsome one anyway."

Link touched his cap and bowed slightly. I looked at Marlene and frowned to let her know I wasn't happy with this change. But I relinquished the oars and moved to the back of the boat. Link stepped in, untied the rope, and pushed us away from the dock.

Marlene tapped him on the shoulder. "I'm Marlene, by the way," she said.

He nodded his acknowledgment and said, "Everybody just calls me Link."

"If that's so, I suppose I will have to call you Cowboy."

"Call me whatever you want, little lady," he said, pulling on the oars in a steady rhythm, "just don't call me late for lunch."

Marlene let go a loud, clear shout of glee that echoed up and down the river. "Oh, I think I like you, Cowboy!" With that, she leaned back against the bow, made a pillow of her arms, turned her face to the sun and closed her eyes. "Now, this is the life," she said with a contented sigh.

I wasn't so sure I shared her sentiments, as I didn't like the idea of rowing the river with a bum. To make me even more uncomfortable, Link sat facing me and I couldn't avoid his gaze. I turned my head so that my face was concealed by the brim of my hat, but still I felt his eyes on me.

After he had rowed for several minutes, I ventured a glance at him. "Why are we going upriver?" I asked.

"That way it's easier coming back."

"Oh. I suppose that makes sense."

He chuckled. I turned away again. No one spoke until the silence itself became awkward. Finally, just to fill the void, I said, "Haven't seen you in a while."

"Been busy."

"Doing what?"

"Looking for work."

"Find anything?"

"Nothing permanent. Just day labor here and there."

"Uh-huh."

Silence.

Then I said, "What were you before, Link?"

"Before the crash?"

"Yes."

He stroked once, twice, three times before answering. "I was an undergraduate at Ohio State," he said at last.

"You were?" I turned to look at him full-on. My eyes widened in surprise.

"Yeah. Funny, huh? Look at me now."

I chewed my lip. "It can't be helped. A lot of people's lives have been ruined by what happened with the market."

"I don't consider my life ruined, just interrupted."

I thought about that, nodded. "What were you studying?"

"History."

"History? What were you going to do with that?"

Link laughed loudly. "You sound just like my father. He was always telling me to study something practical."

"Well, I suppose you could always teach. You could become a college professor."

I gazed at him while waiting for his reply. At the moment, he looked nothing at all like a college professor, with his tattered overalls and scuffed work boots, his shaggy hair peeking out from under his cap, his skin darkened by the sun. I couldn't quite imagine him lecturing at a university.

"Actually," he said at length, "I've entertained the idea of getting my degree and going on to seminary."

"Seminary? You mean, you'd want to become a pastor?" He pursed his lips. "Maybe."

"But . . ."

"But what?"

"Anyone who goes to seminary shouldn't drink."

"Drink?" He frowned and shook his head. "Why do you say that?"

"You asked me for something to drink," I said. "Don't you remember? You asked if we served moonshine at the lodge."

Behind him, Marlene squealed in amusement. "Plenty of that around here, Cowboy," she said.

"Yeah? I'm not surprised."

"They say the county is just bursting with stills," Marlene went on. "People are getting pretty good at making their own spirits."

"Spirits, nothing," Link said. "More like rotgut. Half the stuff that comes out of a still can kill you. Just last week two men were poisoned by White Lightning over next door in Foster."

"How do you know?" I asked.

"I was over there chopping wood for a day. Word gets around."

"They died from drinking it?"

Link nodded. "That's right. It happens. You wouldn't believe what they put in moonshine. Rubbing alcohol, anti-freeze, and even embalming fluid. If it doesn't kill you, it can send you into convulsions or leave you blind. So the thing is, if you're going to drink, at least play it safe and drink the real stuff."

"I don't intend to drink anything ever," I said firmly.

From the front of the boat, Marlene said, "Well, I do! I intend to drink champagne at my wedding!"

Link laughed. I ignored her. Link said, "Probably not much of that around here."

"Probably not much real stuff around here at all," Marlene said. "If you want genuine booze, you'll have to go to Cincinnati. We had one of the nation's biggest bootleggers working out of Cincy, till he was caught and sent to prison. But others have taken over where he left off."

"Yeah? So you think people go all the way into Cincy? I heard there's Scotch and rum floating around here, but I don't know who's serving it up."

Marlene sat up then and shrugged. "I've never heard anything about it."

"Me either," I added. "And I don't want to know."

"Teetotaler, huh?" Link said.

"That's right, I am." I lifted my chin and looked away. "You should be too, if you're going into the ministry."

"I'll be sure to keep that in mind." He lifted one dripping oar out of the water and pointed toward shore. "That's your uncle's mill, right?"

"Oh yes! That's my Uncle Luther's mill, and it was my grandfather's mill before him." I beamed at the imposing wooden structure whose beginnings stretched back into the nineteenth century and whose millstones had sustained my family for generations. The mill produced Pride of Miami flour which, as Uncle Luther was quick to add, was sifted through real silk cloths. I'd toured the mill a number of times with my uncle when I was a child, and I was mesmerized by all the inner workings—the millstones, the wooden shafts, the grinding gears—that extended from the upper-story grain loft down to the sack floor, the stone floor, and finally the meal floor. It was all a great and glorious mystery to me, though what I loved most about the mill was the waterwheel that hugged the outer wall and was turned continuously by the current of the Little Miami River.

"Big operation," Link said. "Bet it earns a pretty penny. I hope he can keep it going."

"Of course he will. Why wouldn't he?"

"I'm afraid things are going to get worse before they get better."

From the bow of the boat, Marlene said, "Hoover says prosperity is right around the corner."

"Yeah, well he's the president," Link said. "He's supposed to say encouraging and otherwise completely stupid things like that."

Marlene laughed out loud while I put a hand to my mouth to suppress a giggle. The bum was growing on me, especially now that I knew he'd been to college.

We rowed on for a short while, enjoying the smooth rhythm of the oars, the warm sun, the strange and unexpected companionship. We had just made our way around a bend in the river when Link said, "Well, here we are."

"Where?" I asked.

"Home sweet home." Once again he pointed with an oar.

I turned toward the riverbank and stared slack-jawed, trying to make sense of what I saw. From the other end of the boat I heard Marlene say softly, "Oh, my word. I'd heard something about this, but I didn't believe it." And even as we saw it with our own eyes, we could scarcely believe the shantytown there by the river, a tent city for the most part with a few tin and cardboard shacks thrown in here and there. Smoke rose up from a half dozen scattered cook fires. Gray laundry hung on lines of rope and over tent poles. Disheveled figures moved ghostlike among the dwellings, their movements slowed no doubt by hunger and a fair degree of hopelessness. A certain despondency hovered over the camp that was evident to us even from a distance.

Link rowed us closer to shore and out of the current, close enough to smell the smoke of the fires and to hear the murmur of men's voices. "This is where you live, Link?" I asked.

"For now."

"But why? Why don't you live with your family?"

"My parents have five children at home. I'm the eldest of six. I'm trying to send money home to help them, if I can."

I shook my head. "But you should be somewhere else, in a city, somewhere where there might be more work. Not out here by the river where there's nothing."

"No, Eve. This is where I'm supposed to be. I'm sure of it."

I looked down the length of the boat at Marlene. She was still staring at the camp. Her lips were parted but she made no effort to speak. It was as though the sight of the place had stolen her words.

"Are there women and children here?" I asked Link.

He shook his head. "No, just men. There are plenty of families in the larger Hoovervilles going up around the country, but this isn't one of those. This is just a little backwater town, compared to some."

"How many men are here?"

"Well, now, that depends on the day you're asking. Men

are coming and going all the time. Some stay longer than others, like me, trying to pick up day jobs around here. Some move on down the rails pretty quick."

I thought of my soft bed in my own room at the lodge, of the hot-water bath between my room and Mother and Daddy's, of the abundant meals Annie cooked that we routinely consumed.

"Link?"

"Uh-huh?"

"What do these people need most?"

"Besides jobs?"

"Yes."

"Food. That's why so many of them show up at the lodge. They know your uncle has an open hand. I wanted you to know why they come."

Reluctantly, I looked back toward the ghosts, wondered how many of them were like Link, intelligent, educated, willing to work but down on their luck.

"Will you take me home now, Link?"

Link turned the boat around and began to row.

Chapter 16

I didn't want to think about the poor people in the shantytown. All I wanted to do was dance with Marcus. Saturday night Uncle Cy brought in a band from Lexington, and once again the dance floor on the island was filled with laughing couples. I wanted to laugh too. I wanted to be young and in love and not alone. There would be time to save the world later. Tonight was mine.

When the band took a break Marcus and I moved to the shadows, lugging along bottles of Coke we'd bought at the Eatery. We sat atop a picnic table, our feet on the bench, and looked out over the river. The surface of the water shimmered under the light of a nearly full moon. I was keenly aware of Marcus beside me; he was, in truth, all that mattered at the moment. Mother was my age when she met Daddy, proving that romance can come early and last a lifetime. I held my breath and savored that thought.

Marcus took a long sip of Coke and settled the bottle on the tabletop. "Well," he said, "the day I haven't been looking forward to all summer is almost here."

I sighed and nodded. "Will you send me a postcard, Marcus?"

"Sure," he said. With a wink he added, "I might even send you two." In the morning, he and his family were leaving for their annual summer trek to Bay City, Michigan, where his father had relatives.

"I hope the week goes by fast."

"Believe me, it can't go fast enough for me," Marcus agreed.

"Don't you like your father's side of the family?"

"I like them about as much as I like my father, which is not very much."

"Do you have to go?"

"Yes." He nodded glumly. "I have to go."

I sighed again.

"But only two more months and then it'll be, so long, family! So long, dear old dad!" He laughed lightly. "At least the old man's letting me go to college. I should be glad about that." He lifted his bottle in the air and straightened his shoulders. "I'd like to propose a toast to rich aunts who pick up the slack where scholarships leave off."

Our bottles met with a clink. We downed the remainder of soda and tossed the bottles in the grass. Marcus had told me about the childless great-aunt whose recent death provided enough inheritance to get Marcus through his freshman year. I thought the timing was a stroke of good luck, and yet . . .

"Don't look so sad," he said.

I shrugged shyly. "I'll miss you."

"It's two months off."

"I know but . . ."

He smiled. "You can't get rid of me that easily, you know. I'll be back."

"And you'll write?"

"Sure I'll write. Of course. You worry too much."

But there would be girls there, pretty girls, and I would be here. Still in high school. Just a kid, compared to them.

"Don't worry," he assured me, as though he knew my thoughts, and there, in the moon shadows on Marryat Island, he kissed me, a brief and gentle kiss—my first.

I believed him that I had nothing to worry about. Everything would be all right now. Everything was unfolding in my favor, and love was possible.

We danced until long past midnight, and I sailed into Sunday on the fragile wings of little-girl dreams.

At a little after nine the next night, the phone at the front desk rang. I was sitting alone on the porch pining for Marcus when Uncle Cy opened the screen door. "Phone's for you, darling."

"For me?" I echoed. "Who is it?"

"She says her name is Marlene. Just don't tie up the line for long, all right?"

Inside, the black receiver lay curled on the desk like a wounded cat. I shivered.

"Hello?"

"Eve, can you come help me?"

"What's the matter?"

"It's Jimmy."

"What's wrong?"

"Just come over."

"Where are you?"

"At the station."

"But it's closed."

"I know that. Jimmy has the key. Please come."

"But—"

The line went dead.

Without telling Uncle Cy or anyone else where I was going, I ran across the street to the station, my mind tumbling with questions. Marlene was waiting for me when I reached the front door. She took my hand and pulled me into the dimly lit room, a stark place with shelves of auto supplies, a lone folding chair, and an ancient wooden cash register that was large enough to hold plenty of money. The place felt oily and smelled of grease.

"What's going on?" I asked as I glanced around suspiciously. My voice quivered and I was finding it hard to breathe.

"I'm scared, Eve. I've never seen him so drunk."

"Who?"

"Jimmy, of course."

"He's been drinking?"

"That's not the worst of it. He's threatening to kill his father."

"Why?"

"For beating him up again."

"His father beat him up?"

She tugged at my hand. "Come on."

My gut told me to run, but I allowed Marlene to pull me into the back office. Jimmy sat on an overturned crate, a bottle of something in one hand, an open pocketknife in the other. Each hand was resting on a knee, and his head hung low, as though he were dozing.

Marlene and I exchanged a horrified glance. My eyes asked, *What in the world?* while hers said, *I told you so.*

Softly I called his name. "Jimmy?"

With effort, he lifted his head. His swollen eyelids opened slowly and reluctantly, like shades that are stuck. He had a split upper lip and a dark bruise across his right cheek. He took a deep steadying breath, though his head bobbed slightly as he said, "Eve. What are you doing here?"

I glanced again at Marlene. She nodded. "Marlene called me over. She was worried."

He lifted the bottle to his lips and took a long drink. He rubbed at his mouth with the back of his sleeve, winced as the rough cloth met the wound. His head went down again.

"Jimmy," I said quietly, "what happened?"

He mumbled something I couldn't hear.

"I didn't understand you." I took a tentative step closer. "What did you say?"

The head rolled up and he struggled to keep his eyes open. When he spoke, his words were slow and slurred. "I said, I'm going to kill the old man. I'm going to kill him."

"What happened, Jimmy?" I asked again.

"I'm tired. Tired of being his punching bag."

"Your father did this?"

Jimmy sniffed out a laugh. "Yeah. That surprise you?"

"But everyone will know. How does he think he'll get away with it?"

"He'll just say I got in another fight. By now I've fought with every kid in town." He lifted the bottle up to the light. "Down the hatch," he said. He emptied the bottle and lowered it to his knee, where it slid down his pants leg and landed with a small thud on the floor.

Marlene moved to him and, kneeling, picked up the bottle. She turned it toward the light so she could read the label.

"This is Scotch," she said. "Real Scotch. Jimmy, where did you get this?"

His head came up with a jerk and his glassy eyes shimmered. "Right here!" he cried. "I got it right here. And I'm covering for that . . ." He swore at his father, a loud barrage of curses that trailed off to mumbled oaths.

I waited till his anger was spent. Then I asked, "Jimmy, what are you talking about? What do you mean, you got it right here?"

His shoulders heaved in a great sigh. He looked first at Marlene and then at me. "I'll show you." He closed the blade of the knife and stuck it in his pants pocket. Then he pushed himself up and staggered on unsteady legs. He stumbled to the door leading to the small bay where they worked on cars. With his hand on the door, he turned back to us. "But wait here a minute. Wait till I call you."

"All right," I said. Marlene nodded.

He went into the bay, and we heard a pounding noise before he hollered, "All right, you can come in."

We ventured in. Jimmy didn't say anything. He didn't have to. One narrow section of the wall between the bay and the front room was not a wall at all but a small storage space filled with crates. Jimmy lifted one off the top and settled it on the floor at his feet. The lid was already missing. He reached inside, dug around amid the straw and pulled out a bottle of Scotch, identical to the one he had just emptied. He unscrewed the cap and waved the bottle dramatically. "That's right, folks! Come on in for a gallon of gas, a pint of oil, and all the booze you can drink." He upended the bottle and drank; it dribbled down his chin and dampened his blood-stained shirt.

Marlene and I stared at him in silence. Finally Marlene managed to whisper, "Jimmy, where does this come from?"

Jimmy stumbled as he turned to look at Marlene. Righting himself, he said, "Canada. Got to be Canada. Goes to Cincinnati. Comes here."

"But I mean, how does it get here?"

"I don't know. It just keeps coming. And the old man keeps unloading it. He thinks I don't know, but I do. Know all about it. I'm not stupid. Cars come in the car wash, roll out with a full tank." He laughed loudly at that, took another swig. "Yeah, he thinks I don't know, but I know. I know what he's doing."

"He's bootlegging," I said.

Jimmy looked at me with his glazed eyes. Spittle flew from his mouth as he hollered, "Bingo! The old man's a bootlegger. I oughta turn him in, have him arrested."

"Why don't you, Jimmy?" Marlene asked. "Why don't you turn him in and have him arrested?"

"Because he'd kill me. Or have me killed. Even if he went to prison, he'd find a way . . ." Jimmy finished by drawing a finger across this throat. "So I stay quiet. Me and Marcus, we don't say anything."

"Marcus?" My eyes widened and a rush of light-headedness rolled over me. "Does Marcus know about this?"

"Sure, he knows. He knows because I told him. Just like I'm telling you." Jimmy's voice trailed off as his expression grew pained. He moaned pitifully and started to cry. "I shouldn't be telling you," he wailed. "The old man's going to kill me."

I went to him and put a hand on his arm. "Jimmy, if Marcus knows, why doesn't he tell his father? His dad's the sheriff, after all. Why doesn't Marcus tell him?"

"You don't know the sheriff, do you, Eve?" he asked,

pulling away from my touch. He sniffed and wiped his eyes on his sleeve. He was angry again. "He's more interested in lining his own pocket than in keeping the law. Marcus and I figure his old man knows. He's just looking the other way. Gets paid off to pretend like he doesn't know nothing. Liquor's flowing through this station, and no one knows about it. Not me, not Marcus, not the sheriff."

He lifted the crate back into the hiding place. Then his foot hit something—I wasn't sure what—and he slid the wall shut. "I'm tired," he mumbled. He looked at the bottle of Scotch in his hand, took a sip and slowly made his way back to the office. There, he pulled the penknife out of his pocket and clutched it in one tight fist. At the same time, he sank to the floor and curled up on his side.

Marlene kneeled beside him. She cried openly now, great silent tears sliding down her cheeks. "Eve, what should we do?"

I moistened my dry lips with my tongue and took a deep breath. "Leave him. He'll sleep it off."

Marlene gently touched a hand to his cheek. His eyes fluttered open. "Don't tell," he whispered. "Don't you dare tell. Old man'll kill me."

"I won't tell, Jimmy. I promise." She bent over him and kissed his brow. Her tears left little pools of grief on his skin. "We're going to get out of here. Soon, Jimmy. We'll leave and never come back."

She drew in a deep trembling breath. Tenderly uncurling his fingers, she lifted the knife from his fist and slipped it into her skirt pocket. After a moment she stood. "I don't want to leave him."

"You can't stay," I said. "Your folks won't know where you are."

She gazed at Jimmy and didn't respond.

"Can you walk home from here?" I asked.

"Yes, it's not far."

"You'd better go."

"What if I leave and he dies in the night?"

"He won't die. Like I said, he'll sleep it off."

"But what about Jimmy's folks? If he stays here, they won't know where he is either."

"Even if he could walk," I said, "do you really think he should go home like this?"

Marlene sighed. She wiped at her face with the palms of both hands. "I hate the old man for what he's done to Jimmy."

I didn't respond, though I had to agree. I'd never met Calvin Fludd, but his signature was written all over Jimmy's face. He was an evil man.

"You can come by in the morning and see for yourself that Jimmy's all right," I said. "Bet you anything Mr. Fludd will be acting like nothing happened."

"All right, Eve." She looked at me, tried to smile. "Listen, thanks for coming over."

I was about to burst at the seams. If I broke into a thousand pieces, every one of them would scream in anger over what I had just learned about the station. And about Marcus.

"You're welcome," I said quietly. "I'll see you tomorrow."

I turned to go. Marlene called me back. "You won't tell, will you?"

I swallowed the bile in my throat. My fists were two tight balls of fury. "I'll see you tomorrow, Marlene," I said again. As I turned and fled, I couldn't know that I would never see Marlene again.

Chapter 17

I had to tell. I had no choice. It was the Jones Five and Ten Law, passed a couple of years earlier. I was well aware of what it said. Anyone who knew of the sale of illicit liquor but didn't report it was just as guilty of the crime, punishable by five years in prison and a $10,000 fine.

I stood in the hallway outside Mother and Daddy's room, lifted my hand to the door, hesitated.

Calvin Fludd deserved to be arrested. He had to be punished both for bootlegging and for beating up his own son. Now that I knew what was happening, how could I let it go on? How could I not turn him in?

Then again, if I told, what would happen to Jimmy? Wouldn't Old Man Fludd notice the missing bottles, the ones Jimmy had pilfered tonight, and from there figure out where the leak was? Surely he would come to realize Jimmy knew about the stash. Not only knew about it but had helped himself to it. If the place was raided and Fludd arrested, no doubt he'd figure Jimmy had turned him in.

And Marcus. What about Marcus? I leaned my forehead

against the door and broke into tears. I had a feeling I was somehow going to lose him over this, and I couldn't bear the thought of it. The cords of my heart were all tied up around him, and I didn't want to have to disentangle myself and step away. He'd made me happy, really happy, in a way I'd never been. And yet, I couldn't deny what was true. At the tip of my anger, the hottest part of the flame, was a sense of betrayal. Marcus wasn't who I thought he was. And he was never going to be who I wanted him to be. He knew the liquor was being sold at the station, and he wasn't willing to do anything about it.

I took one step back from the door just as it opened. Daddy stood there, staring at me with puzzled eyes. "Eve? Darling, what's the matter?"

I fell into his arms and cried even more loudly, burying my face in his shoulder, dripping tears onto his shirt and the strap of his suspenders. He shut the door behind us and ushered me into the room.

"Sweetheart," Mother cried. "What on earth is wrong?"

I sat down on one of the chairs and took several deep breaths, trying to compose myself. Mother handed me one of Daddy's handkerchiefs, then sat on the footstool and put her hands on my shoulders. She was already in her robe and slippers and had been brushing out her hair, readying for bed.

"Sweetheart," she said again, "can you tell us what's wrong?"

Daddy sat in the opposite chair and waited.

My face burned and my head felt heavy, like it had turned to stone. I wiped at my tears and looked at Mother and Daddy's expectant, fearful faces. "It's Calvin Fludd," I began, and by the time I finished my story their faces had run the gamut from concern to disbelief to horror almost equal to my own.

Mother turned to Daddy. "Do you suppose Cyrus knows they're selling liquor right across the street?"

Daddy took a deep breath. "I don't know," he said, "but I'm going to find out."

Mother stayed behind while Daddy and I went off to find Uncle Cy. Thomas, the night clerk, was behind the front desk looking at the guest register. He smiled wanly as we approached him.

"Evening, Thomas," Daddy said.

"Evening, Mr. Marryat."

"Would you happen to know where Cyrus is?"

"I believe he's retired for the night, sir."

"Thank you."

Thomas responded with a slight lift of his chin; his glasses flashed as the lenses caught the overhead light.

Daddy and I moved through the sitting room where the clock on the mantel showed the time to be almost midnight. As we made our way down the hall into the ballroom, I said, "Do you suppose Uncle Cy's asleep?"

"If he is, we'll wake him up," Daddy said. "I don't intend to wait till morning."

Uncle Cy answered our knock right away. He was wearing a sleeveless undershirt and a pair of slacks, and he held a glass of iced tea in one hand. He stared at us a moment, his brows raised, as though he didn't quite know who we were.

"Sorry to bother you at this hour of the night, Cy," Daddy said.

"That's all right," Uncle Cy said, opening the door wider and stepping aside. "Come in."

One of Jones's radios was on, tuned to a comedy show of some kind. Two men talking, a drum roll, people laughing, and then abrupt silence as Uncle Cy turned it off.

"Have a seat," he said.

Daddy and I sat in the two wing chairs while Uncle Cy pulled a straight-back chair over from the table. He set his glass of tea on the floor beside him.

"Jones here?" Daddy asked.

"He's asleep," Uncle Cy answered. "So what's this about? There a problem?"

Daddy leaned forward and squeezed his hands together. "With the lodge, no. Listen, Cy, it's the station across the street."

Uncle Cy's face was passive, though somewhere in the center of his eyes I thought I saw a flash of alarm. He picked up his tea, took a sip, set it back down.

"Calvin's selling bootleg liquor from that place," Daddy said. "Eve saw it tonight, the whole stash. All folks have got to do is pull around back to the car wash, and apparently Calvin loads them up there."

Uncle Cy's eyes slid over to me. "This true, Eve?"

I nodded. I didn't want to tell the whole story again. I was exhausted, my head was pounding, and I wanted nothing other than to crawl into bed and weep myself into a merciful sleep.

Uncle Cy sniffed. He lifted an index finger to his lips and frowned in thought. Finally, he dropped his hand and said evenly, "Listen to me, Drew. We've got nothing to do with Calvin and his station. What he does is his own business. It doesn't concern us."

Daddy sat motionless, a sickish pallor sliding over his face. His Adam's apple moved up and down his throat a couple of times, as though he was finding Uncle Cy's words hard to swallow. Then he said, "Are you telling me to turn a blind eye?"

Uncle Cy nodded. "That's exactly what I'm telling you to do. I'm telling you for your own good. This county is full of bootleggers, and they don't take kindly to snitches."

"That may be so, Cy, but you can't expect me to just sit by and do nothing. This isn't homebrew they're selling over there. It's real liquor, no doubt being smuggled across the border from Canada. We got criminals working right across the street, and you're telling me to leave it alone?"

Uncle Cy sidled forward to the edge of the chair till he was almost face-to-face with Daddy. His eyes grew small, his skin ruddy. "You have no idea what you're getting yourself in the middle of," he said slowly, as though Daddy was a dull-witted child. "I'm telling you to keep your nose out of other people's business."

Daddy was undeterred. When he spoke, a small chill moved up and down my spine. "What Calvin Fludd is doing," Daddy said, "is not a business, it's a crime. And if we sit idly by and say nothing, we're just as guilty."

"So be it, Drew. The laws of Prohibition have made everyone a criminal in one way or another—"

"Not everyone, Cy—"

"And so we run the lodge and keep our noses clean, and we don't worry about what people are doing across the street or up the river or anywhere else for that matter. Do you understand me, Drew?"

The two brothers stared at each other with such intensity

I thought one or the other of them might simply explode. Finally, Daddy stood, reached for my hand, and pulled me up out of the chair.

"Drew?" Uncle Cy said again.

"I thought you would do the right thing, Cy."

"I *am* doing the right thing, Drew. You've got to believe me. I know this town in ways you don't. So we're all going to keep our mouths shut and go on doing what we were doing before this happened tonight."

A small muscle worked in Daddy's jaw. Uncle Cy sighed.

Daddy tugged at my hand and we left without saying another word.

Chapter 18

Are you absolutely sure about this, Eve?"

I looked across the desk at the pock-faced man with the sagging jowls and closely cropped auburn hair. As his blue eyes settled on my face, a ticklish drop of sweat slid down my back between my shoulder blades. I rested my elbows on the arms of the stiff wooden chair and took a deep breath. "I saw it with my own eyes, Captain Macnish," I said.

With that, his small black pupils cut into me like a surgeon's knife, trying to find any indication of falsehood inside. I shivered in spite of the heat. In the single window of his cluttered office, a steel fan worked hard to blow a ceaseless stream of hot air in our direction.

"These are serious charges, you know." Captain Macnish leaned over the desk and clasped his hands together. He was a large man, and his bulky chest threatened to pop the buttons of his shirt.

"We know that, Neal," Daddy said. "You can trust Eve. She wouldn't lie."

I nodded my head in agreement. The penetrating cobalt irises rolled from Daddy to me and back again.

"Who knows you're here, Drew?"

"No one, other than the three of us and Rose."

"Are you sure?"

"Yes."

"Cyrus doesn't know?"

"I didn't tell him we were coming."

"But you told him about Fludd?"

"Yes. He said to keep our mouths shut and our noses clean. In other words, stay out of it."

"Where does he think you are at this moment?"

"At the drugstore getting Rose some headache medicine."

Now the intrepid eyes bore into Daddy. After a long moment, Daddy reached into his shirt pocket and pulled out the packet of headache powder. "I didn't lie, Neal, if that's what you're thinking."

"That wasn't what I was thinking."

"Then what *are* you thinking?"

Captain Macnish glanced at the closed door of his office. His ancient swivel chair creaked in protest as he leaned back and laid his hands across his ample stomach, fingers still entwined. Somewhere out of my field of vision, a fly buzzed loudly.

"The Prohibition laws have been an albatross around my neck for these past five years I've been the chief, Drew. Soon as Prohibition took effect, stills started popping up around here like mushrooms on a manure pile. We've always had moonshiners, of course, but nothing like what we got now. The former chief of police turned a blind eye."

"What about you, Neal? You try to find the stills, close them down?"

"I did. In the beginning. The thing is, there are too many folks willing to wag a tongue to protect the bad guy. By the time my men could reach the moonshiners' camp, the whole kit-and-caboodle had been taken apart and the place deserted. I didn't make many arrests. Some, but not many. I finally decided my men's time and the taxpayers' money could better be spent on other pursuits. Nobody really wanted the moonshiners arrested anyway."

"Are you saying Cy is right, that we should just mind our own business?"

The chair moaned loudly as Captain Macnish pushed himself away from the desk. He stood and began to pace the room. I followed him with my eyes, waiting.

"What Fludd's got at the station isn't moonshine, though, is it?" He turned abruptly and looked at me.

"No, sir," I said. "I saw bottles of Scotch. Jimmy said it's the real stuff. He thinks it's brought to Cincinnati all the way from Canada."

"I always figured somebody was bringing real liquor into Mercy. Never had any proof, though."

"Well, Neal," Daddy said, "now you do. So what are you going to do about it?"

"What do you want me to do, Drew?"

"Raid the place, of course."

"It's not that easy."

"Why not?"

The captain sat down heavily in his chair. His face gleamed with sweat. He placed both arms on the desk and leaned forward. He glanced toward the door again before saying in a low voice, "Because I don't know who I can trust. That's why."

"What do you mean?"

"I mean, of my own men, I don't know who I can trust."

Daddy and I looked at each other. I felt light-headed.

Captain Macnish said, "You shouldn't be so surprised, Drew. There are few men out there who don't want a drink now and again. Even a law officer is only human."

I wasn't quite sure what he was getting at, but Daddy seemed to piece it together. "So you could plan a raid, and one of your men who's buying from Fludd could tip him off."

"That's right." Captain Macnish nodded and rubbed one side of his sagging face with an open palm. "Could and would in the time it takes to say Jack Daniel's."

"I see," Daddy said. "Which reminds me, Eve tells me she thinks Sheriff Wiant maybe knows about what Fludd's doing."

If Daddy expected a look of surprise to flash across his old friend's face, he was disappointed. The captain shrugged. "Sure," he said, "and he's probably getting paid a sizeable cut to put the blinders on."

"That seems to be the case," Daddy agreed. "You know the sheriff's son works at the station."

"Marcus." The captain nodded. "Yes, I know."

"He knows about the liquor, but he's not saying a word."

Captain Macnish looked at me. I nodded. The nausea I'd awakened with that morning rose up and rolled in small waves across my stomach. I never felt well after a night of crying, and Sunday night had been one of those nights.

"Marcus is a good boy," the captain went on. "He's just found himself between a rock and a hard place. I don't envy the kid."

I dropped my eyes and didn't respond.

Daddy said, "So anyway, there's probably no use you taking this to the sheriff."

"No, I can see that. Which pretty much proves my point, Drew. If I can't trust the top lawman in the county, who can I trust?"

"Surely there must be some among your own men."

Captain Macnish nodded thoughtfully but said nothing.

Daddy fidgeted in the chair beside me. He picked up the cap he'd laid across his knee and squeezed it in both hands. "What about the feds, Neal? You don't have any revenuers around here you can turn to for help?"

"Prohibition agents here in Mercy?" Captain Macnish laughed out loud. "You're kidding, right? There are only a few hundred of those in the whole country, Drew. They're stretched as thin as your last dollar just trying to keep up with things in the cities. They're not going to waste their time in a small town like this."

I looked at Daddy. "That's what Jones told me. Remember?"

One side of Daddy's mouth drew back as he nodded. "Yeah, I remember."

Captain Macnish leaned back again in his chair and put both hands behind his head, an unfortunate move as it revealed the two dark moons of sweat under each arm. "Besides," he said, "those revenuers . . ." He clicked his tongue and sniffed loudly. "Their pay is so poor that half of them are taking bribes from bootleggers just to keep bread on the table."

Daddy swallowed hard. He stopped kneading his cap and stared at Captain Macnish. "What's this country come to, Neal?" he said quietly.

The captain sniffed again as he settled his arms on the desk. "I'm telling you, Drew, you try to use a law like Prohibition to put the squeeze on people, and a whole bunch of no-good is going to come out. That's just the way it is." He picked up some loose papers on his desk and tapped them into a neat pile, as though we were finished. He slipped them into a file folder and laid it aside. Then he sighed heavily. "Some days I hate this job, Drew."

"But it's still your job, Neal."

Captain Macnish let out such a long sigh I thought he might shrivel up and blow away. He swatted at the fly that was now buzzing around his head. He looked toward the window, then at Daddy. "You're right, of course," he said quietly. "I'm not arguing with you there. I hate to see the law broken as much as you do." He paused, shook his head. "I knew this badge would show me the ugly side of life, even in a small town like Mercy, but I never thought so much of the ugly would come from otherwise good men. Do you know what I mean, Drew?"

"I think I do, yes."

"Most of my men are honest cops and solid citizens, except when it comes to drink. When it comes to that, I don't know who's in and who's out. Without Prohibition, my job would be a whole lot easier." Under his breath, he cursed the albatross around his neck. Then, sheepishly, he said, "Begging your pardon, Eve."

I nodded and offered him a tiny smile.

"But you'll do something about Fludd, won't you, Neal?" Daddy asked.

"Yes, yes. I'll do something about Fludd." He laid a finger across his lips and looked aside.

Daddy leaned forward in his chair. "You know about those two agents a few years back—Izzy and Moe, right?"

"Yeah." The captain nodded. "What about them?"

"Well, they were always pretending to be someone they weren't. Baseball players. Construction workers. Traveling salesmen. They'd go into a speakeasy, order a drink, and once the liquor came they revealed their badges and arrested everybody in the place."

"Yeah, I know all about it, but if you're saying I should send someone undercover to Fludd's, it won't work. Fludd knows all my men. Everyone knows everyone in Mercy."

Daddy sat back, deflated. After a moment, he said, "There must be one or two revenuers in Cincy who'd come over and make the raid. It's a sure thing, Neal. We already know the liquor's there."

"Maybe. I—" The captain was interrupted when the intercom buzzed. He pressed a button on his desk. "Yes, Miss Dearborn?"

A disembodied feminine voice rose up from the machine. "You're late for your meeting in the briefing room, sir."

"Tell Haskins I'll be right there."

"Yes, sir."

The captain stood. "Drew, don't worry. I'll take care of it."

He held out a hand. Daddy stood and shook it. "Thank you for your time, Neal."

"Of course. Listen, thanks for coming in. And I mean it when I say don't worry. I'm going to take care of this one way or the other."

Outside the tiny police station, as we walked along the sidewalk to our car, I said, "Daddy, do you think you can trust Captain Macnish?"

Daddy thought a moment. We were already in the car by the time he responded. "I've known Neal a long time," he said. "We went all the way through school together."

"I know, Daddy. But do you think you can trust him?"

Daddy stared straight ahead as he started the car. "I surely hope so, darling," he said. He shifted into reverse, looked at me, and tried to smile. "I guess we'll find out."

Chapter 19

For several anxious days, Daddy and I waited for Captain Macnish to act. In that time, a couple of things happened. For one, Jimmy and Marlene disappeared. Rumors reached me that they'd eloped, left town one night in Jimmy's old jalopy, but I had no way of knowing whether the rumors were true. I wasn't about to walk across the street and ask Calvin Fludd where his son had gone. Nor did I want to ask Marlene's folks if their daughter had run off to get married. I figured I would find out sooner or later.

The other thing that happened was Uncle Cy received word that Aunt Cora's health was declining. He told Daddy about it in an off-handed way while Daddy and I were on our way to the dining room for breakfast.

"Well now, listen, Cy," Daddy said upon hearing the news. "Don't you want to go see her? Rose and I can take care of the lodge while you're away."

Uncle Cy shook his head adamantly. He stood behind the front desk sorting incoming mail as he spoke. "If I go out there, it'd be the same as me telling her she's going to die. I'm not going to give her permission. She has to believe she'll get better."

Daddy's brow wrinkled with concern. "But what if she doesn't get better?" He hesitated only a moment before adding, "You can't let her die alone."

My uncle stopped sorting the letters and looked up at Daddy. His expression was one of anger, terror, and sorrow all mixed up together. "She's not going to die, Drew," he said evenly. "Now let me get back to work."

And so we waited. I went about my tasks at the lodge just waiting to find out when Captain Macnish would raid the station, where Jimmy and Marlene had gone, what Marcus would say when he returned from vacation, and whether or not Aunt Cora would die.

Finally, early on Saturday, Daddy came to my door with the morning edition of the newspaper. When I answered his knock, he held up the paper so I could see the front-page headline. One headline wasn't enough for this story; the paper had given it three, laid out across two columns in descending point size.

RAID A BUST!
Police swarm Fludd's Service Station
Find nothing more potent than motor oil

Without saying a word, I took the paper and turned aside into my room. Daddy followed and shut the door. My breath quickened as I stared at the headline and tried to make sense of it. I looked up at Daddy beseechingly. "Daddy, I know what I saw. The liquor was there."

"I believe you, darling," he said grimly. "Obviously, Fludd was tipped off."

"By who?"

"I don't know."

"One of Captain Macnish's men?"

"I don't know, darling, but not likely. Neal pulled the raid with outside help. He went to a couple of state troopers he knew he could trust. No . . ." He shook his head. "It had to be someone else."

I sat down hard on the edge of my bed. I glanced at the paper, but the thought of reading the article turned my stomach and fueled my anger.

"What do we do now, Daddy?"

He shrugged. "Nothing much we can do."

"But won't they just go right back to bootlegging?"

"That's almost a given."

"Will Captain Macnish try to raid them again?"

"I don't know," Daddy said. "Neal came by here briefly after the raid last night." I looked up sharply, brows raised. "You were long asleep. I didn't want to wake you."

"What did he say?"

Daddy shrugged again, rubbed one freshly shaved cheek with his long fingers. "Just said someone had got to Fludd before he did."

"Is he mad at me?"

"No."

"Does he still believe me?"

"Yes. He believes you. 'Course, when something like this happens, it kind of makes the police look bad for a while, like they don't know what they're doing. They may have a little public relations work ahead of them, try to win back some of the respect they might have lost last night. You remember Neal saying he stopped raiding stills because by the time he and his men got there, the moonshiners were already gone?" When I nodded, Daddy went on, "This is the same thing only on a larger scale, because Fludd's playing with the big boys."

"But who's that, Daddy?"

"Don't know for sure." He shook his head. "Neal says Fludd has got to be connected with one of the major bootleggers working out of Cincinnati. Could be any one of a number of them."

"And we can't do anything about them?"

"Cincy isn't Neal's jurisdiction, honey. He has to limit himself to the affairs of Mercy. He did what he could, but he's up against a wall that's just too big. It's hard to enforce a law nobody wants. People want the liquor, not the law, and there's too many willing to lie and cheat to see it's made available. So no, I don't imagine Neal's going to be pulling any more raids anytime soon."

"Does Uncle Cy know what happened?"

"Sure, he knows."

"Was he with you while you were talking with Captain Macnish last night?"

Daddy shook his head. "No, that was just me and Neal. But Cy read the paper this morning. He knows."

"He'll probably say we should have just minded our own business."

"He may not say anything at all. Probably figures we learned our lesson."

"Learned our lesson? As though we were the ones who did something wrong?"

"No, darling, I didn't mean it that way. We did the right thing. We did what we could."

I nodded while turning my gaze to the window. "You know, Daddy, I didn't think living here would be like this. I mean, I thought we were leaving all this bootlegging stuff behind."

I heard Daddy click his tongue. "One thing you got to know, Eve, is people are pretty much the same everywhere you go. Most people are good folks with bad habits. That just seems to be the way of it."

"Fludd should have been arrested."

"Yes, but he wasn't."

"Does he know we turned him in?"

"No. He knows someone did, but he doesn't know who."

"I'm afraid of him."

"Don't be. All he wants is to quietly go on doing what he's been doing."

I looked back at Daddy. "Do you know what happened to Jimmy and Marlene? Did Captain Macnish tell you anything?"

He nodded. "Looks like the rumors are true. The two of them ran off, probably got married somewhere."

"Well, that's one good thing, then."

"What's that, darling?"

"Jimmy won't be Calvin Fludd's punching bag anymore."

Daddy sighed heavily. "Shame they couldn't have had a proper wedding, but it's probably just as well for them to go on and start a new life."

Poor Marlene. I wondered where she was and whether she and Jimmy had really become husband and wife. And if they had, I wondered whether she was sorry she didn't get to wear a wedding dress, walk down the aisle, and toss her bouquet toward the uplifted hands of young girls eager to shed their maidenhood. I wondered what kind of life she and Jimmy would have from now on. With a jumping-off point of liquor and violence, it seemed like the odds were against them, but I hoped somehow they'd be happy anyway.

If, that is, it was possible to be happy in this world. Which, the older I got and the more I knew, was beginning to seem more and more unlikely.

Chapter 20

If Uncle Cy said anything to Daddy about the raid, Daddy never told me. Any confrontation between the two of them had probably turned ugly, and Daddy would have wanted to shield me from that. I did notice, though, that the two men now seemed wary of each other and any conversation between them was stilted and cheerless. As far as his demeanor toward me, Uncle Cy seemed unchanged, as though I'd had nothing at all to do with blowing the whistle on Fludd's bootlegging operation.

The day the news of the raid hit the paper was a busy day on the island, as it was the Fourth of July. Uncle Cy planned a big bash for his guests with feasting, music, dancing, and fireworks. We all went about our business preparing for the party as though nothing at all had happened across the street. Morris made extra runs to the train station, bringing back a crowded jitney laden with both people and luggage of all shapes and sizes. Every one of our guest rooms was full, the suite occupied by the wealthy George Sluder and his wife who came for the weekend. When they arrived on

Saturday at noon, Mr. Sluder appeared uncommonly pale and grim-faced, as though he had a headache or a peptic stomach. Uncle Cy waited on the man personally, carrying refreshments up to the suite and making sure His Highness and the Queen were pampered and comfortable.

By early evening, the lodge, the grounds, and the island were all bustling with folks eager to celebrate the holiday. I was in no mood for merrymaking. When all my chores were finished, I feigned a headache and, accepting a cheese sandwich from Annie for my supper, retreated to my room. There, I tenderly lifted the brass ring out of my treasure box and held it to my heart. Marcus was supposed to arrive back in town in the morning. His father being the sheriff, as well as a possible beneficiary of Fludd's criminal dealings, Marcus probably knew all about what had happened on Friday night.

I clung to what Captain Macnish had said about Marcus: *"He's a good boy. He's just found himself between a rock and a hard place."*

Yes, surely that was true. Marcus was a good person in an impossible situation. He wouldn't know that I had been the one to tell Captain Macnish, but if he found out, maybe he would be glad. Maybe he would even thank me. Surely he hated the bootlegging going on at the station just as much as I did, but with his father receiving a cut, he felt helpless to stop it.

I stood at the window for a long while, nibbling on the sandwich and looking out over the activities below—the guests scurrying back and forth across the footbridge, the arrival of the band and their instruments, Morris and one of the other workers hauling enormous watermelons to the site of the party. As I watched, I discovered that fear and loneliness are magnified by the happiness of others. Had the circumstances been different, I might have been out there too, mingling with the crowd and enjoying the party with Marcus. Instead, I was here in my room and he was gone, and I was afraid of what might happen when he returned. Marcus had been mine for such a brief time, and now that chapter might already be closing, depending on how he reacted to the raid.

As dusk gave way to dark, I slipped out of my shoes and lay down on my bed. Still clutching the carousel ring, I listened. The night air echoed with chatter and laughter; waves of joyful voices rolled up and down the river. Eventually, thunderous fireworks exploded across the sky, their flashing lights reaching into my room like momentary sparks stinging my cold flesh. Then, at last, music. Loud and boisterous and full of cheer. In my mind's eye I saw the dance floor, the flying limbs, the sweaty bodies, the gleeful faces. I should have been out there, dancing under the stars with Marcus.

I wasn't sure I would ever dance with him again.

Sometime after midnight, I drifted into sleep. I awoke in the morning with the brass ring still resting loosely in my palm. Putting it back in my treasure box, I readied myself for church and steeled myself for Marcus's return.

When it happened, it happened quickly and cleanly. Late Sunday afternoon I was on the island, reading in a deck chair by the shore. After the previous night's revelry, the island was subdued, like a drunk sleeping it off. A few people swam, others gathered about the picnic tables, one or two boats were out on the water. I couldn't concentrate on the open book in my hands for thinking of Marcus. I was wondering when I would see him and how it would all play out when suddenly, as though out of nowhere, there he was.

"Eve."

At the sound of my name, I gasped. I turned to look and when I saw him standing there, my heart sprang up in one brief beat of hope that he would think I'd done the right thing. That we would go on from where we'd left off.

I put the book aside and sprang up from the chair but stopped short of reaching out for him. Nor did he reach for me. We stood awkwardly staring at each other, the sun bearing down on us, the dissonance of voices around us receding into the background as my whole world circled down to Marcus and me and this moment. The look in his eyes said he knew exactly what had happened while he was out of town.

Tell me I did the right thing, I pleaded silently. *Tell me you're grateful to me for trying to stop the bootlegging going on at the gas station.*

But when he spoke, I heard the lead in his voice and I knew it wouldn't be so. "I heard about the raid," he said. "And now Jimmy and Marlene are gone."

My own voice betrayed me, scattering in fear. "Yes," I whispered.

"Jimmy told you about the stash."

"Yes." I nodded.

"And you took it to Macnish."

I hesitated a moment before nodding again. My voice still barely audible, I asked, "How did you know?"

"I didn't know. Not for sure. I just figured." He looked at me a long time, and I watched as his breathing grew heavy and his cheeks grew flushed. "Why did you tell, Eve?" he finally said. "Why did you do it?"

166

Why did I tell? *Why did I tell?*

The question ignited my fury like a match on dried kindling. I'd told because it was the right thing, the lawful thing, to do. Didn't he know that? I straightened my back and found my voice. "Why *didn't* you tell, Marcus?"

With that, our eyes locked in contempt; I was determined not to back down. As the seconds passed, my beautiful vision of Marcus began breaking apart, the pieces drifting away like dandelion seeds in a strong wind. There would be no putting my dream back together unless one of us acknowledged a wrong.

Well, it wasn't going to be me. I waited. His lips moved slightly, as though he had something to say, but he didn't say it. He didn't need to. We had made our accusations and that was enough. His mouth became a small dead line, and then he turned and walked away.

Finding Mother alone in her room that night, I broke down and cried at her knee. She listened to my sorrow as she stroked my hair. She crooned, "I know, darling, I know," as I spilled my story into her lap. When I finished, she didn't bother offering empty assurances about other fish in the sea. She simply sang the song she used to sing to me when I was a child.

> *Hush-a-bye, don't you cry,*
> *Go to sleepy little baby.*
> *When you wake, you shall have*
> *All the pretty little horses.*

But instead of comforting me, the lullaby only left me crying all the more, and afterward when I went to bed, I scarcely slept at all.

Chapter 21

Never having had a beau before, neither had I ever lost one. I wondered at the paradox of my heart feeling enormously heavy even though a huge chunk had been torn from it. Of course I put on a happy face for the guests, welcoming them, smiling at them, cheerfully serving them breakfast or lunch while my insides churned with this unfamiliar grief.

At the same time, my thoughts turned outward, and I gazed in curiosity at the people around me. I gazed at the men and women who passed me in the lodge or on the island, and I wondered, *Have they known? Have they felt this too?* It was almost inconceivable to think that every day somebody somewhere was losing someone she loved. And surely not just one somebody but many somebodies so that dozens, hundreds, maybe thousands of people were walking around with shattered hearts. I never knew the world held such sorrow, because it was a sorrow I had previously never known myself.

Such were my thoughts at lunch on Wednesday noon when

I was pouring coffee for a man who had been at the lodge for about a week. I had noticed him, but I hadn't really seen him. It hadn't occurred to me that he was always alone, as he was now, sitting in a secluded corner of the dining room, reading a folded newspaper even while he held his cup up to me for service. Because his left hand was hidden by the newspaper, I couldn't see whether or not he wore a wedding ring.

I tipped the spout of the enamelware pot over his cup. As the coffee neared the rim, I asked, "Can I get you anything else, sir?"

He settled the cup in the saucer and looked at me. He was dressed in a gray double-breasted suit, the jacket buttoned in spite of the summer heat. The gray matched the color of his eyes, which were themselves two round pools of intensity in a hard-luck, leathery face. His cheeks and chin had been shaved raw; a small red nick glistened just above a scar that ran along his right jaw. He reminded me of Al Capone, with his fancy suit, his gray eyes, his slicked-back hair that had begun to recede, leaving his forehead wide and exposed. Except that his single scar wasn't nearly as bad as the three that had earned Scarface his name.

"No thanks, little lady," he said. "I'm fine."

But I knew that he probably wasn't fine, because he was alone. I knew that even as he sat there looking placid and satisfied, he was probably filled with a blistering sadness similar to mine. The thought of it brought tears to my eyes, but the man didn't notice. He had already snapped open the paper, turned the page, and gone back to reading.

As I stepped away from his table, Uncle Cy at the front desk motioned to me with a wave of his hand. I carried the coffeepot back to the buffet and wandered over to the desk.

"This came for you this morning," Uncle Cy said. He reached beneath the counter and pulled out a small white envelope.

I took it, expecting it to be from Ariel up in St. Paul, but my name and the address of the lodge were written in an unfamiliar script. The envelope was postmarked St. Louis, but there was no return address. I ripped it open, wondering who in Missouri would write to me.

Inside were two sheets of hotel stationery covered with small neat handwriting. My eyes fell to the signature at the bottom of the page. My heart pumped harder when I saw who it was from.

Dear Eve, Marlene wrote,

I am Mrs. James C. Fludd now and I'm proud and happy for it. Never in a million years did I dream I'd elope, but what an adventure it was! Maybe someday I'll tell you all about it, if I ever get back to Mercy, which probably won't be soon.

In the meantime there are some things I want you to know. First of all, Jimmy spoke with Marcus on the telephone, so I know Marcus is sore at you for telling. But listen, maybe he'll get over it, but if he doesn't and he just stays angry, then I say you're better off without him. I for one am glad you did it, Eve, even though at the time we left we didn't know you'd already gone to Macnish. We figured you would and that was enough. It forced Jimmy's hand. It got him out of that awful situation he was in with that old man of his. Never again will that dreadful man lay a hand on my beautiful Jimmy.

We decided to run away together the day after I saw you last. We made up our minds and didn't think twice. I went home and packed a suitcase, and in the middle of the night I snuck out and met Jimmy downtown by the movie theater. I jumped in his car and never looked back. We never will look back.

In two days' time we were married by a justice of the peace. I don't have any pictures of the wedding, but it's just as well because Jimmy still had two black eyes and a busted lip, and I don't want to remember that. You'll never believe it, but that JP had a bottle of champagne locked up in his closet. He said he always offers champagne when someone gets married, because he likes to propose a toast to the bride and groom. So think of it, Eve, I really did get to drink champagne on my wedding day!

Jimmy and I are going to make a good life for ourselves, I just know it. Of course Mama and Daddy about had a fit when they got the news, but that's a story for another time. They'll get over it, especially once the grandkids come.

So I wanted to write and tell you I'm happy and I hope someday you're as happy as I am now. Our plan is for Jimmy to find a job, which best be soon, as we've about run out of the money we brought along. Once he gets a job we'll find a place to live and I'll set up housekeeping. I don't know where we're going to settle, but once we get there, I'll write you again and let you know where we are.

> *Your true friend,*
> *Marlene Fludd*

I folded the letter with a smile and slid it back in the envelope. With a deep sigh of relief, I gave a silent word of thanks that Marlene had written me, and more important, that she was happy. Somebody in the world was happy! And she wasn't angry with me for what I'd done, but was glad for it. Finally some affirmation that I'd done the right thing.

As I slipped the letter in the pocket of my skirt, the man in the double-breasted suit stepped out of the dining room, the newspaper tucked under his arm. He nodded curtly at Uncle Cy, who in turn greeted him with a perfunctory, "Good afternoon, Mr. Adele."

That was all that passed between them, and then the man stepped out to the porch where he settled in one of the rockers.

I turned to Uncle Cy with a frown. "Uncle Cy, is that man here all by himself?"

Uncle Cy paused in his shuffling of papers and said, "What man?"

"The one who just passed by."

My uncle glanced toward the door as though an apparition of the man lingered there. "Mr. Adele? *Hmm.* Yes. He takes his vacation here every year."

He went back to shuffling papers—he was forming two neat piles on the front desk—but my curiosity wasn't satisfied. "But, where's his family? Isn't he married?"

Uncle Cy's brows slid lower over his eyes, but he didn't look up at me. "It's not my job to know his personal business," he said distractedly. "I just rent him a room."

"But—"

"Don't bother him, Eve. He's here to rest and enjoy himself. Our job is to see to it our guests get what they need, not ply them with questions. Remember what I told you about rule number one?"

I huffed out a sigh. *"We don't ask questions about the guests."* It was clear I wasn't going to learn anything about Mr. Adele, or any of our other guests, for that matter. I was there to smile at them and change the sheets on their beds and pour their coffee, and that was all. All those things had been easier to do, and far more satisfying, when I hadn't considered the state of their hearts.

"Listen, Eve," Uncle Cy said, "if you're not too busy, would you mind carrying these invoices to Jones?"

I took the pile of invoices. "He's in your apartment?"

A swift nod of Uncle Cy's head sent me off in that direction.

I got sidetracked by the phonograph in the ballroom. I don't know why I was drawn to it, as I hadn't played it since the night we came to the lodge. But now, in a fit of wistfulness, I wanted to listen to music and remember how it was to dance with Marcus. Laying the invoices on the stage, I chose a record, settled it on the turntable, turned on the phonograph, and lowered the needle. At once, the room was filled with the tinny, teasing sounds of Isham Jones and His Orchestra playing "It Had to Be You." One sliver of a warm and starry night rushed over me as I recalled Marcus humming this one in my ear, his hand resting comfortably in the small of my back as he led me around the dance floor.

I clenched my hands together and lifted them to my heart. That was where the wound was, raw and tender. Surely I should have known not to bathe the sore in memories; far better to move on and forget. But I wanted to remember, for a little while, until I was absolutely sure he was never coming back.

It had to be you, wonderful you. . . .

I shut my eyes but, hearing footsteps, quickly opened them. When I did, Jones was there, his hands tucked casually in the pockets of his pants. The pants were held up by black suspenders over a white shirt. The white cotton fabric only accentuated the white of his hair, the paleness of his skin.

"Oh, it's you," he said. He looked toward the phonograph, raised a colorless brow, and added, "Or should I say, it had to be you?"

That made me smile. It felt good to smile. "I guess I'm not really supposed to be playing the phonograph, am I?" I said.

"It's all right," he answered with a shrug. "I just wanted to make sure some kids hadn't gotten in here and decided to tear the place up."

"You don't mind then?"

"No, I don't mind."

Nobody else gave me a thrill, with all your faults, I love you still. . . .

"Do you like to dance, Jones?" I asked.

He briefly stuck out his lower lip. "I don't know."

"You don't know?"

He shook his head. "I've never danced."

"Never once?"

"No."

But of course not. Jones wasn't like other people. He didn't have the privilege of an ordinary life.

I lifted the needle off the record but left the turntable spinning. "Uncle Cy asked me to give you these invoices," I said.

"Okay. Thanks." He took them but made no move to leave.

He seemed to want to say something. I waited. Finally he said, "I have something for you too."

"You do?"

"Yeah." He nodded as he dug around in his pants pocket. "Here, you can have it." He pulled out what looked like a large coin. I held out an open palm and he dropped the coin into it.

Picking it up, I turned it over a few times. "What is it?"

"A St. Rita medal. She's the patron saint of loneliness. I thought you might . . ." His voice trailed off. He shook his head and let out a sigh. "I just thought you might like it."

He knew about Marcus. I was embarrassed, but at the same time touched by his gesture. "Thank you, Jones. It's . . . it's really very pretty. I've never seen anything like it. Are you Catholic?"

He laughed lightly at that. "No," he said. "My father was. My mother too. Devout, both of them. I'm—" Another shrug. "Anyway, a patron saint is supposed to protect you from something. Like sickness. Or accident. Or loneliness."

"Thank you," I said again.

"Yeah, well . . ." He took a step backward. "I guess . . ."

"Jones?"

"Yeah?"

I hesitated, looked at the medal in my hand and back at Jones. "Would you like to dance?"

His eyes widened slightly and his jaw slowly dropped. "Dance?"

"Yes. I mean, I can show you, in case you ever . . ."

"All right."

"All right?"

"Yes. I'd like to try."

I slipped the St. Rita medal into my pocket to rest alongside Marlene's letter. Turning to the phonograph, I lifted the needle and was about to start the music when I heard somebody call my name. "Miss Eve?"

Morris Tweed stood in the doorway at the other end of the ballroom. My index finger held the needle aloft over the spinning record. "Yes, Morris?" I asked.

"Begging your pardon for interrupting, Miss Eve, but Mr. Cyrus said I'd find you here." His black-iris eyes shifted from me to Jones and back again. They were wide enough that those two dark spheres were stranded in a sea of white. I can only imagine what he thought he was interrupting.

"What is it, Morris?" I asked.

"Annie says she needs your help in the kitchen right away. One of the cooks done gone home sick just now."

I swallowed my disappointment. It tasted bitter. "Tell her I'll be there in just a moment."

"All right, I'll tell her. Thank you, Miss Eve."

He gave a small nod and turned away. When he was gone, I looked at Jones. "Well," he said, holding up the invoices, "I've got work to do anyway."

"Yes. I do too, it seems." I placed the needle on the armrest and turned off the phonograph. "Maybe another time, though?"

He nodded stiffly. "Maybe."

My hand went to my pocket where my fingers found the St. Rita medal. I rubbed it like a worry stone as I made my way back to the kitchen.

Chapter 22

The St. Rita medal was oddly comforting to me, even though I wasn't Catholic and I didn't know anything about praying to saints. I sent my nightly prayers straight to God and never doubted that He heard me. Daddy would have said the medal was like a lucky rabbit's foot, mere superstition, which is why I never showed it to him or to Mother. I had no intention of praying to St. Rita or anyone else, though the thought of carrying the medal with me as a sort of seal against loneliness was sorely tempting. But neither did I want to lose it, and in the end I decided to put it in my treasure box for safekeeping. That night, it took its place alongside the elephant from Al Capone and the brass ring from Marcus.

According to the word about town, Marcus was no longer working at the gas station. Sheriff Wiant had got him a job as an errand boy at City Hall in nearby Lebanon, the county seat, where the sheriff himself worked. I was both glad and relieved. That way, Marcus wouldn't be involved in Fludd's bootlegging operation anymore. And that way, I wouldn't happen to see him should I glance across the street. Unless he came back to me, I didn't want to see him. If he didn't come back, I would have the brass ring as a keepsake of my first love.

In the morning, as I passed by the front desk on my way to the dining room, I was surprised to see Morris Tweed appear through a door behind the desk. It wasn't Morris that surprised me but the door. It was perpendicular to the desk and hidden by the wall that held the mailboxes and key hooks. Since Morris was carrying a wooden crate, he shut the door with a small tap of his foot. He moved toward the hall that avoided the dining room and led directly to the kitchen.

"Good morning, Eve," Uncle Cy greeted me. "Sleep well?"

"Morning, Uncle Cy," I said, but I didn't stay to talk. I hurried after Morris and reached him in the kitchen just as he was settling the crate on the table.

"Morris, where did you just come from?" I blurted.

He looked at me, brows raised. "Why, I was just bringing up these canned goods from the cellar, Miss Eve."

Annie said, "And don't you leave until you get the top off that crate, you hear, Morris?"

"I'm doing that right now," Morris said. Even as he spoke he worked the claw end of a hammer between the box and lid to loosen the nails.

"But I've only seen the outdoor entrance to the cellar," I went on. "I didn't know there was a staircase behind the front desk."

Morris nodded. He pried the lid off the crate and pulled out a can of baked beans. "Oh yes, Miss Eve. That way when we need something, we don't have to be going outside when the weather's bad."

At the stove, Annie laughed as she stirred a pot of oatmeal. "What do you find so curious about that, honey?" she asked.

I shrugged. "Nothing, really. It's just, I've been here awhile now and never realized there was a door behind the desk."

"Uh-huh," Annie said. "A door and a long steep staircase. Right, Morris? He should know. He all the time going up and down those stairs."

"That's right," Morris said with a nod. As though to emphasize the stairs' steepness, he took a handkerchief out of his back pocket and ran it along his shimmering brow. "Seems like I'm forever carrying things up and down them stairs. Crates, boxes, bags of flour, all sorts of things."

"Eve, honey," Annie said. She settled the lid on the pot and moved to the Frigidaire, where she pulled out a carton of eggs. "Hester's still sick today. You going to be able to help me in the kitchen?"

"Sure, Annie," I said. "Just let me eat some breakfast with Mother and Daddy first, and then I'll be back."

"All right, honey. Just don't linger too long over your coffee. We got work to do."

"Don't worry about that, Annie. I don't even drink coffee. That stuff's poison!"

Annie laughed lightly as I left the kitchen to join Mother and Daddy in the dining room.

It was nearly noon when Annie peered out the kitchen window and said, "There's one of them men from the camp. Let me fix him a little plate to eat, and you can carry it out there to him, Eve."

She put together a ham sandwich and put it on a plate with

some potato salad and baked beans and handed it to me. "Oh, and take him a glass of nice cold water too," she said, handing me that as well and holding open the door for me.

Link sat by himself on the grass, his back against the stone wall. His hands were behind his head and his eyes were closed, though his jaw worked as he chewed on a long blade of grass that poked out one corner of his mouth. I had to stop a moment just to admire how fine he looked as he sat there soaking up the sun. No denying he was a handsome man. If only the stock market crash hadn't interrupted his life and turned him into a bum, he'd probably be quite popular with the ladies.

"Haven't seen you in a while, Link," I said.

He opened one eye, smiled. He pulled the piece of grass from his mouth and tossed it aside. "Why, hello, Eve. I was hoping you'd come out."

"Where you been?"

"Oh, here and there. Wherever the work is. What have you got there?"

"A ham sandwich. Annie made it. You hungry?"

"Famished." He sat up cross-legged and reached for the plate and fork and the glass of water. He patted the ground beside him. "Can you sit for a minute?"

I shrugged. "I guess. But not for long." I sank to the grass, my legs to the side as I leaned my weight on one arm. As I watched Link take voracious bites of the sandwich, my mind wandered to the camp up the river. Surely it was full of hungry people, some who were maybe even worse off than Link.

The sandwich was almost gone and Link's mouth was full when he said, "I heard there was a raid at the station across the street last weekend."

I nodded and looked out toward the river.

"I wonder what made the cops think there might be illegal liquor stored there. It makes them look pretty foolish, busting into a place like that and coming away with nothing."

He went on but I couldn't hear his words over the sudden rush of emotion that rose up out of my chest and overflowed. "I saw that liquor with my own eyes," I blurted, and the moment the words left my lips, I was sorry. I slapped a hand over my mouth and lowered my eyes.

Link was quiet a moment. Then he said, "You saw the liquor?"

Slowly I dropped my hand from my face. "I shouldn't have said anything."

"Why not? What are you afraid I'm going to do?"

"I don't know."

"You can trust me, Eve."

"Can I?"

"Yes."

Our eyes locked, but only briefly. I had to turn away, back toward the river.

"Now you'll go and try to get some of that liquor for yourself, I suppose," I said.

Link laughed loudly at that. "I'm not going to buy any of that liquor, Eve. What makes you think that?"

"I already told you out in the boat, remember? The first time I met you, you asked if we had any liquor here at the lodge. If you wanted it then, you want it now."

Link shook his head as he pushed his empty plate aside on the grass. "I was just joshing with you when I said that, Eve. Honest. Listen, I don't drink myself, okay? Or, not much anyway."

"What do you mean by not much?"

"Well, let's see." He smiled as he lifted his chin in thought. "It seems when my cousin got married back in '28, I imbibed in a little wine. Didn't get drunk though, if that makes any difference to you."

"Where'd you get the wine?" I asked.

"My uncle's wine cellar," Link said. "There wasn't a bottle at the wedding that hadn't been purchased before Prohibition, which means it was all perfectly legal."

I felt my eyes narrow and my mouth become a thin line. "Are you telling me the truth, Link?"

His face turned serious. "Listen, Eve, I wouldn't lie to you."

"How do I know? I really don't know you very well."

"Then you should get to know me. And I should get to know you. Don't you agree?"

I paused, not quite sure how to respond. Finally I said, "I suppose."

"Good." He nodded and leaned a little closer. "So let's start with your telling me about the raid."

"If I tell you, do you promise not to tell anyone else?"

"You have my word."

As I searched his face, I had the sense that I could trust him. So I told him all that had happened, from Marlene's frantic phone call to Jimmy's showing us the liquor to Daddy and me going to Captain Macnish. I told him about the newspaper article calling the raid a bust, and how Calvin Fludd must have been tipped off and got rid of his entire stash before the cops showed up. And I told him too how Jimmy and Marlene had run away, and how I'd got the letter telling me they were married. While I talked, Link listened intently, never taking his eyes off me. He kept nodding, as though he were filing the story away somewhere in his mind.

When I finished, he said, "Well, I'm sorry you lost your best friend because of this."

At first I thought he meant Marcus, until I realized he was speaking of Marlene. "She's glad for what happened," I said. "She's happy to be married to Jimmy. It was all she wanted anyway."

Before either of us could say more, Annie hollered at me from the kitchen doorway, "Eve! I thought you done wandered off and got lost. You been sitting out there all this time?"

"I'm sorry, Annie." I stood and wiped at the seat of my dress.

"We got lunch to serve and tables to clear and you out there dillydallying." She sounded stern but she was smiling.

I smiled back. "I'm coming right now!"

Link rose too and waved at Annie. "A mighty fine lunch," he said. "Thank you kindly."

"You're welcome, young man. You come on back whenever you need something to stop the hungries."

"Thank you. I'll do that."

I picked up the dirty dishes from the ground, but before I could move toward the lodge, Link grabbed my elbow. "Eve, what about Macnish?"

"Captain Macnish? What about him?"

"Do you trust him?"

"Why . . ." I paused. It was the same question I'd asked Daddy, but now I had my own answer. "Yes, I trust him."

"You don't think he knew about Fludd before you told him?"

"No, I don't think so."

"And you don't think he's getting paid off by Fludd like so

many others? You don't think he was the one who warned Fludd of the raid?"

I frowned and shook my head. "Why would Captain Macnish do that, knowing he'd end up a laughingstock when no liquor was found at the station?"

Link looked at me a long while. Then he said, "I suppose you're right."

"But why, Link?" I said. "Why are you asking me this?"

Link paused a moment, then lifted his shoulders in a small shrug. "No reason, really. You'd best get on inside. Annie's waiting."

With that, he gave my elbow a small squeeze and went on his way.

Chapter 23

But he came back the next day. And the day after that. He came and had lunch at the lodge now whenever he wasn't out working somewhere, which was often. Sometimes he came with several other men and sometimes he came alone, but either way, he always seemed to want me to hang around for a while.

Annie teased me, saying, "That young man ain't coming around just for my cooking anymore, honey. If I didn't know better, I'd say that man has intentions toward you."

"Hush, Annie," I scolded. "Plenty of men from the camp come here to eat, and you know it."

"Yeah, but that one more than any of them."

"He must be hungrier than any of them, then."

"That's what I'm saying, honey. And he done seen a sweet thing he likes."

My face took on color and I suppressed a smile, but even so, I adamantly shook my head. "You can stop your match-making, Annie," I said. "Link's a nice enough fellow, but he's a bum."

"Uh-huh." She chuckled.

"He doesn't have a real job and he lives in a camp."

"Uh-huh. All that's just for a time, Eve, and you know it."

I didn't tell Annie that Link had taken college classes before the stock market crash; that would have only added fuel to her fire. I enjoyed the five or ten or thirty minutes a day I spent with Link, but still, I couldn't imagine introducing a dirty-clad, tent-dwelling day laborer to Mother and Daddy as a possible suitor. I didn't want him as a suitor. I didn't want any more suitors, and I didn't want any more broken hearts. I wanted only to concentrate on doing well in school, once it started up in the fall, so I could go on to college and devote my life to helping people.

Funny thing was—and I scarcely admitted it even to myself—but the more Link came around, the flimsier and more ghostlike the image of Marcus became in my mind. Before long, the boy who had been my first love had very little substance at all, as though he'd never been real.

Toward the end of July I was washing the lunch dishes with Annie when Morris entered the kitchen carrying a crate of canned goods. I paused with a plate in one hand and a dish towel in the other, and in that moment I heard the Reverend Kilkenny quote one of the verses about mercy that he was so fond of quoting: "He that hath mercy on the poor, happy is he."

I looked at Morris carrying the canned goods, and I looked out the window at the handful of men from the camp that had come for a plate of food, and I finally connected the two.

"Morris," I said, "you told me there's a lot of food in storage down in the cellar, right?"

Morris nodded. "That's right, Miss Eve. About near enough to feed Noah, his family, and his whole boatload of animals till the flood clear up, I'd say."

"Why, honey?" Annie chimed in. "What you thinking?"

"I'll be right back!" I yelled. Leaving the plate and dish towel on the counter, I rushed down the hall to the front desk.

Uncle Cy was there as usual, registering a family with three small boys. While he spoke with the father, the phone rang, and when he excused himself to answer that, I blurted out, "Uncle Cy!"

He held up an index finger in my direction, had a brief conversation with the person on the phone, dropped the receiver into the cradle, and turned back to the father.

"Uncle Cy!"

"Excuse me, Mr. Danby. Eve, what is it? Is the kitchen on fire?"

I laughed out loud, giddy at my own idea. It was such a good idea Mr. Danby could wait. "No, the kitchen's not on fire," I said. "I want to take some food to the people in the shantytown. Can I?"

"You want to feed the people in the shantytown?"

"Yes, they need food more than anything."

"But, Annie already—"

"But I mean, I want to take it *to* the camp—"

"Eve, I'm awfully busy right now." The phone rang again. "Excuse me just another minute, Mr. Danby."

"But can I, Uncle Cy?"

"What, Eve?" He put his hand over the telephone mouthpiece. "Yes, yes, take them some food. Fine, fine." He waved me away and said into the phone, "Marryat Island Lodge. This is Cyrus Marryat speaking. . . ."

189

I clasped my hands together in victory and hurried back to the kitchen. "Morris, Uncle Cy said we can take some crates of food to the camp!"

Morris's eyes widened and he scratched his ear. "You just now asked him, Miss Eve?"

"Uh-huh. And he said yes. I'm sure we can take anything we want."

"Well, now," Annie said. "That's right nice of Mr. Cyrus, though I'm not surprised. He's a good man."

"What do you want to be taking, Miss Eve?" Morris asked.

"Beans, fruit—I don't know. Whatever's down there. I'm sure the people living in the camp will be glad for whatever we bring them."

"So you want I should just pack up the truck with this and that and haul it on out there?"

"Yes, but I want to go with you."

"I don't know about that, Miss Eve. Might be dangerous, you going out among all those drifters and all."

"Oh no, Morris, I don't think so. The men who come here for meals are very nice."

"Especially one," Annie interjected.

"Hush, Annie," I said. "I've gotten to know several of them. There's Freddy and Bill and Cecil and—"

"And Link," Annie said.

I sighed. "Yes, him too."

"Listen honey, if you go on out there," she went on, "you'd best be taking your daddy with you. Morris, you, and your daddy, then that's all right." She nodded.

"I can't go today, Miss Eve," Morris said. "Got runs to make to the train station and too much other work around here. But you go on and ask your daddy. Maybe we can make a run on out there tomorrow, if you think your daddy can take time away from the Eatery."

"I know he'll do it. Daddy always wants to help people. Up in St. Paul, we worked at the mission all the time. I don't know why I didn't think of this before!"

The next morning, Morris and Daddy carried up a dozen crates, cardboard boxes, and bags of fruit from the cellar and loaded them into the back of the pickup truck. After they tied everything down with cord, the three of us crawled into the cab and headed for the shantytown. None of us had been there, but we knew we'd simply have to follow the railroad tracks to find it.

Morris put the truck in first gear—I had to snuggle close to Daddy on the hot vinyl seat to avoid the gearshift—and turned right onto the road that ran behind the lodge. The road stretched out between the railroad tracks and the river, a bumpy narrow avenue between steel and water. A warm wind blew in through the truck's open windows.

"Eve, darling," Daddy said, speaking loudly into the wind, "you're sure Cy said we could take these goods out to the camp?"

"Of course I'm sure, Daddy. I already told you that a hundred times."

"Well, so long as we take note of what we're giving away so Jones can restock, I guess it won't be a problem."

"I wrote down what was in each crate and box as you and Morris carried them out. See?" I reached into the pocket of my chemise and pulled out a piece of paper and a stub of pencil. "Canned peaches. Baked beans. A bag of apples. Flour. Cooking oil—"

Daddy stopped me with a nod of his head. "All right. Give that list to Jones."

"I will."

We picked up speed and the truck whined as Morris shifted into a higher gear. The inrushing air pulled the short ends out of my braid and whipped them across my face. I squinted against the assault.

"That Mr. Cyrus," Morris said, "he's a generous man. Always helping folks out. Always doing good round the town. Don't worry, Mr. Drew. He won't pay no never mind about a few canned goods and whatnot. He always glad to give to them that's needy."

I gave Daddy an I-told-you-so look, then pointed out the window. "Look, Daddy, there's Uncle Luther's mill."

Daddy glanced outside, nodded curtly, moved his eyes back to the road. As I watched, the muscles of his face seemed to stiffen, and his expression grew stony. Then I remembered and understood. Uncle Cy had the lodge. Uncle Luther had the mill. Daddy had run away from it all and come back with nothing.

No one spoke again until we arrived at the camp, which thankfully was just ahead, beyond the bend in the road. Morris eased the truck onto the grass, and we bumped along until we came to rest at the edge of organized squalor. There'd been a thunderstorm during the night, leaving the paths between the tents a maze of muddy walkways. The tents themselves looked on the verge of collapse, as though beaten down by the rain. Ill-clad men sat here and there on cinder blocks and tree stumps, huddled around campfires that left the air gray with smoke. The place smelled of ash and mildew and things I knew nothing about because I had never been homeless.

Several men stepped forward to meet us as we climbed out of the truck. One of the men appeared to breathe out a sigh of relief when he recognized me. "Good morning, Miss Eve," he said. "What brings you out this way?"

"Hello, Cecil," I said. "We've brought a little food from the lodge to pass around."

With that, the men took a step closer. Heads began to poke out of tent flaps and around corrugated tin doorways. The figures clustered by the fires rose one by one, hesitantly. Undoubtedly driven by hunger but at the same time cautious, they moved slowly toward us through the mud.

"Cecil," I went on, "I'd like you to meet my daddy, Drew Marryat."

He was a large man, Cecil, with hands the size of dinner plates, which he tried to wipe inconspicuously on his overalls before extending one to Daddy. "Glad to meet you, Mr. Marryat."

"Likewise, Mr. . . . ."

"Gutermuth. Cecil Gutermuth."

The two men shook hands, while the others nodded and muttered greetings.

Daddy said, "My daughter here got the idea you men might appreciate a few extra provisions."

Cecil glanced at me and I smiled. "Yes sir," Cecil said. "That's mighty kind of you."

"So we have just a few items in the truck, if you don't mind helping us distribute them." Daddy nodded toward Morris, who hopped up onto the bed of the truck and started untying the cord. Daddy hopped up behind him to help.

I stepped closer to Cecil. "Is Link here this morning?" I asked.

He shook his head. "He got himself a couple days' work up near Lebanon. I saw him leave the camp before daybreak."

I smiled to hide my disappointment. "Well, would you mind putting a few items in his tent for when he gets back?"

"I don't mind at all, Miss Eve. We're much obliged."

I stepped aside then and watched as the men lined up while Daddy, Morris, and Cecil formed an assembly line of sorts to hand out the food. Those wearing overalls stuffed apples in their pockets and canned goods behind their bibs. The others made slings of their shirttails and carried off the goods that way. The whole procession was done in a quiet and orderly manner, men taking whatever was offered without complaint and with a word of thanks. Still, I could see the conflict in their eyes, the clash of pride with gratitude as they found themselves in the place of accepting charity through no fault of their own.

Some of the men I recognized from their visits to the lodge; others I'd never seen before. Each one acknowledged me in some way—a small nod, a few mumbled words. I smiled and nodded in return.

Morris's face glistened with sweat as he took the claw hammer to the final crate. With a grunt, he pulled off the lid and dug through the straw inside. Suddenly—back bent, head down, left hand resting on the side of the crate—he froze.

"Morris?" Daddy said.

"Sir?"

"What's the matter?"

Morris cleared his throat. He didn't speak and he didn't rise. The few remaining men beside the truck began to mutter among themselves. Daddy moved closer to Morris. Curious, I jumped up onto the truck bed and made my way among the empty crates and boxes till I too was at Morris's side. I gazed at his profile, waiting. His eyelid twitched and the corner of his mouth trembled as though a wave of fear was moving across his face. Quietly, so as not to be heard by anyone else, he said, "That don't look like no canned peaches I ever seen, Mr. Drew."

Nestled in the pink palm of his brawny hand was an expensive bottle of professionally manufactured Canadian whiskey.

Chapter 24

━━━━━━━━━━━⟨∽◦⦅◦∾⟩━━━━━━━━━━━

On the way back to the lodge, Daddy, Morris, and I made a pact of sorts not to breathe a word about the whiskey to anyone. Not Mother. Not Annie. No one.

I knew instinctively that Daddy was going to have it out with Uncle Cy, but beyond that I could only imagine what was going through his mind. Whatever he was thinking, his downturned mouth told me it wasn't good. Neither was he interested in Morris's attempts at finding some sort of explanation for the liquor.

"Excuse me for saying so, Mr. Drew, sir," Morris said, his hands nervously clutching the steering wheel, "but maybe that crate got down in the cellar by some sort of mistake. Or maybe it was the only crate of whiskey down there, and I just happened on it."

"Maybe," Daddy said. His jaw worked and his narrowed eyes stared straight ahead.

"Or maybe it was left from before the law changed over," Morris tried again. "Used to be Mr. Cyrus served liquor at the lodge and wasn't breaking no laws."

Daddy sniffed. "Maybe. Though it seems strange he'd keep his whiskey in a crate marked canned peaches, doesn't it, Morris?"

One great drop of sweat broke out at Morris's hairline and eased its way down the side of his face. "Yes, sir," he mumbled.

"Daddy," I said, "that's the same kind of whiskey and the same kind of crate I saw over at Fludd's."

Daddy lifted his chin in a sort of nod. "I figured as much."

"But since everything—I mean, our goods for the lodge and the liquor for the gas station—since all that comes into the train station, maybe there was a mix-up of some sort. Maybe that crate was meant to go over to Fludd's."

Daddy looked at me a long moment, looked away. "Maybe," he said again, his voice a whisper.

We were silent then, the three of us sitting like strangers in a waiting room, anticipating the worst as we bumped along the road toward home.

Daddy insisted on confronting Uncle Cy without me. He waited till late that night when everyone was asleep, including Mother. I lay in my own bed, tossing with fretful dreams, the all-too-familiar nightmare of the man shot down on the sidewalk ahead of me. Only this time in my dream I got close enough to look into the man's eyes and see that he wasn't quite dead. His lips moved. I bent closer.

"I'm sorry," he said. "Tell them I'm sorry."

"Who?" I asked.

But he didn't say. I heard the death rattle in his chest and the light went out of his eyes and then he was gone.

I awoke with a feeling of dread. My stomach turned and I could eat only a bite or two of breakfast. Daddy told Mother he and I were going to spend a couple hours on the river enjoying the morning. I put on my sun hat and joined Daddy at the dock. Neither of us spoke as we rowed far downriver from the lodge.

Finally Daddy eased up on the rowing and let the boat drift a moment. He looked at me and I looked at him. My heart pounded as I waited for him to speak. He wore a pained expression and he looked years older than he'd looked just yesterday. "We can't stay here, Eve," he said at length.

I drew in a sharp breath. "Where will we go?"

"Back home, most likely." He looked down the river, up at the sky, back at me. "Mother got a letter from Cassandra yesterday. She, Warren, and the girls are coming down to see us in another week or so. I'll talk with Warren then about heading back to St. Paul. He can help us get resettled there."

I couldn't believe what was happening. Return to St. Paul? "Why?" I asked. "What's going on? What did Uncle Cy tell you?"

Daddy looked away but not before I saw the flash of anger in his eyes. "Lies, at first. He wanted me to think that crate got there by mistake. He's never been able to lie to me, though. I can always tell. Luther too. Back when we were kids they were always telling me stories, figuring I'd believe anything. They thought I was plain stupid because I didn't do well in school, because I couldn't read like everybody else. Maybe I couldn't read letters, but I learned to read faces. I got good at that."

I nodded when he fell silent and waited for him to go on.

"I finally got Cyrus to tell me the truth."

"How, Daddy?"

"Never mind how. The important thing is I found out what's going on around here."

I'd been resting my hands on the sides of the boat, but now I brought them together in my lap. "What did you find out?"

"I found out what I already knew—what you probably already knew—the minute we saw that bottle of whiskey in the back of the truck."

My fingers clasped each other until my knuckles turned white. I said, "Uncle Cy's working with Calvin Fludd, isn't he?"

Daddy nodded. "Yes, Eve, he is."

"Uncle Cy's a bootlegger."

"I'm afraid that's the long and the short of it."

"Does he store the liquor in the cellar, the liquor that comes in from Cincinnati?"

Daddy nodded again. He sighed heavily. "Here's the way it is, darling. Cyrus is one small link in a very large bootlegging ring. At the center is a man working out of Cincinnati. I don't know his name. Cyrus wouldn't tell me. At any rate, he's a lawyer and yet he runs one of the largest bootlegging operations in the Midwest. Some years back he wanted to extend his operations east to Warren County and beyond. He sent his men out to find people who would help. In exchange for their cooperation, he promised to pay those people well."

"So Uncle Cy's doing it for the money."

"He claims to be doing it for Cora."

"Aunt Cora?"

"He says he was in debt to every doctor from here to Columbus, trying to get her cured of the consumption. Now she's out at that highfalutin sanitarium in New York State where you pay a year's wages in a month's time just to breathe

the mountain air. You don't afford a place like that on what you make running a lodge, even in the best of times. Now with the economy the way it is and all . . ."

His words trailed off. I said, "Maybe when Cora's better, he'll stop selling liquor."

"Don't count on it," Daddy said. "When I asked Cyrus how he could put us all in danger, he said he was doing it to keep us all alive. He said without the extra income he wasn't sure he could keep the lodge going, what with the country in the trouble it's in."

"So not all the money goes for Cora."

"No, not all."

"Uncle Cy must get a lot for selling liquor."

"No doubt the man he's working for has deep pockets. He has to, to keep an operation like this going. He's got a whole lot of people to pay off for one thing or another."

"Like Uncle Cy and Calvin Fludd."

"Yes. But here's how it works. Uncle Cy doesn't sell the liquor. Fludd does that. Cyrus just warehouses the stuff. The lodge is a liquor transfer station."

"A liquor transfer station?"

"That's right. Cyrus has got the room and Fludd's got the opportunity. They work together. See, when the liquor comes in on the train from Cincy, it's picked up and carried to the lodge, where it's stored."

"Who picks it up?"

"Morris does."

"Morris?"

"He's not in on it. He's hauling it not knowing what it is."

"Poor Morris! They made him part of the ring, and he doesn't even know it."

"Yeah, well, he knows it now."

I stiffened in alarm. "Is he going to have to leave too? Will he and Annie both be out of a job?"

"No. Morris will stay. They'll both stay."

"But—"

"Listen, Eve, to some folks Negros aren't quite human. They're no more of a threat than a dog. It doesn't matter what the Negro help knows. Cy's one of those people."

I couldn't respond. I thought of Annie, sweet Annie, singing in the kitchen while she made her cinnamon rolls. Then I thought of Uncle Cy, and the corner of my heart that belonged to him hardened to stone.

"But, Daddy—"

"Now hear me out. The crates with the liquor are labeled something else, of course, but they're marked in some way so that the men who work the tunnel know which they are."

"The tunnel?"

Daddy nodded impatiently. "Listen, Eve, some years back a tunnel was dug between the cellar and the station so the liquor can be moved between the two underground. Usually one or two men are working the station, keeping an eye on the liquor, bringing more over when the supply runs low. Fludd has a steady run of customers coming through. Like Jimmy told you, they go back around to the car wash and that's when the liquor is loaded into the cars. It's a pretty smooth operation all the way around. Things were going off without a hitch till Jimmy sampled the goods enough to get drunk and spill the beans."

Of all people, I was the one to whom Jimmy had spilled the beans. Me and Marlene.

I suddenly had a terrible thought. "Daddy?"

"Yes, darling?"

"After I found out about Fludd, we told Uncle Cy."

"That's right."

"So Uncle Cy probably warned Calvin Fludd about the raid."

Daddy's head bobbed reluctantly. "That's right, he did. They weren't sure it was going to happen, but they decided to clear everything out of the station for a time just in case. They brought the whole stash at Fludd's back on over to the cellar, so when Macnish and his man showed up, the place was clean."

"And the cellar was dirty."

"In a manner of speaking. We were sitting right on top of the liquor they were looking for."

"I can't believe it."

"I wish it weren't so, but it's true."

Daddy lowered the oars back into the water then and slowly started rowing back toward the lodge.

"Daddy," I said, "does Uncle Cy want us to leave?"

He took a deep breath. "He says it'd be better for us if we did, now that we know what's going on around here."

"What does he mean?"

He hesitated another moment before answering. "Let's just say, knowledge can be a dangerous thing. We—you and I—are now carrying knowledge around that certain people out there don't want us to have."

At the thought of that, I wanted to reach down inside myself and yank that knowledge out, tossing it far, far down the river. I didn't want to carry anything so awful inside of me, especially if it put Daddy and me in danger. As we moved over the placid water, the air full of birdsong, I shivered in terror.

Daddy went on, "Only two people were ever supposed

to know anything about this, and that was Cy and Calvin. The more people who know about a secret, the less likely it's going to stay a secret. Now too many people know."

"Who besides us *does* know? Does Aunt Cora?"

"Cy says she doesn't. She was here when the whole thing started, but Cy claims he never brought her in on it."

"And Uncle Luther neither?"

"He doesn't know."

"What about Jones?" I asked reluctantly. "Does he know?"

Daddy sniffed and looked aside. "Yes. He knows. He was with us last night in the apartment. Didn't say much but didn't leave either. I guess he figured we might need a referee, if fists started flying." He chuckled at that.

"But . . ." I hesitated, but I had to ask. I wanted to know. "Is Jones in on it, or does he just know about it?"

"I think he knows about it and looks the other way. Kind of like what Cy hopes you and I will do now until we can leave the lodge. He did offer me a cut for a time, to keep my mouth shut. I told him to keep his money; I didn't want it."

I tried to swallow but my mouth was dry. My hands went on wrestling each other in my lap. "What are you going to tell Mother?" I asked. "I mean, about why we're leaving."

"I haven't quite figured that out yet. Something'll come to me, though. She can't ever know what went on here." He looked at me hard, seemed to be searching my face. "You understand that, don't you?"

I nodded. I was quiet for another moment as I pondered the hardest question of all. Then I said quietly, "Daddy?"

"Yes, darling?" He stopped paddling again and leaned toward me.

"The Jones Five and Ten Law?"

Daddy's mouth became a thin line. "Yes, darling."

"If you know about the selling of illegal liquor, you're just as guilty of the crime as if you were selling it yourself."

"Yes."

"And it's punishable by five years in prison and a ten-thousand-dollar fine."

"That's right."

"But you're not going to turn in Uncle Cy, right?"

Daddy lowered the oars, stroked once, stroked twice. "I wrestled with that question all night long, Eve. Lord knows I've done plenty that's wrong in my time, though as I've grown older I've tried more and more to come down on the side of right. If it were anyone else, I'd know what to do. Turning in Fludd was easy. But we're talking about my own brother here. Not just my brother but the man who took us in when we needed help. May God forgive me, darling, but no, I'm not going to turn him in. I just can't bring myself to do it."

I nodded. "Daddy?"

"Yes?"

"I can't do it either. I can't do that to Uncle Cy, even though he's doing wrong."

"Eve, darling," Daddy said, "we stumbled into this by mistake, but we're going to get out of it on purpose. Soon as we can, we'll take our leave of this place. Until then, we'll keep our mouths shut and go on about our business."

Our eyes locked. I'm not sure either one of us could quite believe what we were doing. We had just agreed to break the law. And so, in those few quiet words of complicity, Daddy and I became felons.

Chapter 25

W e docked the boat and, in silence, walked across the island and over the bridge to the lodge. I averted my eyes from the guests we passed, not at all sure that they couldn't see inside of me, all the way to the secret I carried there. By the time we reached the bottom of the porch steps, I felt so weak from the weight of that awful knowledge that I took Daddy's hand in case I should stumble on the way up.

He squeezed my fingers, and we entered the lodge together. As expected, Uncle Cy was behind the desk. He stopped what he was doing and looked at us, his gaze a wall that brought us up short.

"Good morning, Drew," he said evenly.

"Morning, Cy." Daddy's voice was equally passive, as though the morning were like any other.

Uncle Cy turned to me and nodded. "Eve," he said.

"Hello, Uncle Cy."

An uneasy hush followed. I could scarcely bring myself to look at my uncle. In that moment, I hated him. I had decided to protect him, and yet I hated what he was doing and what Daddy and I were doing because of him. I clenched my teeth so hard my jaw hurt. Daddy squeezed my hand again, a gesture of empathy.

Finally, Uncle Cy said, "Everything all right, Drew?"

Daddy cleared his throat. "Everything's fine. We've just been out on the river awhile. It's a beautiful morning."

Uncle Cy nodded. Something unspoken had just passed between the two men, some understanding of where we all stood. Now we would all go on about our business, each of us carrying a piece of the lie.

"Listen, Drew, take the day off. It's Saturday. Take Rose and Eve into town for the matinee or something. Have some fun." He sounded magnanimous, like he was offering us some great gift, and he even tried to smile as he spoke.

After a moment's hesitation, Daddy said, "All right." He tugged my hand. "Come on, darling."

I cast a last glance across the desk. When my eyes met his, Uncle Cy sighed. He seemed to know without my saying so that the familial bond between us had been broken and that, even if I lived to be one hundred, I would never forgive him for what he had done.

Getting away from the lodge for the day turned out to be a good idea. Mother, Daddy, and I had cheeseburgers and chocolate malteds at Huey's Diner on Main Street. The only theater in Mercy was showing *The Public Enemy* with Jean Harlow and an actor we didn't know, James Cagney. Because it had to do with gangsters, we opted to go to Lebanon instead, where the theater was showing *City Lights* with Charlie

Chaplin. It felt good to laugh and to forget, for a little while at least, that Daddy and I had landed on the wrong side of the law. I envied Mother, who didn't know what we knew. I longed for the bliss of ignorance, which I would never have again, because even after we left the lodge I would know what was going on there. I was an insider now, and there would be no getting out.

The next morning as we walked into church, Daddy and I once again held hands in mutual support, knowing we would probably hear something in the sermon we didn't want to hear. I sat between him and Mother, fanning myself with the church bulletin as Reverend Kilkenny ascended to the pulpit. The church was always warm, this being summer, but today it seemed unusually so, in spite of the open windows and the overworked ceiling fans. My cheeks burned and perspiration moistened my skin wherever my body made contact with the wooden pew. I was uncomfortable in body and soul as I awaited the Reverend's words of condemnation.

Oh, God, I'm a criminal, I thought. *A lawbreaker, a liar, every inch as bad as Uncle Cy and Calvin Fludd. How can you love me now, God? How can you love me now?*

The Reverend rambled on for a time, undeterred by the waves of fidgeting and fanning going on among the congregation. Daddy's head began to bob, though he tried valiantly to stay awake. Mother dabbed at her neck with a small white handkerchief. I silently begged Reverend Kilkenny to wrap it up so we could move out of the crowded sanctuary and into the open air. I felt suffocated by the warmth and by my own sense of shame. I longed to go to the island and take a plunge in the river. I imagined myself sitting in the shade of the Island Eatery, drinking a bottomless glass of ice-cold lemonade. Anything to bring relief from the heat. Anything simply to bring relief.

I didn't realize that my own chin had sunk down low. With some effort, I lifted my head and looked up at Reverend Kilkenny. He had made a fist of one hand and was beating it against his chest. "And the publican," he was saying, "did not even dare to lift his eyes to heaven but bent low because of his sin and beat his breast, saying, 'God be merciful to me a sinner.'"

He paused and looked out over his wilting audience. I, for one, sat up straighter.

"The Pharisee was thanking God for his own righteousness, you see. 'Thank you, God,' he said, 'that I am not as other men are, extortioners, unjust, adulterers, or even as this publican.'" Reverend Kilkenny's arm went straight out, and his index finger pointed over our heads as though the publican was behind us at the far reaches of the narthex.

He held his pose for a moment, then slowly dropped his arm and smiled down at us. "It's all about mercy, my friends. We are sinners, all of us, but God is merciful."

I drew in a breath and as I did, my right hand rose to my heart. I laid my fist there, over the place where I kept the lie. *Oh, God,* I thought, *be merciful to me, a sinner. Oh, God, please be merciful to me, a sinner.*

Chapter 26

As I walked through the sitting room and down the hallway to the ballroom, I was keenly aware of the illegal stash beneath my feet. Shivers of terror moved up my spine at the thought of it all. I was more afraid now than I had ever been in St. Paul, knowing evil men were traveling through the tunnel, back and forth between our cellar and the gas station, carrying the goods that put money in the pockets of Uncle Cy, Calvin Fludd, the bootlegger in Cincinnati, and any number of otherwise law-abiding citizens of Mercy who took a bribe to look the other way. I felt all tangled up in the web of crime that Prohibition had created, and I sensed that in the end nothing good could come of it.

I was on my way to find Jones. I hadn't seen him except in passing since Friday—the day we took the food to the camp—and now it was Monday night. Jones seemed to me a kind of fellow victim of Uncle Cy's wrongdoing. He too was forced to keep the secret, and by doing so, to break the law.

The door to the apartment was open as it so often was to allow the air to move through. And, as he so often was,

Jones sat at the cluttered table surrounded by his radios and his books. So deeply absorbed was he in one of those books that he jumped when I knocked on the doorjamb.

"Sorry, Jones," I said. "I didn't mean to scare you."

He pushed his glasses farther up his nose. "That's all right. I just didn't hear you coming."

"Are you busy?"

"Not really. I'm just reading."

"Can I come in?"

"Sure."

I pulled a chair around from the end of the table so I could sit beside him. "What are you reading?" I asked.

He closed the book to show me the cover. "It's about the Alaskan Territory."

"Oh yeah. I noticed that book here before. Why are you reading about Alaska?"

"Because I'm going to go there someday."

My eyebrows rose sharply. "You are? What on earth for?"

"To live. To make a life for myself."

"In *Alaska*? Why do you want to live up there? Why, there's no one there but the Eskimos!"

His expression told me I'd answered my own question. "That's right," he said. "Mostly. There's not many people and there's plenty of wide open space up there."

"But what would you do? How would you make a living?"

"I don't know yet. I suppose I'd have to live off the fat of the land for a time. You know, hunt, fish, gather berries." He paused and gave a small laugh. "I'll figure it all out once I get there."

"But how will you even get to such a faraway place? You'd need a whole lot of money to travel so far."

"Maybe. Yeah, I suppose. But I'm going to get there some-day, even if my wallet's as empty as it is now. I'll work on the way up, if I have to. I'll travel awhile, stop in some town or another to work, travel a little more."

I frowned in thought as I pictured him making his way north through the wilds of Canada. How would people treat him when he showed up in a small town looking for work? With fear? With disdain? With violence? I wanted to warn him not to go, to stay here in Ohio or to go back to Chicago, but not to venture such a great distance through territory that might be far from friendly. But it wasn't my place to say so. Instead, I said simply, "I never knew you wanted to go to Alaska."

"Does it seem so strange?"

"No." I shook my head. "Well, yes. It's just . . . I never imagined you wanting to do something like that."

"Well . . ." He smiled and lifted his shoulders in a shrug. "We all have dreams, don't we?"

"Yes, I guess we do." I gazed at Jones, at his red eyes blink-ing behind the thick lenses of his glasses. "I suppose you want to get as far away from Uncle Cy as you can."

"Why would I want to do that?"

"Because of, you know." I looked down at the floor and up again.

He stared at me for a few uncomfortable moments as he reg-istered my meaning. A small nod told me he understood. "I'm sorry you and your father ever found out about it," he said.

"I'm sorry Uncle Cy got himself mixed up in something like that. I'm having a hard time believing it of him."

"Why? Because no one with Marryat blood would ever break the law?"

"I thought my uncle was a good man, not an outlaw."

"So what's your definition of good, Eve?"

My back stiffened and my jaw grew tight. I lifted my chin and said defiantly, "Someone who keeps the law and works to help people, not hurt them."

Jones narrowed his crimson eyes at me. His pale cheeks took on color and his mouth tightened, as if there were words inside he wasn't sure he wanted to let out. As much as I wanted to be friends with him, we seemed always to end up just inches from an argument. I waited for him to blow, but he must have talked himself out of the fight because when he spoke, his words were quiet.

"Look, Eve," he said, "I'm keeping my mouth shut for Cy for one reason and one reason only, and that's my mother. What he's doing, he's doing mostly for her sake. There were so many medical bills. You wouldn't believe how many doctors she'd gone to, trying to find some cure. With all those bills Cy might have lost the lodge, and worse, my mother might have died a long time ago if it weren't for the extra money. The offer from Cincinnati came at just the right time, and Cy grabbed it. I'd probably have done the same thing, if I was in his position."

"So you approve of the bootlegging?"

"I approve of Cy's efforts to take care of us. I approve of anything that helps my mother."

I was quiet a moment. "You really love her, don't you, Jones?"

"Of course I love her. And lucky for us, Cy loves her too. That's the one thing about him I can appreciate. But just because he's married to her, it's not like he and I are father and son or anything even remotely like that. I'm here because

I'm part and parcel of what Cy got when he married her. That doesn't make him and me close. Far from it. He thinks I'm a freak, just like everybody else. I think he'd rather I wasn't here, wasn't hanging around to scare the guests when they see the red-eyed devil."

He turned his face away from me then. He took off his glasses and rubbed his eyes. I thought he might be trying not to cry, but when he turned back to me there was no sign of tears. Only anger. Layers and layers of that.

"I think you're wrong, Jones," I said. "Surely Uncle Cy doesn't think of you as a freak."

"Why wouldn't he?" Jones snapped. "It's what I am. I'll never be like everyone else. Cy would rather I'd stayed in Chicago with relatives there, but since I'm here he tries to make the best of it. He gives me work to do that'll mostly keep me back here and away from the stares of the guests." He pulled the Alaska book closer to him and ran his ghostly hand over the cover. "Soon as Mom's better and back here with Cy, I'm going to try to take my leave."

"But . . . your Mom won't want you to leave, will she?"

"I'm a grown man, Eve. It's time for me to be out on my own. Somewhere where the sight of me won't bother too many people."

I felt my heart constrict. No wonder Jones had given me his St. Rita medal. St. Rita would never do him any good; he would always be alone and lonely, as long as he lived. I wanted to throw my arms around him and take away the sting of his separateness, but I was as helpless as St. Rita to change what was. Lamely, I said, "Your mother will miss you terribly, after you're gone."

"She'll have a good life here. I can go knowing she's being

taken care of. At least Cy has done that much for me." He cleared his throat and put his glasses back on. "Listen," he said, "I'm really thirsty. You want some iced tea? I've got some in the fridge."

"Sure," I said. "I'd like some."

"I'll be right back."

When he left, I idly reached for the book, thinking I'd thumb through it while he was pouring the tea. But I didn't get any farther than the inside front cover where a name was written in a tight, left-leaning script. I gasped. In the next instance, Jones stepped out of the kitchen with a glass of tea in each hand. When he saw the look on my face, he stopped.

"Your name," I said, "is Jones O'Brannigan."

His eyelids fluttered but his gaze held my own. "That's right."

I was momentarily speechless. Then, "Why didn't you tell me?"

"You didn't need to know."

"Your father was the flower-shop owner."

"Yes."

"And a gangster."

Jones nodded. "But that wasn't important. That wasn't what mattered to me. He was the best father, he was—"

"But that's all you've ever known," I interrupted. "He was a bootlegger, just like Uncle Cy."

"My father wasn't like Cy at all. To him, I wasn't a freak." Jones moved to the table then and set one of the glasses in front of me. He sat down. "I didn't tell you because I knew you wouldn't understand. You'd see everything bad about him and none of the good, and you'd judge me as his son by your own impossible standards. But I *was* his son, see, and the only thing that mattered to me was that he loved my mother and me both. He was a good man, Eve. You've got to believe me."

I closed the book and slid it across the table to Jones. He was right. Had he told me before, I wouldn't have understood. But now . . .

I lifted my eyes from the book and looked at Jones. "Will you excuse me?" I said. "I have some thinking to do."

He nodded.

I left the tea untouched and left the room without a word.

Chapter 27

Annie stood on tiptoe at the kitchen window, peering out. "Someone here for you, Eve, honey."

I looked out over her shoulder. "He's here for something to eat, and you know it, Annie."

"Uh-huh. That too," she said. "I'll fix him up a tray of these leftovers."

He sat on the grass, watching me nonchalantly as I approached. "Hope you don't mind warmed-over oatmeal and toast," I said, handing him the tray. "You're early today. Lunch isn't ready."

"Beggars can't be choosers." He winked. "Can you sit for a time?"

I looked at the kitchen window where Annie was waving me down to the grass. "I guess I can. For a little while."

We sat in silence for a few minutes while he ate the oatmeal. I couldn't help staring at his hands as he lifted the spoon to his mouth. They were fine, strong hands, and they were probably equally at home holding a book, a hammer, even a gun. I remembered how he'd shot the ducks at the carnival while Marcus had missed. He'd gone to college and read who-knew-how-many books about history. Now, he was doing day labor.

Who are you, Link? I wondered. I didn't even know his name.

"So is there anything new with you and the folks?" he asked, scraping the last of the oatmeal from the bottom of the bowl.

"New?" I echoed.

"Yeah. Haven't seen you in a few days, so I was just wondering."

I shook my head, looked away. "No. Nothing's new."

"Nothing?"

"No. Why?"

"No reason." He took a bit of toast, chewing thoughtfully. "I'm just making conversation, Eve."

I cleared my throat, thought a moment, finally settled on something to say. "My sister's coming to visit soon."

"That right?"

"Yeah. Maybe you can meet her."

"I'd like that."

"She's married."

"Uh-huh."

"She's got two kids."

He nodded, finished off the toast. He set aside the plate and bowl and wiped his hands on the bib of his overalls. "Bet she's not half as pretty as you are."

My heart thumped. No one had ever told me I was pretty before, not even Marcus. The words sounded strange in my ears. I lifted my eyes to Link's and when they met, I had to admit to myself what I'd been trying to suppress ever since

Daddy told me we were leaving. Of all the things I didn't want to leave behind in Mercy, Ohio, the one thing I didn't want to leave most of all was Link.

"You're just saying that," I whispered.

"I never say anything that isn't true."

"Cassandra's beautiful. You just wait and see."

"I don't have to wait for anything. I already know."

I fidgeted on the grass, looked out toward the river. Soon I would tell him we were leaving, though I would never be able to tell him why.

"I heard you and your father brought some food out to the camp last Friday."

"Yeah, we did." I nodded.

"That was good of you. The men appreciated it."

I shrugged. "It was Uncle Cy's food."

"But your idea."

One I wished I'd never had. If only we could have gone on living without knowing. It was the knowing that changed everything and was driving us away.

"I asked Cecil to hold some back for you. Did you get it?"

"I did, thanks."

I took a deep breath. My heart had settled back into rhythm. "You got work today?" I asked.

He fingered a pebble he'd found in the grass, tossed it across the lawn. "Not today. Prospects aren't always very good around here."

"I don't know why you stay."

"It's where I'm supposed to be."

He'd told me that before. I didn't understand it then and I didn't understand it now. It seemed like someone in his position could travel just about anywhere.

"How long do you think things are going to be the way they are now? I mean, in the way of jobs?" I asked.

"A good long while, I imagine. The future looks pretty bleak."

I had to agree. The country's future. His future. Mine.

"Do you think you'll ever go back to college?"

"God willing and the Little Miami don't rise." He laughed lightly at that. Then, more seriously, "I don't intend to be a bum my whole life, you know."

The crash had made him a bum, but he was a beautiful bum. I wanted to touch the hand that had held the spoon, but I didn't dare. I hardly dared look at him, knowing which way my heart was leaning.

"Well, I'd better get back to helping Annie with lunch." I rose.

"Eve?"

I waited but didn't respond.

"You sure you're all right? You seem . . . I don't know . . . distracted or something."

"Sure. I'm all right."

"Nothing's wrong then?" He unfolded himself to his full height and cupped my chin in the palm of his hand. He lifted my face so that I had to look him in the eye. "You can tell me," he said.

"Nothing's wrong," I whispered. I wanted to sink my head into his shoulder and take refuge there. I wanted to feel his arms around me and to hear him tell me I didn't have to be afraid. But instead I withdrew, turning away.

"Eve . . ."

"It's all right, Link. I've got to go. I'll talk to you later."

One day he'd go back to school and make something of

himself. One day he'd marry a beautiful woman and have beautiful children, and he'd be happy. I hoped so. For his sake, I hoped so.

I moved across the lawn toward the kitchen, wondering at all the marvelous things people might be, if not for the circumstances that pulled them down.

Chapter 28

The knock on the door was so subtle I thought perhaps I had dreamed it. Eyelids half open, I listened a moment before rolling over in bed in the still-dark room. Another knock, louder this time, followed by my mother's voice. "Eve?"

I moaned, sat up in bed. "Come in, Mother."

The door to our adjoining bathroom opened and Mother padded across the room in her slippers and light cotton robe.

"What time is it?" I asked sleepily.

"Nearly six," Mother said. "Listen, Eve, we've just received some bad news. . . ." She paused as she sat down on the edge of my bed. In those few seconds, I envisioned every possible scenario, most of them revolving around the secret, all of them having to do with tragedy.

"What is it?" I pressed.

"Aunt Cora died in the night."

I lifted both hands to my mouth and squeezed my fingers together. "Oh no," I whispered. "How awful. Does Jones know?"

"Yes. Cyrus received the call about a half hour ago. He's already packing and getting ready to go."

"Go? Go where?"

"New York. He'll accompany her body back on the train."

"He's leaving this morning?"

"Yes. On the first train out. While he's gone, Daddy and I will cover at the front desk. Your help will be needed down at the Eatery. It's just for a few days, of course."

"Sure, Mother," I said. "Whatever I can do to help."

"You might want to get up now, so you have time to give your condolences to Uncle Cy before he leaves."

I nodded and pushed back the covers.

Mother stood and wrapped her arms around herself. "Poor Cyrus," she said. "It'll be the second wife he's buried. Such a hard lot for a good man like him. With no children of his own, he has so little to ease his grief."

"I wonder," I said absently, almost to myself, "what Jones will do now."

Mother looked at me in the dim light and shook her head. "Stay here, of course. Keep doing what he's doing. Why should that change?"

"He isn't Uncle Cy's son."

"No, but I should think he'd always have a place here, if I know Cy."

But you don't know Uncle Cy, I thought. *Not really. Not like I do.*

Mother let her hands fall to her side and seemed to steel herself with a deep breath. "Well," she said, "get dressed and meet us downstairs so we can see Cyrus off to the train. Daddy's going to give him a lift and then he'll come on back and we can have breakfast."

Ten minutes later I was on my way downstairs. Mother and Daddy were at the front door waiting. Daddy fingered his car keys while Mother dabbed quietly at her eyes with one of Daddy's handkerchiefs. Uncle Cy was at the desk, giving last-minute instructions to Thomas. He was dressed neatly in a gray cotton suit and wing-tip shoes; a single suitcase sat on the floor at his feet. His cheeks were crimson and his mouth drawn down, and he spoke with a certain urgency and like a man who was angry, which he very well might have been. He'd been dealt a rotten hand, after all.

Finally he picked up his fedora from the desk and settled it on his head. He turned and looked startled as he realized for the first time that I was there. For a moment neither of us spoke. His expression became one of annoyance, as though I were little more than a roadblock between him and the door.

I drew in a deep breath and said, "I'm very sorry about Aunt Cora, Uncle Cy."

He nodded curtly. "Thank you, Eve. Did your mother tell you about the work arrangements?"

"Yes, she told me."

"Do whatever needs to be done and don't cause any trouble while I'm gone."

I was taken aback and momentarily silenced. Then I said, "I won't cause any trouble, Uncle Cy." I wasn't a child who needed a reminder to behave. I hadn't caused a moment of trouble since we'd arrived, and I had no intention of causing any while he was away.

Only as his gaze bore into me did I begin to understand. Of course. The secret. The knowledge. I realized the power I had in that knowledge, and I realized too that Uncle Cy was afraid. One word from me to the right people and I could bring this whole place down.

He picked up his suitcase and stepped around me to the door. "You ready, Drew?"

"I'm ready. But don't worry, Cy. There's plenty of time before the train pulls out." Daddy kissed Mother's cheek and settled his own worn fedora on his head. Then the two men disappeared through the front door.

"Poor Cy," Mother said again.

"Jones isn't going with him?"

"No. Cy's going alone."

"How come?"

"How come Jones isn't going?"

I nodded.

"Apparently, he wanted to stay here."

"Sure he did," I whispered.

"What, Eve?"

I hesitated. "Nothing."

Mother sniffed and tucked her handkerchief into her skirt pocket. "Well, I'm going to see if Annie has the coffee on. Do you want to join me?"

"In a few minutes."

She stopped briefly to talk with Thomas on the way back to the kitchen. He smiled at her politely as they exchanged a few murmured words. When she left, Thomas peered at me over the round lenses of his glasses. His smile had disappeared, and the look in his eye told me he'd be watching and waiting for me to do something wrong in my uncle's absence. I narrowed my eyes at him and turned away to the window.

Like Mother, Thomas had no idea. Uncle Cy wasn't telling me to be good; he was telling me to be quiet.

The door to the apartment was closed. On the other side, a radio played something fierce and loud. I heard violins screeching, horns bellowing, cymbals crashing.

I knocked. No answer. I thought maybe Jones couldn't hear me over the music, so I knocked louder. Still no answer.

I almost turned away but something told me to stay. I knocked again. The music stopped abruptly. "Who is it?"

"It's me. Eve."

Silence. Then footsteps as he walked across the hardwood floor. The door squeaked open a crack and there was Jones, his red eyes staring out from behind the magnifying lenses of his glasses. He looked at me but said nothing.

"I've come to tell you how sorry I am about your mother." I waited. It was obvious he wasn't going to invite me in. "I just wanted you to know that," I finished awkwardly.

"Thank you, Eve."

His voice was strained and barely audible, but he hadn't cried. That much I knew. He appeared more ghostlike than ever, as though all the lifeblood had been sucked out of him, but he hadn't yet shed a tear.

"Uncle Cy didn't want you to go with him, did he?" I asked.

"It wasn't discussed," Jones said flatly.

"He should have let you go. She was your mother."

He shrugged resignedly. "My going with him wouldn't change anything. She'd still be dead."

I had no response.

He removed his glasses, folded them, and slipped them into his shirt pocket. "When are you leaving?"

"What?"

"You know, going back to St. Paul."

"Oh." I nodded. Of course he knew. He'd been there when Daddy had confronted Uncle Cy and our future had been set. "Soon. A week, maybe less. We'll probably caravan with Cassandra and her family on their way back up."

He lifted his chin a notch. "You'll be here for the funeral?"

"I . . . I don't know. When will it be?"

"Soon as the body gets here, I suspect."

I grimaced at his choice of words. "How long will Uncle Cy be gone?"

"Four, maybe five days."

"Then I imagine we'll be here."

"I'd like it if you were at the service."

I smiled sadly. "Then I'll try to be there."

He looked down, shifted his weight from one foot to another.

"Jones?"

"Uh-huh?"

"What will you do now?"

He looked up, not at me but somewhere over my shoulder. "Some wide open spaces out there are calling my name, with nothing holding me back now. I best get busy." He held out a thumb like he was waving down cars. He actually smiled.

"I think I'm going to miss you, Jones."

He sniffed shyly. A corner of his mouth drew back. "I think you'll be all right."

"Jones?"

"Uh-huh?"

"Can I hug you good-bye?"

"I'm not leaving yet."

"Can I hug you anyway?"

"What for?"

"Because that's what people do when someone dies."

Jones hesitated, rubbed his jaw. "I guess they do. All right, then."

He opened the door a little wider. I took a step toward him and lifted my arms around his neck. He didn't hug me back, but he let me cling to him for a long moment. The way his shoulders trembled I was sure it was the first time he'd been held by anyone other than his own mother.

Chapter 29

The stars shimmied and winked over the Little Miami. Uncle Cy had booked a band from Cincinnati to play the final Friday night of July, and even though he wasn't there, the band kept the date. Orson Albright and his musicians had played the island before, and they knew Uncle Cy was good for the money.

At a little after nine o'clock, their buoyant music enticed me from the lodge and drew me down to the pavilion. I stood in the shadows off to the side of the dance floor, watching, listening, drinking in the joy of couples dancing to "Happy Days Are Here Again." The song was popular just then because our country needed it; while it played, whenever it played, for those three minutes people could pretend that the days really were happy, in spite of everything. How I would miss that about the island, the live music rising up in the open air, spreading delight, reaching so far as to leave even the stars dancing overhead, their jubilance mirrored on the water.

I stood tapping my foot, my hands behind my back. I didn't want to leave the island to go back to St. Paul, but neither did I want to stay. All I knew for sure was there wasn't a place in the world that matched my dreams. For as long as I lived I would never stop pining for Paradise, but the gates had been shut and bolted long before I was born. I knew that now. The heartsickness of life outside of Eden was everyone's lot, including mine.

But it will be all right, I told myself. *We'll go back to St. Paul, and I'll make the best of it.* Ariel, at least, would be glad I was there. I'd return to school in another month as though I'd never been gone, and I would graduate next spring with the classmates I'd known since grade school. Yes, everything would be all right.

As I stood there consoling myself, someone tapped my shoulder and spoke quietly in my ear. "Want to dance?"

Marcus! I thought. But it wasn't Marcus; it was Link. Link towering over me, his smile vaguely apparent in the dim light.

"What are you doing here?" I asked.

"Same as you. Enjoying the music. So do you care to dance or not?"

The band was playing a swinging rendition of "Nobody's Sweetheart," which seemed somehow appropriate. I looked over the bobbing hands of the dancers to where Orson Albright waved his wand at his men, pulling the music out of them as though by magic. I turned back to Link. He stood expectantly, his thumbs hanging idly from his suspenders.

Don't do it, I told myself. *Lie. Tell him you're needed back at the lodge. Anything. Just don't spend the evening dancing with Link.*

And then I smiled at Link and said, "Sure. Why not?"

He let go of the suspenders and grabbed my hand. He

pulled me out of the shadows and, with his usual vitality, began to spirit me around the dance floor. I couldn't help but laugh. For an hour we forgot the world, though somehow the joy of the music and the dancing and of each other seemed more real than anything the world had to offer. When the band took a break, I was sorry for the interruption, but I invited Link to follow me to the Eatery. My cousin Earl, Uncle Luther's oldest son, was working the stand, and with a nod and a wink, he gave us a couple of tall cold glasses of lemonade free of charge.

We chose a table in the breezeway where we could sit and enjoy our drinks. The welcome iciness of the lemonade moistened my throat and sent shivers down my spine and out my arms.

"So when's your sister coming?" Link asked. He pushed his unruly curls out of his eyes. He remained sorely in need of a haircut.

"Tomorrow. They should arrive sometime toward evening."

"Well, I hope you all have a nice visit together."

"Uh-huh," I said. "Don't bother getting your hopes up too high. My sister and I aren't exactly the best of friends. On top of that, we have a funeral right in the middle of their visit."

"A funeral?"

"Yeah. Haven't you heard?"

"Heard what?"

"My Aunt Cora died. Uncle Cy's wife. He's in New York right now, bringing her back so she can be buried here."

Link shook his head. His expression became serious. "I hadn't heard. I'm sorry for your loss."

I shrugged. "I didn't know Cora, really. I met her only once, at the wedding about five years ago."

"Well, it's a terrible loss for your uncle."

"Yes, I guess it is. It's the second wife he's buried. The first one died of the Spanish flu and now Cora's died of tuberculosis."

Link gave out a low whistle. "Some people have it rough, don't they?"

I nodded but didn't say anything.

Link asked, "So when is the funeral?"

"Daddy and Uncle Luther have been making plans. Last I heard it's supposed to be held on Thursday."

"Will it be at a church here in town?"

I shook my head. "Aunt Cora was Catholic. It'll be up in Lebanon at the Basilica of St. Matthew."

Link nodded, dropped his eyes, became intent on his lemonade. No one wants to interrupt laughter to acknowledge death. Certainly I didn't. I finished my drink, feigning interest in the people milling about us, wishing I hadn't mentioned Aunt Cora's funeral.

At last the band returned from break. When we heard the opening notes of "On the Sunny Side of the Street," Link looked at me expectantly. Visions of Aunt Cora and the funeral drifted off and disappeared. Link and I were animated again, living in the buffer zone of youth, eager simply to be alive.

"Ready for another go-round?" he asked.

"Ready." I smiled.

For another hour, maybe more, we danced ourselves into a sweat, danced until our feet hurt, danced until our lungs ached for air and our hearts burst with happiness. And then . . . then the band eased into "After You've Gone," a slower song that called for dancing cheek to cheek. I couldn't reach Link's cheek, he was so tall, but he held me closer than before—a gesture that broke the spell I'd been under all evening. I didn't belong here—not in Mercy, not on the island, not in Link's arms. I'd be gone soon and it wasn't likely I'd ever come back.

I struggled in Link's grip, just slightly, just as though I were seeking cooler air, but he held on tight.

"Say, Eve?"

"Yeah?"

"How old are you?"

"Seventeen."

"Oh." He seemed to think about that a moment. Then he said, "When will you be eighteen?"

"September."

"September what?"

"Twenty-first. Why?"

"I'm just thinking."

"Thinking about what?"

"Thinking about when it might be appropriate to ask your father if I can call on you."

I gasped. My feet were suddenly rooted to the floor. Link stumbled, righted himself. "What's the matter, Eve?" he asked. At last, he loosened his grip. He frowned at me. The band began to play "Let Me Sing and I'm Happy."

"Link, I can't—"

"I know I'm not working a steady job right now, Eve, but—"

"You don't understand. I . . ."

I never should have accepted the first dance. I should have known better, *did* know better and hadn't heeded my own warning.

"Listen, Eve, I just want the chance to spend some time with you, get to know you."

"I can't. It won't work. It won't—"

"But why not? Whatever you're afraid of—"

I wiggled out of his arms, bumping into the couple dancing behind us. The man glared at me a moment before whisking his partner away. I started to cry.

Link reached for me. "Eve!"

"I'm sorry, Link. I'm just . . . I'm sorry."

I fled the dance floor and stumbled back to the lodge. To my relief, Link didn't try to follow.

Chapter 30

I didn't sleep much that night for thinking about Link. Two months at Marryat Island—two broken hearts. Things seemed not to be working out in my favor.

Maybe I should have explained. Maybe I should have told Link we were leaving, but he'd want to know why, and I couldn't tell him. Besides, I wasn't supposed to know myself that we were leaving. Daddy planned to sit down with Mother, Warren, Cassandra, and me sometime in the next few days to announce his decision to return to St. Paul. I was to act as surprised as the others.

Just before dawn I slipped out of bed and sat by the open window. The view was of the side yard and the wall where Link took his meals when he came. I wondered now whether I would ever see him again. I decided it didn't matter. Another few days and I'd be heading back to St. Paul, and that would be it.

The world outside was gray shadows. In some unseen place, the sun was just beginning to rise. As light seeped in, trees, shrubs, the wall where Link sat became more distinct, their edges defined. Colors, once only suggestions, began to bloom. The morning air drifting in through the open window was cool and sweet. It chilled the tears on my cheeks and made me shiver.

I leaned my elbows on the windowsill, listening. I could almost hear the rush of the Little Miami. The trees were choir lofts of birdsong. And down below, somewhere toward the back of the lodge, came the sound of gravel crunching as someone walked the unpaved drive leading to the road. I pressed my nose to the screen and waited to see who it was. Probably Morris Tweed on an early morning errand to who-knew-where.

When at length the figure came into view, I saw it wasn't Morris but someone else. I couldn't see the face, but I knew the hat. The safari hat that Jones wore out in the sun. He had his hands stuffed deep in his pants pockets, and his shoulders were drooped as he walked. He was headed in the direction of town. I'd never known Jones to go into town, or even to leave the grounds of the lodge at all, except when he was out on the river.

I wondered what his destination was at this early hour.

I watched him, small and lonely, until he'd crossed the road and disappeared from sight.

Mother sang hymns of joy in the bath that morning. I heard her as I stood at the dresser braiding my hair. Cassandra and her family would arrive by nightfall. I didn't consider that anything to sing about, especially since their coming signaled my leaving. My eyes were still red and puffy from a night of crying, though I'd washed my face twice in cold water and soothed it with lotion warmed between my palms.

I dragged myself downstairs to breakfast. Mother's excitement was salt on a wound, and I was glad to finish eating and go to the kitchen to help Annie. Uncle Luther had sent Earl and Jason to cover at the Eatery while Uncle Cy was away, which freed me up to do other things. Working with Annie was what I preferred over all the other tasks I did at the lodge.

All morning I was drawn to the window that looked out over the side yard and the wall. In between cooking and cleaning and washing dishes, I stood there wondering whether Link might come for lunch with some of the other men of the camp.

I wondered too how anyone could want and not want something so desperately at the same time.

No matter what I wanted, he didn't show. The day hobbled along on wounded feet. At dusk a car pulled up to the lodge with Minnesota plates. Cassandra and her family had arrived.

Mother and Daddy rushed out to meet them while I trailed behind. I walked solemnly across the graveled lot toward the laughter, the hugging and handshaking, the cries of "Grammy! Grandpa!" from my nieces.

When Effie and Grace saw me, they squealed loudly, "Aunt Eve!" They ran to me and I kneeled down on the hard gravel and took them both in my arms. They were hot and sweaty and sticky and oh-so-sweet as first one then the other pressed her cheek to mine and filled the air with kisses. Only then did I realize how much I'd missed them.

Grace clung to my neck until Warren came and gently pried her away. "You have all week to be with Aunt Eve, so give her room to breathe," he said with a laugh. "Hello, Eve, by the way. It's good to see you."

I rose from my kneeling position and stretched my legs. "Hello, Warren. Have a good trip?"

"Tolerable," he answered. "I suspect it'll be an early night for all of us. It's a long way from Minnesota."

I nodded. Out of the corner of my eye I could see my sister reaching in through the open car window to retrieve her pocketbook. At the same time she was talking animatedly with Mother.

"Your room's all ready for you," I assured him. "Soon as you have some supper, you can fall right into bed."

"Lovely place here," he said, looking around. "Should be quite a nice week."

"Yeah." I nodded again, even as I imagined the tunnel that ran under our feet to the gas station across the road. "No better place to take a vacation."

I hardly realized I was looking at the station until Warren followed my gaze. "Well, that's convenient," he said. "A place to gas up and get the car washed. It's filthy after the drive down. I assume you know the fellow who owns the station."

"Oh sure," I said. "Calvin Fludd. Go on over tomorrow and he'll get you all fixed up."

"All right. Looks like Drew's ready to haul in the luggage. Guess I'll go help him."

The girls were gathering pebbles at my feet. As Warren went to help Daddy with the suitcases, Cassandra and Mother left the car and casually moved toward me. I told myself to smile.

While they were yet several steps away, Cassandra raised her arms. "Eve!" she said. "I've missed you something awful!"

In the next moment, I was being squeezed in her embrace. I tried to breathe. When she let go, I scrambled to remember how to speak.

"I-I've missed you too," I stuttered.

She wrapped her arm through mine, locking elbows. "We have so much catching up to do," she said as she pulled me toward the lodge. "Even a week is hardly going to be enough time. Oh, isn't it wonderful to be here! I want you to tell me everything about your summer. . . ."

As we strolled arm in arm, Cassandra chattered like a magpie. At one point, I stole a glance over my shoulder at Mother. Her expression was one of quiet victory, as if the day she had long been waiting for had finally arrived.

Chapter 31

For two days I went along with it all. In this dizzying game of make-believe, the lodge was simply a lodge, Uncle Cy stored only canned goods in the cellar, the train from Cincinnati carried no surprises, the gas station sold only gas, and the car wash was clean as a whistle. Any trouble in Mercy, Ohio, was caused solely by wayward chickens and gophers that carried the remains of our ancestors through the streets of the town. Other than that, all was right with our world.

Neither did I have a broken heart, as no one—not Mother, not Daddy, not even Annie—knew about what had happened between me and Link.

For those first two days, while we waited for poor Uncle Cy to bring his dead wife home, we were a family enjoying a holiday. We cooled ourselves in the river. We picnicked on the island with Uncle Luther and the cousins. We played croquet with Cassandra's girls, took them rowing in the boats and drove to the ice cream parlor in town to indulge in hot fudge sundaes.

At night, after the girls were asleep, Cassandra hurried across the hall to my room and, sitting cross-legged on the bed, acted as though we were boarding-school roommates chatting about our lives. She untangled my long braid and brushed out my hair. She suggested I might want to cut it on my eighteenth birthday, as a bob with a permanent wave would make me look more grown-up. She asked if she could paint my face with rouge and lipstick, and so I let her. She turned her head this way and that and stuck out a pouty lower lip as she studied her artwork.

"You've become quite pretty, you know, Eve," she said admiringly.

"I have?" I held the hand mirror in front of my face and thought how strange I looked with the added color.

"Of course, silly," she said with a wave of her hand. "Don't you know that?"

When she idly asked me about going to school at Mercy High, I told her I was enrolled—which I was—and I pretended as though I would be starting there in just another month. We talked about the lodge as though it was my home. We talked about the town as though I belonged there. We talked about my future in Mercy as though I had one.

At times it was a pleasant place to be, this nest of lies. For certain stretches—sometimes minutes, often hours—I could pretend it was all real. Other times, I was amazed at how different the truth of our existence was from the staged scenery we wandered through. I was always mindful that Uncle Cy wasn't the only lawbreaker in the family: Daddy and I were too. Simply because we knew. Jones Five and Ten hung heavy over my head.

Finally, on Monday night, a break in the charade came

when Daddy called us all to the dining room after Effie and Grace had been put to bed. The kitchen was closed till morning and the lighting in the dining room was dimmed, though the tireless ceiling fans whirled faithfully overhead. The numerous windows were thrown open against the heat, and all the night sounds drifted in—the chorus of crickets and tree frogs, the creaking of rocking chairs, and the soft murmur of voices as guests settled on the porch to enjoy the evening.

We gathered over glasses of iced tea, and from where I sat I could see Thomas leaning idly on the front desk, waiting for the phone to ring or for a guest to stop by with some request or other. The tables around us were empty, but Daddy spoke in low tones anyway, as though he feared being overheard.

"I've got something I'd like to talk with all of you about," he began. He had both hands wrapped around his sweaty glass of tea.

"What is it, Daddy?" Cassandra asked. "Is something wrong?"

Daddy shook his head. "No, nothing's wrong. I've just been thinking, is all."

"About what?" Mother asked. She cast Daddy a worried glance.

Daddy sniffed and cleared his throat. My heart thumped in my chest. I knew what was coming. After what seemed an interminable amount of time, Daddy said, "I believe we made a mistake, coming here."

"What?" Mother cried. "A mistake? What do you mean, Drew?"

She looked at me. I looked away, down at the table.

Daddy said, "You know I've never belonged here, Rose. That's why I left all those years ago. When Cy invited us down, I felt compelled to give this place another chance, especially since I needed a job, but I've decided coming here was wrong. We don't belong in Ohio. We belong in St. Paul. That's our home and I think we ought to go back."

"But, Daddy," Cassandra exclaimed, "where will you live? What will you do?"

"I haven't quite figured all that out yet, darling," Daddy confessed. "I was hoping maybe you and Warren might have some ideas, since you're still there."

Warren fidgeted in his chair, took a long sip of iced tea. Then he said, "Well, Drew, we have an extra room at our place. You all could stay with us for a time, till you get yourselves settled."

Cassandra's jaw dropped and her eyes widened a notch, but she said nothing.

"That'd be more than kind of you, Warren—"

"But, Drew," Mother interrupted, "I'm not sure we should impose."

"Oh, no imposition, Rose," Warren rushed to assure her. "After all, you're family. We maybe should have made the offer before you came all the way down here, but we thought your minds were made up."

Daddy nodded. "My mind *was* made up, but now I've changed it."

"But that's what I don't understand, Drew," Mother said. "What changed it? I know we were both hesitant at first, but everything seemed to be going along so well for us here."

"Rose, there are some things I don't expect you to understand. One of them is how a man feels about being the man of the house and providing for his family. I want to make us independent again. Sure, we'll be beholden to Warren and

Cassandra for a time, but eventually we'll have our own place again. I promise you that."

A leaden silence followed Daddy's announcement. While I waited for someone to speak, I happened to look at Thomas, who was looking at us. Though he couldn't possibly hear what we were saying, I had the feeling he knew exactly what we were discussing. He impatiently tapped at the front desk with the eraser end of a pencil, as though he wanted us to hurry up and come to a consensus about leaving. I was sure he was beating out the minutes until he could be rid of us.

Mother broke the silence. "Well, I don't know, Drew," she said. "I mean, you've caught me off guard. I had no idea you were thinking about going back to St. Paul. I don't know if we should. I don't know if it's right for Eve. I simply don't know. . . ." Her words trailed off.

Warren said, "Listen, Drew, I'll ask my father if there's anything you can do at the company. I should think there must be something."

"I'd be grateful to you, Warren. I'll do anything, anything at all, so long as I can win my independence back."

Warren nodded. "I'll telephone Dad tonight. We'll get this thing settled as soon as we can."

Cassandra flopped back in her chair, limp as a rag doll. "Well, I just can't believe it," she said. "You're all settled in here. You've got jobs here. Now you want to uproot yourselves again and go back up to where you have nothing?"

"We've got plenty there, darling," Daddy said. "We've got you and the kids, for one thing. We stay down here, we won't get to see our grandkids grow up."

"Yeah, but *St. Paul?* What's St. Paul compared to this place? I mean, the island is such a great place to live."

"It's a nice place to visit," Daddy said. "But like I say, St. Paul is our home. That's where we belong."

Mother put a hand on Cassandra's shoulder. "Listen, honey, I can understand if you don't want us staying with you. Maybe we can—"

"No, no, no, Mother. It isn't that. It's just . . ." She sighed and looked around the table. She offered us all a tentative smile. "I guess I'm just surprised, is all."

Mother frowned at Daddy. "So am I. Why didn't you talk to me about this before, Drew?"

"Honey, I don't know. I guess it's really only been in the last few days that I've known what I want to do. It kind of hit me all of a sudden that leaving—going back home—is what's best for the family."

Mother opened her mouth, but before she could speak Warren jumped to Daddy's defense. "I understand how you feel, Drew." He patted Cassandra's hand as he added, "It's just something you ladies can't appreciate, this burden of trying to do what's best for the family."

I couldn't help it. I snorted out a chuckle at that, knowing full well the weight of Daddy's burden. Just as quickly I tried to look somber, as though contemplating our move.

Still, Mother turned stern eyes in my direction. "What's so funny, Eve?" she asked.

I feigned innocence. "Nothing's funny."

"I thought you laughed."

"Me? No, just clearing my throat."

"Well, what do you have to say about leaving here?"

I sat up primly. "I'm willing to do whatever Daddy thinks is best."

"It's settled then," Daddy said, with a look around the

table. "We're going home. We'll leave when Cassandra and Warren leave—"

"But, Daddy, we're leaving next Saturday!"

"That's right, Cassandra, and we'll be ready to go by then. It's not as though we have a whole houseful of possessions to pack up. We can caravan to Minnesota and keep an eye on each other while we're on the road."

"I agree," Warren said. "Best if we all plan on going back together."

God bless Warren for being so agreeable. He made it easy for us to escape.

I felt a little lighter when I went to bed that night. One lie had been mercifully removed. No longer would I have to pretend we were going to go on living in Ohio. All I would have to pretend now—and for the rest of my life—was that, other than Daddy's fickleness, I had no idea why we would ever want to leave such a beautiful place as Marryat Island.

Chapter 32

Warren and Daddy swam with the girls while Cassandra and I sat in beach chairs set back from the river's edge. Between us, on a small wicker table, were two tall glasses of lemonade, the ice long gone. The August sun was a scorcher, its heat tempered only by an occasional cloud or, even rarer, a reluctant momentary breeze.

Cassandra read a *True Detective* magazine while fanning herself with the August issue of *Ladies' Home Journal*. She wore a modest navy blue swimsuit, as modest as my own, but she didn't hesitate to stretch her long sleek legs out in front of her, her painted toes digging in the pebbly beach. Her floppy sun hat hid her face from my view.

I closed Agatha Christie's *The Man in the Brown Suit* and pushed my sun hat high on my forehead. The island was alive with laughter; it was a living, swarming throng of swimmers, boaters, sunbathers, picnickers. Sitting in the midst of it, I felt my rib cage swell with something bittersweet. I loved this place for its visible snapshot of fun and pleasure and rest; at the same time I hated it for the corruption festering beneath the surface. In a few days, when I left Marryat Island behind, I would take away joyous remembrances, and I would be haunted by terrible memories.

And long after we left this place I would think of Link, and wonder.

"Say, Eve?"

Cassandra turned to me. She'd let *True Detective* fall to her lap, though she went on fanning herself with the *Journal*.

"Yeah?"

"Mother told me this morning about your boyfriend, and I wanted you to know . . . well, I'm sorry. I know how much it hurts."

I squinted out over the water, trying to imagine how Mother had learned about Link. "My boyfriend?" I asked.

"Yes. Maybe I shouldn't have said anything, but . . . oh, I hope you don't mind Mother telling me about Marcus."

I laughed lightly. "Oh, him."

"Oh him?" She sniffed. "Well, I can't say you sound very brokenhearted to me."

I shrugged. "I can do better than Marcus."

"Of course you can," she said brightly. "And you have plenty of time to find just the right one. And common sense too. Between the two of us, you were always the one with common sense."

I frowned at her, but she had turned away to look out over the water. "Just look at that Gracie, will you?" she said, sitting up and resting her elbows on her knees.

For a moment we watched the child as she tried to swim, her long skinny arms turning like windmills, her tiny feet splashing up a squall in the otherwise placid water. She threw her wet curls back and laughed openly at the sky. It was a song of unspoiled joy.

"She's really growing up fast," I said. "Effie too."

"I can hardly believe they aren't little babies anymore. Seems like just yesterday they couldn't even crawl, much less swim."

"Hmm."

"It's nice to see the girls having such fun with Daddy and Warren, isn't it?"

We watched the foursome play in the water. Warren's shoulders had turned pink in the sun, but he didn't seem to notice. Daddy was much more at ease today, now that our leaving was settled. He'd come down to breakfast whistling.

"Do you think you'll have more?" I asked.

"More kids? No. Two's enough."

"Oh. Well, then . . ."

"What?"

"When Gracie was born, didn't Warren hope for a son?"

Cassandra thought a moment, shook her head. "He never said so. He's a wonderful daddy to the girls, both of them."

Even Effie, I thought, *who wasn't his own.*

"Daddy wished I was a boy," I said.

She looked at me sharply. "Why on earth would you say that?"

"Well, you know." I paused and shrugged. "To make up for the one who died between us."

"That's not true, Eve. I can't imagine how you ever got that idea."

"It only makes sense."

"It doesn't make sense at all. When you were born, Mother and Daddy were thrilled. Nothing was ever said about wanting a son instead. They were just thankful you were healthy and strong."

I had to let that sink in. "Really?" I asked.

"Of course, silly. I should know. I was there, after all."

Cassandra reached for her glass of lemonade and took a long drink. She looked thoughtful—and older and more serious than the sister I had left in St. Paul. "You know, Eve," she said at length, "Gracie is the spitting image of you at age three."

I studied my niece, smiled at her cherubic little-girl face, her head of blond ringlets. "Really?" I asked again.

Cassandra nodded. "It's uncanny, actually. I look at her and sometimes I think I'm looking at you. I even call her Eve sometimes."

"You do? Well, I don't know. I can't see it myself."

"You just don't know what you looked like at three, except for a picture or two."

"I guess not."

"But when you were three, I was eleven. Old enough to be aware. Old enough to know better. Sometimes I look at Gracie and I see you, and I feel such terrible shame."

I cocked my head and my mouth fell open. "But why?"

Cassandra delayed answering by picking up the glass of lemonade and taking long leisurely sips. At last she said, "You're angry with me, aren't you?"

I drew in a breath. I felt my eyes narrow. "Of course not," I said.

"Tell the truth, Eve. You're angry, and frankly, I don't blame you. I treated you something awful when we were kids."

"Well—"

"It's just . . ."

"Not always, though. I remember some good times."

"How could you possibly?"

"Well . . ." I paused to think. "I remember being here, on the island . . . we had fun together. You danced with me when a band came and played in the pavilion. I was very small but I have a vague memory of you twirling me around."

"Oh." She leaned back in the chair and sighed deeply. "I suppose I tried, early on. But it was no use."

"What do you mean, it was no use?"

She shook her head. "I didn't know how to handle . . . well, see, I was eight years old when you were born, and I was used to being the only child. When you came along, I was so jealous. It was as though I became invisible to Mother and Daddy. Everything was Eve, Eve, Eve. I guess, after they'd lost the other baby . . . and I remember that, you know. I remember how heart-wrenching and miserable that was. All the tears! They tried to hide their grief from me, but . . ." She shook her head again and lifted her hands to her ears. "I thought the crying would never stop. And then, after all that, there *you* were. A beautiful, healthy baby. And Mother and Daddy were happy again. And I was forgotten."

I sat up straight in the chair and looked hard at my sister. "That's not true, Cassandra. They always loved you."

She drew back one corner of her mouth before looking away. "I know that now. I didn't know it then. So I took my anger out on you, because I considered it your fault. If you hadn't been there, I would have gone on being an only child. And that would have made me special."

"But . . ." Incredulous, I was having trouble gathering my thoughts. My sister, my tormentor, had always seemed to me genuinely happy and self-satisfied. And beautiful. And popular. "Cassandra," I said quietly. When she turned her eyes to me, I saw they were glassy with tears. I understood then what I had never understood before. "You say you were jealous of me, but I spent my whole childhood jealous of *you*."

"Of me?"

I nodded.

"Why?"

"Because you were so beautiful. You had so many friends and boyfriends. I pretended to be disgusted by you, but I wanted to be just like you, and I knew I never would be. You were the swan and I was the ugly duckling."

We looked at each other. I saw the corners of her mouth twitch, and in the next moment we were laughing loudly together.

"Holy buckets," she cried. "You mean we spent all those years being jealous of each other?"

I threw up my hands. "I guess so!"

We went on laughing loud and long, until Cassandra started fanning herself again with the *Ladies' Home Journal*. She handed me *True Detective* so I could cool my own laughter. And my surprise and regret at all the hurtful years.

After several minutes, she sighed and shook her head. "You know, Eve," she said, "we never knew the boy, but I think he affected our lives more than we can imagine."

I nodded in agreement. "I always felt like I had to make up for his death somehow. You know, do something special to kind of make everything okay for Mother and Daddy."

"Yes." Another deep sigh. "And I always felt there wasn't anything at all I could do to make everything okay for Mother and Daddy, because I simply wasn't there anymore."

After a moment's silence, I said, "Maybe when we get back to St. Paul, we can kind of start over. You know, be friends this time around."

She smiled at me and nodded. "I'd like that."

"I wonder whether we might have been friends all along, if the boy had lived?"

"Who's to say?" Cassandra lifted her shoulders in a shrug. "Maybe a lot of things would have been different if he'd lived."

"You know, I've never known anything about him. I'm not sure I would have known he'd been born, if you hadn't told me."

"You mean, you never heard Mother and Daddy mention him?"

"Never. And I never asked. Did he have a name?"

"Oh yes. They named him after Daddy. Andrew Lyle Marryat Jr. He was born perfectly formed, a perfect little corpse. He never so much as took his first breath."

A large cumulus cloud covered the sun and cast us into shadow. A couple in a rowboat drifted lazily on the river, he pulling leisurely at the oars, she sitting at ease under a white parasol. I envied them, yet at the same time I wondered whether they were happy or whether there was some gnawing sadness beneath the surface of things.

Daddy lifted Grace to his shoulders and started walking toward shore.

"Cassandra?"

"Yeah?"

"There's a whole world of hurt out there, isn't there?"

My sister nodded slowly. "And then some," she said.

Daddy came and settled Grace in her mother's lap. Cassandra put her arms around the little girl and held her close.

Chapter 33

Cassandra took the girls back to the lodge for their afternoon nap while Daddy and Warren traipsed off to the Eatery for a snack and something to drink. Daddy invited me to go but I wanted to be alone.

Once everybody left I realized I was still clutching Cassandra's *True Detective* magazine. Thumbing through it, I settled on an article about the smuggling of rum from Jamaica. Fifteen minutes later, my jaw came unhinged and my wide eyes gazed unseeing out over the river.

Tossing the magazine aside, I headed for the lodge in search of Jones.

I stopped by my room first to change out of my bathing suit and into my usual cotton dress. I didn't want to confront Jones without being properly attired.

He was in the apartment, not at the radio table but at the desk on the opposite wall. The windows were thrown wide open against the heat. Two oscillating fans blew air at each other from opposite ends of the room, rustling several piles of paper on the desk that would have gone sailing had they not been held down by paperweights. Jones was bent over an open checkbook; I could hear the tip of his pen scratching its way across the paper.

"Jones?"

He looked up, magnified eyes blinking. "Oh. Hello, Eve."

"You busy?"

"Just working my way through a pile of invoices. Trying to get caught up before Cyrus gets home tonight."

"He'll be here tonight for sure?"

"According to his latest telegram, yes."

I shivered as I thought about Uncle Cy traveling home with Aunt Cora's body. I couldn't begin to imagine what Jones must be feeling.

"Um, Jones?"

He grunted. He tore off a finished check and slid it into an envelope.

"Can I ask you something?"

He licked the envelope and sealed it. "I guess so."

"You don't have to tell me, but I was just wondering."

My pulse escalated and I could feel my heart pounding in my chest. I took a deep breath to calm myself.

Jones looked annoyed. "Well, I can't tell you anything if you don't ask your question," he said.

"Um." I took a few steps closer. He didn't invite me to sit down. I would have declined anyway. His pen was scratching out another check. "It's about the radios," I said.

He nodded. He picked up another bill and studied it. The pen moved in rapid strokes as he scribbled something on the invoice.

I took another tentative step toward the desk. "You were receiving information. I mean, from Cincinnati. Weren't you?"

The scratching stopped. The pen slowly dropped to the desk. Jones turned to face me. "What do you mean, Eve?"

With another deep breath, I admonished myself not to back down now. "Those bedtime stories you listened to. They were coded messages, weren't they, telling you when you could expect the next shipment of liquor to come in on the train."

The red eyes narrowed behind the lenses. "Why do you think that?"

I swallowed. I felt the spittle slide down my throat, leaving my mouth dry. "I read about that kind of thing in a magazine just now." My voice had weakened but I compensated by lifting my head higher.

"You did, huh?"

I nodded.

"What magazine was that?"

Because I didn't want to admit to the name, it came out in a whisper. "*True Detective.*"

He laughed. One swift cutting laugh. "And you believe what you read in a rag like that?" He took his glasses off and rubbed his eyes. "Anyway," he added, "what difference does it make?"

"It doesn't make any difference. Not really. I just want to know."

"Uh-huh." He slid his glasses back on and pulled another statement from the pile.

A bead of sweat slunk down my back. "If you don't tell me otherwise, Jones, I'm going to believe you were helping

Uncle Cy with the bootlegging, that you didn't just know about it but you were telling Uncle Cy when the liquor was coming in on the train."

Blood rose to his pale cheeks, turning his skin eerily red. When he spoke he didn't look at me. "It doesn't matter what you think, does it, Eve? Another few days and we'll never see each other again."

"I know that, Jones, so I just want to know why. Uncle Cy never treated you like a son. He never even treated you like a real member of the family. Why did you help him?"

"I didn't help him!" Jones yelled. I gasped as he banged the desk with an open palm, pushed back the chair, and stood abruptly. He walked to the window and looked out. The view was of the gas station, where even now the illegal liquor sat in its hiding place, awaiting customers.

"Then why did you do it, Jones?" I asked quietly.

He leaned his head back and took a deep breath. "I did it for her. For my mother."

I didn't respond. I waited. After a moment, he turned from the window and looked at me. "I did it for my mother," he said again, "because we needed the money to try to save her."

And now she was dead, her body riding in a casket halfway across the country, heading home for burial. "I'm sorry," I said. "I'm not judging you, Jones. I understand why you'd do it. I really do."

He feigned a smile. "Thank you, but I doubt it. You can't possibly understand. My mother loved me. She was the only person who ever did. She and my father. Now they're both dead."

I felt something terrible in my chest, an actual constriction of my heart because I knew what Jones said was true. To everyone other than his own parents he was the red-eyed devil, the freak, the boy to be hushed up and hidden away.

I fumbled for something to say. I made several false starts, but Jones cut me off by asking, "When are you leaving?"

"You mean, to go back to Minnesota?"

He nodded.

"Saturday."

"Good." He walked back to the desk and sat down. "You know, you can tell the police about my involvement, but it won't matter. Not anymore."

"I have no intention of telling anyone anything. You know that. That's why we're leaving. So Daddy and I don't have to live a lie."

He looked at the wall and I looked at his profile. His head bobbed slightly; he appeared deep in thought. Finally he said, "Go on home and forget you ever came here. Just forget about this place, Eve. That's the best thing you can do."

A silence settled between us, weighted with sadness. As I had so many times before, as I had when his mother died, I wanted to throw my arms around Jones and comfort him.

Hesitantly I said, "I mean it when I say there's one good thing I'll never forget about this place, and that's you, Jones."

Slowly he turned his gaze to me. We looked at each other for what seemed a very long time. His face relaxed, and though his eyes were sorrowful, one corner of his mouth turned up in the smallest of smiles. "You take care of yourself, Cousin Eve."

I breathed deeply and nodded. "You too, Jones O'Brannigan."

I moved to the desk and put my hand over his. He looked at it, then circled his fingers around my own and squeezed gently. He hung his head, as though against some inner pain. For a moment I thought he might kiss my knuckles or press my fingers to his cheek. But he didn't. He pulled his hand from my clasp and picked up his pen. I dropped my hand to my side and left the room.

Chapter 34

His mother's funeral called for one of Jones's rare excursions from the lodge. On the morning of the service, he slipped into a gray linen suit, slicked his white hair down with Murray's pomade, and ventured forth to endure the stares of those who had come to pay his mother their last respects.

At his request I sat beside him in the church, lost in the tangle of candles, holy water, incense, and a volley of Latin that left my head reeling. Jones appeared unmoved; the only indication that he was aware of anything at all was a nervous twitching of his right thumb.

I heaved a sigh of relief when the choir started singing something about paradise and the casket was carried out of the church. There was still the burial to get through, but at least we were making progress. At the grave site, I stood beside a still stony-faced Jones. I longed to comfort him, but his rigid husk seemed impenetrable. The few tears that sprang to my eyes weren't for the aunt I'd never known but for her hapless son and the open-ended question of what would become of him. The world was not a kind place for someone like Jones.

I tried to pay attention as the priest intoned a few prayers and sang words of Scripture. The coffin was lowered into the earth and sprinkled with holy water while we silently recited The Lord's Prayer. Finally the priest uttered the parting words in English, something I could at last understand: "May her soul and the souls of all the faithful departed through the mercy of God rest in peace."

Jones rode home from the cemetery with Uncle Cy and promptly disappeared. He completely sidestepped the food-laden reception in the dining room that the ladies of Mercy had spent days preparing. It was not his way to mingle, nor, I realized, would the townsfolk have wanted him to. Awkward enough to be at a funeral without having to express one's sympathy to a boy they had never once spoken to before. On top of that, they would not have been able to look him in the eye without flinching.

No sympathy was wasted, though, as the citizens of Mercy heaped it in great piles upon Uncle Cy. Though he was genuinely grieving, my uncle's hangdog look annoyed me. I didn't think he deserved the comfort and condolences of the crowd that had gathered at the lodge. For one swift moment, as I was reaching for a glass of fruit punch, I felt the urge to stand in the center of the room and holler, "Cyrus Marryat is a bootlegger! His stash of liquor is in the cellar right beneath this room!" I nearly laughed out loud just imagining the wave of horror that would follow my announcement, knocking the expressions of grief right off this throng of sweaty faces, replacing it with wide-eyed shock and contempt. What an instant change in atmosphere, if only these people knew the truth.

But of course I held my tongue. I chose a glass of punch, looked around the room, listened to snippets of stilted conversation, and moved in a haze of heat and fatigue from one end of the dining room to the other. As I passed by a second punch bowl at the back of the room, I witnessed a scene that brought me up short. Two tidy, well-dressed men were chatting amiably when one reached into his jacket's inner pocket, pulled out a thin silver flask, poured a dollop into his glass of punch and another into the glass of his companion. That done, the flask was then returned to the unseen pocket in one swift and uninterrupted motion while seemingly no one noticed or, if they did, no one cared. It was just as though the two men had lighted cigarettes or bitten into wedges of tomato sandwiches rather than indulging in something illegal.

Only then did I realize, in a sudden bolt of clarity, that any number of the men and women gathered at the lodge were the very people who drove through Fludd's Service Station, carrying away something in their cars other than a few gallons of gasoline. Who, after all, would Calvin Fludd be servicing but the fine people of Mercy and the neighboring towns? Not all of them, of course, but surely some. And maybe many. Rather than the outrage I had imagined just moments before, any announcement on my part about liquor in the cellar would probably produce a riotous stampede in that direction.

I swayed slightly and felt a ripple of nausea roll across my stomach. The air in the lodge was stifling; I couldn't breathe.

The intrepid ceiling fans turning overhead were no match for the soaring temperatures and the close proximity of so many bodies. I had to get out. I elbowed my way through the dining room and hurried to the porch.

I had barely stepped into the open air when Cassandra was beside me. "What are you doing out here, Eve?" she asked, pinching my elbow playfully. She was fanning herself with a funeral parlor fan she'd picked up at the service.

"It's too hot inside."

"It sure is, and I've had quite enough of all this. What do you say we go down to the island and put our toes in the river?"

I looked at her and smiled. "Let's go."

She tossed aside the fan, I set down my glass of punch, and together we hurried down the steps and across the bridge to the island. The place was deserted; Uncle Cy had closed it off to guests for the day. We giggled like children as we rushed along the path to the beach, where we kicked off our shoes and stepped barefoot into the river.

Cassandra tilted her face toward the sky and smiled. "It's just delicious!" she cried, wiggling her toes in the water. "I couldn't wait to get away from the crowd. I thought I would die of the heat and the long faces and all the kowtowing to Uncle Cy. 'Oh, she was such a dear woman,' and 'Oh, what a loss to the town.' I bet not one of them ever gave Cora the time of day when she was alive."

I sniffed out a laugh and said, "I don't know, Cassandra. Maybe they liked her, some of them. After all, we never came to visit while Cora was here, so we don't know what went on."

"No, but I know people. They all want something. Even when they do nice things for you and act as though you're all they care about in the world, the bottom line is what's in it for them. I . . ." She stopped herself and took a deep breath. "Well, never mind, Eve. You haven't seen the things I've seen, and that's good. You won't end up so cynical."

I picked up a small rock and tossed it into the water. With one hand shading my eyes, I looked up and down the river. "I think I understand what you mean. At least a little bit. I've seen a few things myself."

Cassandra laughed. She didn't believe me. That was all right. "You're lucky to be young and innocent," she said, "and . . . I don't know . . . pure, I guess."

"Pure?"

"Yes. You know, you haven't run off to speakeasies and gotten drunk and been with the boys the way I used to. You haven't made a mess of things. You've always been a good person, Eve."

I dropped my hand to my side and shook my head. "I used to think I was," I said quietly.

"What?"

"I said, I used to think I was a good person. Once."

She laughed again, splashed the water with her feet. "You're so funny. What have you done that's so awful? Kiss Marcus?"

I smiled wistfully. If only I were as innocent as that! Maybe I would never join the dash for illegal liquor, but neither would I reveal the hiding place. What was the difference? One transgression was the same as another. I picked up another stone, threw it more forcefully, watched the water ripple away from where it landed. I wanted to steer the conversation away from me, to talk about other things.

"Aren't you happy, Cassandra?" I asked. "I mean, with Warren and the girls?"

She paused in her splashing and appeared deep in thought. Finally she said, "Having them is more than I deserve. So while things aren't perfect, yes, I guess I'm nearly as happy as a person can be. Still, it doesn't erase the past. I've been thinking a lot lately about the day I'll have to tell Effie that her daddy isn't her daddy. Not her real one, anyway."

"Do you think you have to tell her?"

"It's only fair that she knows. Wouldn't you want to know?"

I shrugged. "I guess I would."

"Yes." She sighed heavily. "It will be a confession of sorts. 'Look what your mommy did. Look at what a bad mommy you have. . . . '"

Her voice choked up and she looked away.

"She'll forgive you," I said gently.

"Do you think so?"

"Yes."

"Why should she?"

"Because she loves you."

She turned to me, brushed away a tear, smiled. "You sound like Daddy."

"Do I?"

"'Love shall cover the multitude of sins.' Remember?"

"First Peter 4:8," I said.

"Yes."

"One of the Bible verses he made us memorize when we were kids."

She nodded. "And I heard him say it a thousand times himself. Though I don't even really know what it means."

I drew in a breath. I looked at the river, at the lodge, at Cassandra. "Maybe it's mercy," I said.

Cassandra tilted her head. "Mercy?" she asked.

I nodded. Yes. What Reverend Kilkenny had been preaching about all summer.

Lord, have mercy on me, a sinner.

"Well," Cassandra said, "maybe so. I don't know much about that sort of thing. But I hope you're right about Effie. I hope she'll forgive me."

"She will," I said. "I'm sure of it."

Cassandra smiled and, to my surprise, threw her arms around me and held me close. "I'm glad we've had a chance to . . . you know, talk about things. And become friends."

"I hope you'll still think so in a few months, after we've lived with you and Warren for a while. You don't mind too much, do you?"

"That you'll be living with us? No, of course I don't mind. I don't understand it. I mean"—she let me go and threw open her arms over the river—"how Daddy could want to leave here to go back to St. Paul." She shook her head. "I guess there's a lot about Daddy I've never understood, but don't worry about coming back with us. It'll be all right. We'll make it so."

We stood in silence for a while, enjoying each other's company, enjoying the coolness of the water. I was comforted by the refreshing shivers that traveled up my legs and out my arms. It *was* delicious, and lovely, and serene. Standing here in the river with Cassandra was the first sweet moment of the day.

But only a short time later, Cassandra nodded over my shoulder and said, "Uh-oh. We've been found out."

I looked back at the bridge and saw Link crossing over to the island. I gasped.

"Do you know him?" Cassandra asked.

"Yeah."

"He kind of looks like a bum."

"He is. He lives in the camp up the river."

Her eyes widened. "Is he safe?"

I laughed. "Oh yeah, he's perfectly safe. He's actually a very nice person. I know him well enough to say that for certain."

"Oh?" A smile spread slowly across my sister's face as Link came closer. Quietly, she said, "Well, Eve, he's rather handsome too, isn't he? For a bum, I mean."

Before I could respond, Link was there. He didn't smile. "Hello, Eve."

"Hi, Link. Um, this is my sister, Cassandra."

He nodded politely. "Nice to meet you."

"Cassandra, this is Link."

She smiled—rather playfully, I thought—and said, "I've heard such wonderful things about you. I'm glad to finally meet you."

My jaw dropped. Link looked at me, his eyes flashing bewilderment. But he smiled at Cassandra and offered her another brief nod.

"Well, I'd love to stay and chat," Cassandra went on, "but Warren's been watching the girls for the past couple hours, and it's about time I go give him a break. Maybe I'll see you again later, though, um . . . Link, is it?"

"Yes. Yes, maybe I'll see you."

"But—" I started, to no avail. Cassandra blew me a kiss and moved away, and I was left alone with Link.

I didn't want him to think I'd been gushing about him to my sister, but I couldn't quite figure out how to explain. I fumbled for the right words, but as though he'd already dismissed Cassandra's innuendoes, Link jumped in and said, "Listen, Eve, I have to tell you something. It's important."

We spent a few awkward seconds staring at each other, each waiting for the other to say something. Then I blurted, "So tell me. What is it?"

He fidgeted, shifting his feet on the pebbly beach. He didn't seem to know what to do with his hands, though he finally settled on hooking his thumbs in the pockets of his worn tan slacks. "I don't know how to say it, so I'm just going to say it."

I waited.

He drew in a deep breath, all of which rushed out as he said, "Come Saturday night, I want you to be in your room by ten o'clock, and once you're there I don't want you to come out again until morning."

Just as quickly as he started, he stopped. His jaw snapped shut and beads of sweat broke out along his brow, as though his announcement had raised his temperature and ignited a fever. For a moment I didn't respond, but then a loud sharp laugh escaped me that surprised us both. "What are you talking about?" I cried.

"I can't explain but—"

"You want me to go to my room on Saturday night and not come out?"

"Yes. I can't explain, Eve, but—"

"Well, it just so happens that I'm not going to be here on Saturday night because we're leaving Saturday morning." As soon as I spoke, I gasped and raised a hand to my lips. But it was too late; the words were already out in the open.

Link frowned so deeply all his features seemed to gather at the center of his face. "You're leaving on Saturday?"

I nodded hesitantly.

"Where are you going?" he asked.

I lowered my hand from my mouth. When I spoke, it was in a whisper. "We're going home. When Cassandra leaves, we're going back with her."

"You're going back to Minnesota?"

"Yes."

"But why? Why are you going back?"

I didn't want to lie but I had no choice. "Daddy wants to go home, is all. He's not happy here."

His eyes spoke of disbelief as his face reddened. "Why didn't you tell me you were leaving?"

"I . . . I don't really know, Link."

"When did your daddy decide to leave?"

"Some days back. About a week ago, maybe."

"Well, were you ever going to tell me or were you just going to disappear?"

I shook my head. Tears pressed against my eyes. I couldn't answer.

Link looked aside and kicked at the stones at his feet. When he looked back at me, his eyes were steely. His mouth twitched. "Maybe it's for the best," he said. "Good-bye, Eve."

He turned and left before I could respond. Through my tears, I watched him walk away, a lone figure moving in waves across the island.

Chapter 35

I spent Friday saying good-bye. Good-bye to my room, to the view out the window, to the green lawn where the guests lounged and strolled and played croquet. Good-bye to the dining room, the front porch and its rocking chairs, the footbridge arching over the narrow tributary to the island. Good-bye to the island itself, the pebbly beach, the vast cool waters of the Little Miami, the boats and picnic tables, the pavilion and the dance floor. Good-bye to ghosts and good-bye to memories. Good-bye to the dream of a safe place. Eden's gates were locked and the key was beyond my reach.

Good-bye too to Annie Tweed, as we stood together at the sink, washing and drying the lunch dishes.

"Shame you have to go, child," she said. "I'll miss you."

"I'll miss you too, Annie."

Did she know why we had to go? After all, Morris knew. He'd been the one to find it, the bottle of Scotch in the box marked canned peaches. I studied Annie's face to see if there was any knowledge there, but it was impossible to tell.

"It's been real nice having you here, having you help around the kitchen."

I nodded as I wiped a plate with a dishcloth. "I'm glad I could be of help, Annie. I wish we could stay."

"Well, you'll be back to visit us, I suppose."

"I guess so," I said, though I knew we'd never be back.

She was scrubbing a pot, but she paused and looked out the window at the stone wall. "Someone else going to miss you, Eve," she said, "'sides me."

Though there was no one there now, some of the men from the camp had gathered by the wall at lunchtime. Link had not been among them.

"No," I said, "I don't think so. Anyway . . ." I shrugged, lifted the plate into the cupboard. I didn't want to think about Link.

"Shame you have to go," Annie said again.

I nodded. We finished the dishes in silence.

That night I packed my suitcase. I laid it open on my bed and folded my clothes into it. I tucked in my photographs and scrapbooks. I lifted my treasure box from the dresser and, without opening it, held it in my hand for a moment. I didn't want to look at what was inside: the elephant from Al Capone, the brass ring from Marcus, the St. Rita medal from Jones.

I would say good-bye to Jones in the morning. I would say good-bye to Uncle Cy too, though I would refuse to look him in the eye. It would take me a long time to forgive him, if ever.

Latching the suitcase, I set it aside. I would finish packing my few belongings in the morning. Now, it was time to sleep. We would pack up the cars and be on the road by daybreak. We had a long hot trip ahead of us, and I wanted to be rested.

When I awoke, the room was full of light. There was a moment of panic, the sense that something was wrong. My first incoherent thought was that I'd slept through Mother's knock on the door and the family had left without me.

I scrambled out of the bed, threw on my robe, and glanced at the clock. Almost eight already. I rushed through the bathroom to Mother and Daddy's room. The bed was made. No one was there.

Throwing open the door to the hall, I hurried out and rushed nearly headlong into Cassandra, who was carrying a glass of something in each hand. "Slow down, Eve," she snapped. "You almost drenched me in Coke."

"What's going on?" I asked.

"The girls have been sick all night. Fever and vomiting, both of them. Obviously, we're not going to be going anywhere today." She sighed and pushed a strand of hair out of her eyes with the back of one hand. She was dressed in the clothes she'd worn yesterday, and I suspected she hadn't slept at all.

"What's the matter with them?"

"I don't know. The doctor's on the way."

"Is anyone else sick?"

She shook her head impatiently. "Not that I know of. Listen, I'd love to stay and chat but I've got to get back to the girls."

"All right. So—" I wanted to ask her what I could do to help, but before I could get the words out she'd already stepped into her room and closed the door.

I went back to my own room to get dressed. I suddenly had

one more day to say good-bye to everything all over again. It made it all seem rather anticlimactic.

Dressed, with hair pulled back into a braid, I went downstairs to breakfast.

The doctor decided the girls were suffering from a simple case of stomach flu. He said to keep them comfortable, cool and hydrated, and they should be able to travel in a few days.

We were relieved it was nothing more serious, but we were all annoyed with the doctor's prognosis of "a few days." By now, we were ready to go, and no one wanted us gone more than Uncle Cy. He didn't say as much, but I could tell by the look on his face when he got the news. On top of that, he let off the deepest sigh I'd ever heard. As far as Uncle Cy was concerned, the longer Daddy and I were there, the greater the chance one of us would slip up and give the secret away.

Mother and I spent the day taking care of the girls while Cassandra and Warren napped in Mother and Daddy's room. We kept the girls cool with cold compresses draped across their foreheads. We encouraged them to drink water and juice and to nibble on soda crackers. By midday, the nausea had largely passed, but both Effie and Grace were weak, tired, and cranky. Mother tried reading from their favorite storybook and singing lullabies and hymns to lull them to sleep, which they did fitfully for short periods of time. I was appointed the task of running back and forth to the kitchen for whatever they needed.

Late in the afternoon, I was searching the Frigidaire for something soft for the girls to eat when I heard Morris's truck crunching over the gravel outside.

"About time Morris got back from the train station," Annie said. "Must have had a big load of supplies come in today."

I found a bowl of strawberry Jell-O and shut the refrigerator. "Can I take some of this to the girls?" I asked.

"Sure you can, honey. Whatever you need." She stood at the screen door, looking out. "Your Daddy's out there helping Morris unload the truck. Think I'll take them both a nice cold glass of lemonade. Hot day like this, I'm sure they could use some."

When she stepped to the refrigerator, I moved to the door and peered out through the screen. Both Daddy and Morris were hauling crates off the truck and stacking them onto dollies. More supplies to be rolled down to the cellar for storage. I wondered if any of the crates were marked canned peaches. Or maybe the men in Cincinnati packed the stuff in different boxes this time? Maybe that was part of the code picked up by Jones when he listened to the bedtime stories. Maybe the information that came in over the airwaves was not just about when a shipment was coming in but how the crates would be labeled. Today, canned peaches. Tomorrow, cooking oil or applesauce or canned sardines.

Annie hummed to herself as she poured the lemonade and carried it outside on a tray. She couldn't know, of course. No, Morris surely wouldn't tell her. Morris would see, hear, speak no evil, and Annie would go on living in sweet ignorance of what went on beneath our feet.

I dished up the Jell-O in two small bowls and put them on a tray with spoons and napkins. Just as I turned away from the counter, Jones stepped into the kitchen. When he saw me, he stopped short. His eyes widened.

"What are you doing here?" he asked. "I thought you left this morning."

I shook my head. "The girls are sick with the flu. We can't leave until they're better. No one told you?"

"No. I've been working at my desk all morning. I didn't know."

"Seems like Uncle Cy should have told you."

"Yeah, well, he doesn't tell me much."

"Anyway, I wouldn't have left without saying good-bye."

He walked to the refrigerator, trying to look nonchalant. I knew there was something on his mind.

"What's the matter, Jones?" I asked.

He shrugged as he pulled open the refrigerator door. "Nothing. I . . ."

I waited a moment. Then I said, "You what?"

He grabbed a bottle of milk and shut the door. "So you're not leaving today?"

"No, we can't. Like I said, the girls can't travel right now."

His mouth disappeared into a small tight line. He walked to the screen door and looked out. Annie was lingering by the truck as the men drank from the glasses of lemonade. Jones squeezed the neck of the milk bottle so hard I thought he might crush it, the glass breaking into a dozen pieces in his hand.

He turned back and looked at me. Our eyes met. We both knew what came in such shipments as that one. Neither of us would speak of it.

"Eve . . ."

"What is it, Jones?"

He drew in his breath; his jaw worked. Finally he said, "Just stay safe, all right? I mean, on your trip home."

"Um, sure." I frowned. "I'll tell you when we're leaving.

It'll probably be Monday, maybe Tuesday, but I'll let you know. So we can say good-bye."

He nodded hesitantly. "Yeah, all right." He glanced at the tray in my hand. "I don't mean to hold you up."

"It's all right," I said. "Though I guess I'd better get this to the girls. I'll see you later, okay?"

He nodded. He didn't move. I felt his eyes on me as I walked out of the kitchen into the dining room. At this time of day the room was usually empty, but today four men were gathered there, two of them playing what looked like poker at the table closest to the front window. A third man with a droopy moustache sat at the table with them while a fourth, smoking a cigarette, stood at the window peering out over the lawn where the croquet game was set up.

The man at the window pulled the cigarette from his mouth and laughed abruptly. "Well, I can tell you one thing," he said, "The old man can't hit worth a hill of beans, that's for sure. The little lady's got him beat by a landslide."

He laughed again as I tried to make my way through the room unnoticed. I was only a few steps from the front hall when the man with the moustache snapped his fingers. "Hey, miss!" he hollered. "You work here?"

I gritted my teeth but tried to smile as I made my way to the table. "Yes, I work here. Can I help you?"

"Yeah. Would you mind bringing us something to drink?"

One of the men playing poker must have seen the alarm in my eyes. He jumped in and added, "Water. He means water. Can you bring us a pitcher with ice? It's hotter than blazes today."

I looked from face to face and nodded. "I'll bring you some."

The man at the window crushed out his cigarette on the sill. "That man couldn't hit the side of a barn from a foot away with that croquet ball!" He followed up his announcement with an expletive that underscored his amusement.

"Hey, Bert." Moustache man frowned at cigarette man and waited for him to turn around. "There's a lady present."

Cigarette man looked at me sheepishly and cleared his throat. "Beg your pardon, miss."

"That's all right," I said, though I hoped he heard the disdain in my voice.

He had stepped aside from the window enough that I could see who was outside playing croquet. It was George Sluder and his wife, both dressed fashionably in white croquet clothing as though they were at a country club. He wore neatly creased slacks, a short-sleeved shirt, and a white straw hat with a black band; she, a narrow sundress and floppy brimmed hat that sported feathers on one side. They laughed and chattered freely, unaware that they were entertaining the men in the dining room.

I looked back toward the table. "I'll be right back with your water."

"Thank you, miss. Much obliged," said moustache man.

Why they couldn't see that I was already in the middle of running an errand was beyond me. Mother and the girls had been waiting an unreasonably long time for the Jell-O. I huffed as I made my way back to the kitchen and was relieved to see Annie at the sink. "Annie, the men in the dining room need a pitcher of ice water. Would you mind taking it to them?"

"Sure, honey," she said as she wiped her hands on her apron. She looked wide-eyed at the tray in my hands. "You'd best run that Jell-O upstairs before it melts and the girls have to be drinking it with a straw."

I thanked her and hurried back to the dining room. The man at the window was lighting another cigarette. Moustache man was pulling on his moustache. One of the men playing cards folded while the other pulled a pile of chips toward him with a shout of triumph.

"Annie will be bringing your water in a minute," I told them.

Moustache man nodded.

I turned to go. When I reached the threshold to the front hall, cigarette man snorted out another hearty laugh. "Yes, sir, gentlemen," he announced merrily. "I believe this one's in the bag."

Chapter 36

By nightfall, Cassandra was sick, which left us playing a sort of musical chairs with our sleeping arrangements. She and Warren stayed in Mother and Daddy's room. Daddy took the single bed in my room, and Mother and I took the second double bed in Cassandra and Warren's room so that we could be with the girls.

The night was hot and sticky. We had the windows thrown open and two oscillating fans blowing air about the room. Effie and Grace managed to fall asleep about nine o'clock, both stripped to their underwear and cuddling cold water bottles. For Mother and me, sleep didn't come so easily. We abandoned the top sheet early on and lay sweating in our cotton gowns.

"Mother?" I whispered.

She rolled toward me. "Yes, Eve?"

"Are you glad to be going back to St. Paul?"

She was quiet a moment. "Yes, I think I am. It seems more like home than Ohio does."

"But we didn't really have the chance to get used to Ohio. You know, to make it home."

"No, I suppose not."

She rolled over again, away from me.

"Mother?"

"Hmm?"

"Do you know why Daddy wants to leave?"

"Of course. He feels our place is in St. Paul."

I pushed a strand of sweaty hair off my forehead. "But, I mean, the real reason. Do you know the real reason he wants to leave?"

Mother sighed. "If you're talking about Daddy and his brothers, Eve, it's no secret he feels out of place here. He thinks he can't live up to their success. We probably never should have come to Ohio in the first place. Your father hasn't really been happy since we arrived."

So Mother still had no idea about the bootlegging. Daddy hadn't slipped up and told her. Would we ever tell her, I wondered?

No. Probably not. Better for her not to know.

"Do you think Daddy will be happy again in St. Paul?"

"Yes. Eventually." She turned onto her back again. "You don't want to go, do you, Eve?"

Of course I didn't want to go. And yet, we couldn't stay. Maybe once we reached St. Paul and I was free of the black secret in my heart, I would feel light again. And young. And hopeful. "I'll try to make the best of it," I said.

"You'll be all right." Mother looked at me and smiled. "You can go back to the school you know and graduate with all your friends. I should think you'd be glad about that."

"Yes. I guess I have that to look forward to."

After a moment, Mother turned her face toward the ceiling. She shut her eyes and said sleepily, "And besides, Eve, you don't really have any reason to want to stay here, do you? I can't imagine what Mercy has to offer that St. Paul doesn't have."

I thought of Link, had been thinking of Link ever since he left me standing alone on the island the day we buried Aunt Cora. If things had been different, I might have loved him.

A tear formed at the corner of my eye and slipped down the side of my face. "No," I said. "I don't have any reason to stay here."

Mother yawned loudly. "I didn't think so. Now let's try to get some sleep, all right?"

"All right. Good night, Mother."

She rolled over one last time, and I could soon tell by her breathing that she was asleep. I thought about Link and shed a few more tears until I too drifted off to a place of fitful dreams.

Several hours must have gone by, but I was wading through such shallow sleep that when Grace moaned quietly, I sat straight up. "Gracie? What's the matter?"

"I'm so thirsty, Auntie Eve." Her voice was small and hoarse.

"I'll pour you some water," I said, moving toward the pitcher on the dresser.

"But I want lemonade."

"Lemonade?"

"Please, Auntie Eve?" She gave off a weak pathetic wail.

"Shh," I said. "You'll wake up Effie and Grandma. You know I have to go all the way down to the kitchen to get lemonade, don't you?"

"But I want it."

I sighed. "All right." I lifted my cotton robe off the hook

on the back of the door. "But try to be quiet until I get back. I'll be as quick as I can."

The door squealed on its hinges. I stepped into the hall and closed it gently behind me, making sure it latched. I looked down the length of the dimly lit hall and sighed again. The kitchen seemed a long way off at this hour. Plus, I'd have to pass by Thomas at the front desk, and I didn't relish the idea of walking by him in my nightclothes. For whatever reason, I'd begun to feel increasingly uncomfortable around that strange little man.

But Grace was waiting for her lemonade and I didn't want to disappoint her, especially if that was the only thing that would encourage her back to sleep. I padded quietly along the hardwood floor in my bare feet, hoping to go unheard by the guests who were no doubt sleeping as restlessly in the heat as I had been.

Halfway down the hall, I stopped and listened. There had been something outside. . . . Tires on gravel? Footsteps somewhere? I wasn't sure. I looked back over my shoulder, then forward again. I must have been hearing things. After a moment, I moved on.

I was at the top of the staircase—my hand was reaching for the banister—when the front door to the lodge flew open, banging in fury against the wall. I gasped loudly and froze. In the same instant someone yelled "Stop!" and I was grabbed from behind and pulled to the floor, but even as I was going down I saw a swarm of men rush into the front hall with weapons drawn. I had just enough time to register that some were police officers in uniform while others wore plain clothes with red armbands, but I had no time to ponder what it all meant. At once, a shot rang out from the sitting room, and one of the officers went down while another swung his tommy gun around and sent a hail of bullets back.

Thomas, at the desk below, reached down for something and came up shooting. A plainclothesman went down, but he had hardly dropped to the floor when a second barrage of bullets sent Thomas flying back against the mailboxes, his hands in the air, his shotgun spinning away from him as he screamed and sank to the floor. The next few seconds were a muddle of men swarming the first floor, some disappearing through the cellar door, others pounding up the stairs and spreading out across the second floor, shots ringing out below me as well as somewhere down the hall behind me, and oddly, a wild tangle of camera bulbs flashing. Someone—no, several men were downstairs taking pictures of the unfolding carnage while a man who reeked heavily of cigarette smoke held me in his grip, both arms around me so that I was nestled in a tight cocoon. I wiggled but he wouldn't let go. I didn't know whose side he was on and whether I might end up with a bullet in my brain, but even if I didn't die of a gunshot wound, I felt as though I might drown beneath his stifling bulk. I gasped for air as waves of fear sent shivers all the way through me.

Panicked guests tumbled out of their rooms and filled the hall behind us with screams of terror. A deep-voiced someone yelled, "Federal agents! Everyone get back to your rooms!"

"Let me up," I begged. "You're hurting me. I can't breathe."

Loosening his grip only slightly, he said, "Not yet, little lady. Not until the coast is clear." I recognized the voice. And the smell. It was cigarette man, the man named Bert who'd stood at the window and laughed at the Sluders playing croquet.

I wiggled again, but he was too strong for me. "What's happening?" I asked.

He didn't answer.

"Bert!"

"Here!"

"See Mrs. Treadwell out, will you?"

"You got it." Quietly, he said to me, "Okay, I'm going to let you go now. But you're not going down those stairs. You understand?"

I nodded. At last his arms relaxed and his weight was lifted off of me.

Free of him, I drew in several deep breaths. My heart pounded in my chest and my ears rang in the aftermath of the machine-gun fire. Trembling, I pulled myself up to my knees, leaned toward the railing, and grabbed a baluster with each hand. The shooting had stopped, and down in the front hall someone was leaning over the wounded officer. The officer was alive still and writhing in pain. The other man down, the plainclothesman, lay motionless in an ever growing circle of blood. Thomas, also dead, lay alone behind the desk, his glasses askew on his face and his mouth hanging open as though he had died mid-scream.

I shut my eyes against the sight, but even so the image of Thomas lingered there behind my lids. Nausea swept over me. I hung my head and gave off a low cry that ended in a whispered prayer, "Oh, God, help me." Rocking forward on my knees, I pressed my lips into a small tight line and waited for the nausea to pass.

Finally I ventured a look over my shoulder at the people milling about in their doorways, clutching their robes, ashen-faced. Making his way through the crowd was Bert; he had a hand on Ada Sluder's elbow as he led her toward the stairs. She appeared wraithlike in a white floor-length nightgown, her eyes wide, her hair disheveled from sleep. When they passed me and headed down, I saw the cuffs that held her slender hands behind her back. I watched slack-jawed as she was led away like a criminal and wondered why the man had called her Mrs. Treadwell. Bert and Ada Sluder were followed by two other men, the poker players, escorting a handcuffed and obviously agitated George Sluder down the stairs. Looking vulnerable and slightly ridiculous in his bathrobe and slippers, he hollered threats about calling his lawyer while one of the poker players repeatedly told him to shut up.

Somewhere down the hall, a woman shouted, "They're dead! Oh, dear God, they're dead!" And a man's voice responded, "Get her outta here, will ya?"

My head spun as though I was in the middle of a nightmare, one from which I couldn't wake up. I didn't know what was happening or who might be dead. Everywhere, upstairs and down, pandemonium reigned. Footsteps went on beating the floor, women wailed, men shouted in angry voices, and in the next moment, sirens screamed outside and surrounded the lodge like a gathering of banshees.

I didn't dare move from where I was. I clutched the balusters until my hands ached, waiting for it all to end and wondering whether it ever would. Then, seemingly out of nowhere, Mother and Daddy were beside me. "Eve, are you all right?" Mother asked, her eyes roaming over me as though looking for wounds. "You're not hurt, are you?"

I shook my head and she knelt and pulled me into her arms. I buried my head in her shoulder and clung to her like a child. "Someone is dead down the hall, Mother," I cried. "Who's dead? Is it Cassandra and Warren?"

"No, Eve, no. Of course not. They're all right. I just spoke with them."

"Then who's dead, Mother?"

"I don't know." She looked up at Daddy.

He too knelt down beside me and put a hand on my shoulder. "Stay right here until this is all over, all right?"

I nodded.

He stood and started down the stairs. Mother hugged me tightly once more and, kissing my cheek, rose to follow him. They were halfway to the bottom when Uncle Cy, himself in handcuffs, stumbled into the front hall, a man on either side of him gripping his elbows.

"Cyrus!" Daddy yelled, picking up his pace.

Uncle Cy looked over his shoulder at Daddy but didn't respond. Both men holding him looked up as well, and I recognized Captain Macnish. An array of camera bulbs flashed and all three men blinked. In another moment, Uncle Cy was taken out the front door. Daddy and Mother followed.

More footsteps pounded through the hall below and another handcuffed figure appeared. Jones. Escorted by two men in plain clothes and red armbands, he walked docilely with his head down. He hung his head further as the flashbulbs went off. I wanted to cry out to him, but my breath caught in my throat. Tears pushed at the back of my eyes. "Dear God," I whispered, and in those two words were a thousand pleas I'd never be able to give voice to. And then he was gone.

A couple of ambulance attendants rushed in through the front door and gently lifted the wounded officer onto a stretcher. The man who had been bending over him stood and watched, still holding a shotgun in his right hand. He was not a police officer; he wore dark slacks and a long-sleeved shirt with the sleeves rolled up. On his right bicep was the red armband. After the attendants whisked the stretcher out the door, he went on standing there in the sudden silence. As quickly as the raiding men had come, they now dispersed. Even the photographers had disappeared. The front hall was empty, save for the two dead men and the lone figure holding the gun.

I watched as he moved to the dead man lying in the pool of blood. He stepped gingerly around the blood and felt the man's neck for a pulse, a futile gesture. His fingers left the man's neck and traveled to his eyes to close the lids.

He stood and sighed heavily. I didn't hear it, but I saw his shoulders rise and fall. Moving to the front desk, he laid down his gun. And then he looked up. Our eyes locked. I gasped; his name escaped me in whispered disbelief.

"Link!"

For a moment, he didn't move. Then, in long strides, taking the stairs two at a time, he hurried to my side. He raised a hand to my face, as though to see if I were real.

"Are you all right?" he asked.

I nodded. "Yes." A tear slipped down my cheek. He wiped it away with his thumb.

"You told me you wouldn't be here."

My heart was still racing and my words came out in a trembling rush. "The girls were sick. We couldn't leave."

"Is everyone all right?"

I looked down the hall. I didn't know where Cassandra and Warren were, or the girls. They weren't among the crowd now moving about more freely and chattering among themselves. "I think so," I answered.

I looked back at Link, first at the badge pinned to his breast pocket, and then directly into his eyes. "You told me you were a bum," I said. "But you're not. You're a Prohibition agent."

A smile began to play about his lips. "Bum. Prohibition agent." He shrugged. "Most people consider them the same thing."

For the first time since Grace had awakened, I smiled. "You've been undercover all this time?"

"Yes."

"And you were just posing as one of the men at the camp?"

"That's right. I was sent over from Cincinnati where we've been working to shut down a huge bootlegging ring for a while. We knew the booze was being distributed through transport stations throughout the state, like your uncle's lodge."

"They arrested Uncle Cy and my cousin Jones."

"I'm afraid so. Along with others. Including the big guy himself."

"The big guy?"

"The owner of the whole operation."

"Who's that?"

"George Treadwell. You may know him as George Sluder."

Stunned, I shook my head at the thought. "Yes, I know who he is. They arrested his wife too."

Link nodded. "Sure. She's an accessory."

"You knew all that?"

"Eventually we did."

"But . . ."

"But what, Eve?"

"You knew about the lodge?"

"We found out."

"How?"

Link glanced away. "It doesn't matter."

"But—"

He laid a finger to my lips to quiet me. "Listen, Eve, your uncle's probably going to be gone for a while. You understand that, don't you?"

I thought a moment, then nodded. "Uncle Cy is going to prison, isn't he?"

"I'm afraid so, yes. So . . ." He paused and cleared his throat. "So he won't be around to run the lodge, and that being the case, I'm wondering, do you think your father might take over and, well, you know, you'd all end up staying here?"

I frowned at that. "I don't know," I said truthfully. "I have no idea what Daddy will want to do now."

"Okay, well." Link paused and looked away a moment. Then he looked back at me and said more forcefully, "I'm going back to my original plan. If you stay, I'm going to ask your father if I can call on you. And don't you say no, all right?"

I offered him a tentative smile. "But what if we leave?"

"In that case, I'll have to follow you. I'm in the market for a new job anyway."

"You are?"

"As of tonight, I am. A man can get himself killed going after bootleggers. We can't have that happening now, can we?"

"No," I agreed. "We can't have that happening."

He reached for the badge on his breast pocket and unpinned it. "From now on, I'm plain old Charles Hoppe."

"Charles Hoppe?"

"My real name. Charles Lincoln Hoppe. I needed a cover so I decided to go by Link."

I laughed lightly. "I will have to get used to calling you Charles."

"I hope so," he said.

"Hoppe!" A uniformed figure hollered up from the front door.

"Here, sir!" Link answered.

"You're needed outside."

"Be right there."

The officer left. Link turned back to me. Taking my hand, he gently uncurled my fingers and laid the badge in my palm. "Someday, I'll trade this for a ring."

I looked at the badge and blinked back tears. "You sound pretty sure of yourself," I whispered.

"I am. Will you wait for me?"

I nodded. "Yes, I'll wait."

He kissed me then, a brief and tender kiss that shattered all my fears. For the first time in a very long time, I felt safe. He gave me one last smile and hurried down the stairs into what was left of that dark and beautiful night. I lifted the badge to my heart and watched him go.

Epilogue

May 1981

The words are a tarnished gold against a fading blue: "U.S. Prohibition Service—Treasury Department." It somehow seems smaller than I remembered, nestled there in the center of my palm. Maybe it's because the skin of my hand is loose and wrinkled now, the knuckles enlarged. Deep in memory, I stare at the badge until my grandson interrupts my thoughts.

"Did he ever give you the ring, Grandma?"

I look up, startled. "What? Oh yes, of course." I lift my left hand for him to see the wedding band. "I've worn it for forty-six years now."

Sean lets out a small whistle. "That's a long time."

"Yes, it is," I agree. "A good long time."

I tuck the badge back into the wooden box that lies open on my lap. "Thank you for finding my box for me."

"Sure, Grandma." Sean claps his hands together as though to rid them of dust, then wipes his palms on his shorts. "How come you never told me before about Grandpa being a federal agent?"

I think about that, then shake my head. "I don't know, Sean. I guess because it meant telling you all the family secrets."

He looks around at the cluttered attic, at the boxes in disarray that we had just dug through. To him, we had been sorting through junk. For me, we had been resurrecting the dead.

Sean sniffs, sneezes, and then sits down on a box beside me. "So what happened to Uncle Cy and everyone?"

"Well . . ." I take a deep breath. "Uncle Cy went to prison. He did five years in the Ohio State Penitentiary."

Another low whistle. "I bet he sighed about that."

I glance at Sean and chuckle. "I well imagine he did, a time or two."

"And then what? Did he come back here?"

"No, he never came back. Once he got out he just kind of disappeared. I guess he figured it was dangerous to come back."

"Dangerous?"

"Well, he probably assumed George Sluder—or Treadwell, rather—would seek revenge for what had happened. But by then, there was probably nothing to worry about. Old George was still in prison when Uncle Cy got out. George did seven years, the last one in Alcatraz. By the time he was released, he was a broken man. Sick in body and soul. He lived only about another year after that. I heard he died almost penniless."

"Really?"

"That's the story, anyway. Prohibition was long over by then, and he had no way to make a living."

"What about his wife?"

I lift my shoulders in a shrug. "I'm not really sure what happened to her. She somehow avoided prison, but what became of her, I don't know."

"Maybe she found another rich man to marry."

"Maybe. Yes, probably. Marrying rich men was most likely her vocation. Some women are just born to that."

The late afternoon sun slants in through the attic windows. Dust dances like dandelion seeds in its rays. Sean sneezes again.

"Bless you," I say. "Do you want to leave now?"

He shakes his head adamantly. "I want to know what else happened."

"Like what?"

"Like, what happened to Jones? Did he go to prison too?"

"Jones." I smile at the name. "No, he didn't. Jones, like Uncle Cy, simply disappeared. Except that he disappeared on the night of the raid. No one ever saw him again after that night."

"How'd he do that?" My grandson's eyes grow wide as nickels.

"He had a little help," I say as I pull the St. Rita medal out of the box.

"The saints helped him escape?" Sean asks incredulously.

I laugh. "No, not the saints. The feds."

"The feds?"

"Yes. Jones was the informant. He gave it all away. At first I didn't know that, but your grandfather finally told me all about it. After his mother died, Jones really had no reason to stay on at the lodge. He was ready to go after his dream. So he made a deal with the feds. The information they were looking for in exchange for safe passage out of the States."

"Really? Where'd he go?"

"He went to the Alaskan Territory, just as he'd hoped. Back then, Alaska wasn't a state. It was the ends of the earth, as far as we were concerned. I think Jones figured he could go there and be safe and simply live a normal life, or at least a different life from the one he was living here."

"But are you sure he got there?"

"Oh yes, I'm sure. Some years after the raid I received a package from Alaska. There was no return address and no name inside, but I knew it was from Jones."

"How?"

I look at the medal in my hand once more. "It was another medal. This one was for St. Zachary."

"Who?"

I smile at Sean. "St. Zachary. The patron saint of peace."

He returns my smile. "So maybe Jones was happy."

"I think so."

"Maybe he married an Eskimo woman and had a bunch of Eskimo kids."

"Maybe. I hope so. At any rate, I knew he was all right."

"It was nice of him to let you know."

"Yes, Sean, it was."

"And what about your friend Marlene? Did you really never see her again?"

"No, I never did, though we stayed in touch for many years. She and Jimmy made their way to California, where they eventually settled and had six kids."

"Six kids!"

I nod. "They named their youngest daughter Eve, which I always thought was nice. We eventually lost contact, though. Kind of a shame, but life gets busy when you're raising a family."

We sit quietly a moment. Then Sean says, "So after the raid, that's when you took over the lodge."

"Well, not me exactly. Daddy and Mother took over. They became part owners with Uncle Luther. Finally Daddy had something he felt he could be proud of. He did a fine job of running the lodge. And as you know, your grandfather Charles came to work for us while he went to college in Cincinnati part-time. Eventually, as you also know, he went on to seminary and became a pastor."

"And you finished high school."

"Yes."

"And never went to college."

I shake my head. "No, I never did."

"Why not?"

"Once I got engaged, my dream changed. I was content to become a pastor's wife."

"I think that's a good thing to be, Grandma."

"So do I." I touch my wedding ring briefly. "I stayed here at the lodge and worked until your grandfather Charles and I got married. Then we made a home of our own and started having children. Your uncle Charlie first, then your daddy, and then lastly your aunt Sarah. With your grandpa in the ministry we moved those poor kids around a lot, but we finally settled in Illinois, where we've been the last twenty-some years. Anyway, when I became a bride and moved out of the lodge, I left some of my things here, including this box, and it eventually ended up in the attic. That's what brought us here today."

Sean smiles at me, but then his face shifts into a frown. He looks around the attic and shivers in spite of the heat. Quietly, he says, "What about the stories of the lodge being haunted? You know, by the ghosts of all those people killed here that night?"

I chuckle. "We don't believe in ghosts, Sean. You know that. Though people seem to be amused at the thought of places being haunted. Daddy always played it down, but Uncle Luther said the stories were good for business. Those rumors started up right after the raid, of course. Five people shot to death in one night—that's some good fodder for all sorts of stories. Only the brave dared sleep in the suite after that night, since George's two bodyguards were shot to death in the front room while George and Ada were asleep in the back bedroom."

"I don't guess they were asleep for long after that, were they, Grandma?"

"No, not very long. They had a rather rude awakening that night, I'm afraid."

"And then that night clerk, Thomas—he was killed, right?"

"That's right."

"And then the other guy—the one that Grandpa closed his eyes."

"Yes, he was a Prohibition agent out of Cincinnati who'd come to take part in the raid."

Sean wiggles his fingers, counting. "Who was the fifth?"

"The fifth was Mr. Adele, if that was his real name. He was the man who used to come to the lodge by himself that summer. I always felt sorry for him because he was alone.

It turns out he was simply one of the armed guards George Treadwell had watching the lodge. There were all sorts of men keeping an eye on things, men I was hardly aware of, watching the lodge and the gas station both. And the tunnel. There were two men watching the tunnel on the night of the raid, and they were both arrested."

"But what happened to Mr. Adele?"

"Oh, he was in the sitting room when the raid started. I guess he'd pulled night watch that night because he was armed and apparently awake. When the police swarmed in, Mr. Adele fired the first shot. He was killed right away. After that, we had to replace the couch in the sitting room because that was where he landed. There was just no getting the bloodstains out of it."

"Wow! And what about all the bullet holes?"

"Bullet holes?"

"Yeah, didn't some of the walls get shot up?"

"Yes, well, we fixed most of those, though we left a couple in the suite. Kind of a memento, I guess. Now that I think of it, it seems a funny thing to do. But like the ghost stories, those bullet holes drew business. People liked to come to the lodge just to see those holes and the room where George Treadwell and his wife were arrested."

"I'd like to see the bullet holes myself!"

"All right." I nod. "You can see them on the way out."

"Okay. But there's one more thing I want to see first."

"And what's that?"

"The elephant from Al Capone."

"Of course," I say. "I almost forgot."

"You can't forget that, Grandma."

"No, you're right. I must never forget."

I lift the little ivory elephant out of the box and hand it to Sean.

"Wow!" he exclaims. "I can't believe you got this from Al Capone! Public Enemy Number One!"

I chuckle at his enthusiasm. "Yes, one of the most notorious men in the world. And yet he was kind to a little girl."

Sean lifts his shoulders nonchalantly. "So maybe he wasn't all bad."

"No, I'm sure you're right. He wasn't all bad, just as none of us is all good. Though it can be tempting to think of ourselves that way."

Sean isn't listening. He is turning the elephant over and over in his hands. Our fascination for the notorious never ends.

"I want to tell you something, Sean."

"Yeah?" He doesn't take his eyes from the little figurine.

"In recent years, I've read some of the books written about Al Capone."

"Yeah?"

"He was arrested for tax evasion, you know. Not for murder. Not even for bootlegging or for running brothels."

Sean's brows meet. "Brothels? What's that?"

"Never mind," I say. "Forget I said that. Anyway, he went to prison and eventually ended up in Alcatraz."

"Like old George."

"Yes, like old George."

"That's where they sent the worst of the worst. That's what Grandpa told me."

"Yes, it's true. Alcatraz once held the worst of the worst, before the whole prison was shut down. It was a dreadful place."

"So did he escape?" Sean asks eagerly.

"Oh no, he never escaped. But what I want to tell you is this. One Sunday at Alcatraz a visiting pastor was holding a church service. A large number of the prisoners attended, including Al Capone. Well, when the pastor asked who felt in need of prayer, Capone raised his hand. Then the pastor said that anyone who felt in need of a savior should stand up. Capone stood up."

"He did?"

"Yes, he did."

"Do you think he prayed to Jesus?"

"I do. I think he prayed to ask Jesus to forgive him."

"How come we never hear about that? We only hear about how he killed people and all that."

"Well." I take a deep breath. "First of all, it would ruin the whole picture of the tough guy, you know? He's an American icon and we don't want to change his image. On top of that, the people who did know about that Sunday at Alcatraz didn't take it seriously. See, by that time, Capone was already sick with a serious illness that affects the mind. One of his friends said that because of the sickness Al was 'nutty as a fruitcake.'"

"Oh." Sean thinks about that for a moment. "Then maybe he really didn't know what he was doing."

I lean toward him and catch his eye. "But you see, I think he did."

"You do?"

I nod. "Because it didn't end there. Once he was out of prison, he went to live at his mansion in Florida. He was still sick, of course. He was sick right up to the end of his life a few years later. But when people came to visit him, he would tell them about how he was sorry for what he'd done in the past. And he told people he'd accepted Jesus as his savior in Alcatraz."

"Really?"

"That's what's written about him. More than one of his biographies tells about his conversion, though perhaps even the authors of those books don't believe it themselves, since Al was nuts, after all. It's easy to chalk it all up to a mind gone crazy."

"So no one believes he really did pray to Jesus?"

"Well, the thing is, he was buried in a Catholic cemetery, in what's considered consecrated ground. The church has a rule that the unbelieving can't be buried there. But they allowed the remains of Capone to be laid to rest beside his father. When one of the Catholic priests was asked by reporters why this was allowed, he explained that the Church recognized Capone's penitence and the fact that he died fortified by the sacraments of the Church. Do you know what his headstone says?"

Sean shakes his head. "No. What?"

"It says, 'Al Capone. My Jesus, Mercy.'"

Sean studies the elephant in his hand a moment before looking back at me. "So, you mean, you think he went to heaven?"

I smile and pat Sean's hand. "I think God's mercy is big enough for anything."

Sean takes one last look at the elephant before offering it to me. "No," I say, "you keep that now. As a reminder."

"A reminder of what?"

"A reminder that 'love shall cover the multitude of sins.'"

Sean scratches his head and I laugh lightly. "Someday, you'll understand," I assure him.

"All right," he says at length. "But listen, Grandma, hold on to it till we get home. I don't want to lose it. That thing's got to be worth a million bucks!"

Through the open windows comes the sound of tires crunching on gravel followed by a horn honking. "Listen," I say, "it's Grandpa Charles come to pick us up. Time to go, then."

I tuck the elephant into the box and ease myself up from the crate. Sean goes about the attic closing all the windows, and when he's done we head downstairs. As I descend to the second floor—one hand on the railing, the other clutching the wooden box—I hear voices again, reaching me from long ago. But this time there are only two. Jones's voice and mine. We are out in the boat on the Little Miami on a hot summer day in 1931.

"You sound like that man who said he believes the law can regulate morality and make upstanding citizens out of everybody."

"His name is Volstead and that's right, I do agree with him. If people acted decent and nobody drank, this country would be a whole lot better off."

"You mean, if everyone was as perfect as you, this country would be a whole lot better off."

"I didn't say that."

"No, but that's what you meant. You've got a lot to learn about being human, missy."

Jones was right. And before the end of that strange summer, I had learned what it means to be human. *O God, have mercy on me, a sinner.*

Sean rushes ahead of me to the suite. In another moment, he hollers, "Hey, Grandma, I found them! I found the bullet holes!"

But I've reached the top of the stairs leading to the front hall, and my attention is turned elsewhere. I am watching a beloved figure climb the stairs. He's not as quick as he used to be, and yet, he still takes the stairs two at a time all the way to the top. His once curly hair is now wispy and gray. His face is wrinkled, his chin slack, his forehead freckled with age spots. But his eyes—those are the eyes of the man I fell in love with fifty years before.

"Hello, Link," I say.

He smiles. "Haven't heard that name in a while. Did you find what you were looking for?"

"I did." I reach into the box and pull out his badge.

He takes it and turns it over in his hands. "Well, I'll be. Guess I was Link when I wore this thing, huh?"

"I guess you were, yes."

"I'll be," he says again. "Those were some interesting times. A man can get himself killed chasing bootleggers, you know."

"I know. Thank God you weren't killed."

He nods. "Wouldn't have been able to marry my sweetheart if I had been, and that'd have been a shame."

"Yes." We share a smile.

He hands me the badge and I tuck it away. "What else you got in there?" he asks.

"You won't believe me if I tell you."

"Try me."

I smile coyly. "I've got an ivory elephant that Al Capone gave me."

He stares at me blankly a moment before bursting into laughter. "Oh, sweetheart, that's good! And I'm the proud owner of one of his diamond belt buckles!"

Sean runs toward us from down the hall. "What's so funny, Grandpa?" he asks.

"Just something your grandma said."

"What?"

"She says she has an ivory elephant from Al Capone."

"Oh, but she does, Grandpa! I saw it!" Sean reaches for his grandfather's hand, and together they start down the stairs. "Let me tell you all about it. See, one summer when Grandma was little she wanted a pair of roller skates, so her daddy bought her a pair, and . . ."

I smile as I listen to my grandson talking excitedly. The Marryat Island Ballroom and Lodge will soon be torn down, but the stories remain. I take one last look around the old lodge before descending the stairs and following my husband and grandson out into the sweet Ohio air.

Acknowledgments

My special thanks to Colonel Robert Lindsey, retired, Jefferson Parish Sheriff's Office, Louisiana, as well as my next door neighbor and friend, with whom I have shared endless cups of tea. I appreciate the hours you spent instructing me about law enforcement and imagining with me "what might have been" and "what might have happened" in a time neither of us knew firsthand. Without your invaluable input, this book would be completely different—or might never have been at all.

Thanks too to Maggie Lindsey, Bob's wonderful wife, who read the manuscript in rough draft for me. You two are a blessing.

Ann Tatlock is the author of the Christy-Award-winning novel *Promises to Keep*. She has also won the Midwest Independent Publishers Association "Book of the Year" in fiction for both *All the Way Home* and *I'll Watch the Moon*. Ann lives with her husband, Bob, and their daughter, Laura, in Asheville, North Carolina.

More Stirring Inspirational Fiction from Ann Tatlock

To learn more about Ann and her books, visit anntatlock.com.

Jane Morrow is devastated when her fiancé returns from the Iraq War severely injured and convinced their relationship—and his life—is over. With the help of a retired doctor, seeking redemption of his own, can she hold on to her hope for love?

Travelers Rest

Tillie Monroe has lived a long, full life. But the greatest thing she may ever do is offer her selfless love to protect a little girl and her family from an unspeakable danger.

Promises to Keep